A Message in Poison

Center Point
Large Print

Also by BJ Magnani and available from Center Point Large Print:

The Queen of All Poisons
The Power of Poison

A Message in Poison

A Dr. Lily Robinson Novel

BJ Magnani

CENTER POINT LARGE PRINT
THORNDIKE, MAINE

This Center Point Large Print edition
is published in the year 2025 by arrangement with
Encircle Publications.

Copyright © 2022 by BJ Magnani.

All rights reserved.

This book is a work of fiction.
While the science and toxins are real, names,
characters, places and events are products of the
author's imagination or are used fictitiously, and
any resemblance to actual persons, living or dead, or to
actual places or businesses, is entirely coincidental.

The text of this Large Print edition is unabridged.
In other aspects, this book may vary
from the original edition.
Printed in the United States of America
on permanent paper sourced using
environmentally responsible foresting methods.
Set in 16-point Times New Roman type.

ISBN: 979-8-89164-472-4

The Library of Congress has cataloged this record
under Library of Congress Control Number: 2024949802

*To my father—whose wisdom and guidance
has served me well over the years.
I thank you, and I love you.*

A Message in Poison

I'm okay with death. In some ways, it brings peace and quiet. There's little conflict once you cross the River Styx and leave the Earth behind. Cool waters separate the living from the dead, yet I dare not dip my hand in this mythical body and bargain for life renewed. I only ask that a small token be paid to Charon to ferry my soul to its final resting place and that I may be forgiven for my past sins.

CHAPTER 1

The Republic of Jokovikstan

Beibut Khan, President of Jokovikstan, sat by the fire, his book in his lap and his wolfhound by his feet. His much younger wife was spending the weekend with her sister, giving him precious alone time for rest and recuperation while he remained under the watchful eye of his house staff. Only a hundred pages into *The World of Economics and Power*, he was finally getting to the part of the book that underscored the benefits of democracy. Using diplomatic connections, his staff had obtained an advanced reading copy written by the well-regarded American authority on political economy. In Jokovikstan, new ideas had often been blocked before they could grow wings, an unfortunate side effect of being caught in the middle of Russia and China's challenges to the small nation's sovereignty. Yet the newly-minted country had already begun to orchestrate the unwind from its greedy neighbors, and banked on selling the valuable precious ores deep within its mountains on the global market. From a monetary standpoint, Jokovikstan was in an excellent position to divest and stand on its own two feet.

After reading through chapter 13, the head of

state began to feel warm and nauseous. The heat now creeping throughout his body propelled him to push the chintz-cushioned chair away from the fire, disturbing his dog from her coiled position. He regretted having had the extra portion of *solyanka* and wondered if that was the cause of the impending explosion in his belly. A favorite dish, filled with a variety of meats, cabbage, potatoes, onions, and carrots, he thought the final addition of the fish heads in the broth was what made his stomach spin. The president rose from his chair, grabbed hold of the arms to steady his balance, and made his way to the bathroom, where he vomited his entire dinner. His heart was racing. *Not just soup. It must be the antibiotic,* he thought, *that is making me sick.* The urge to move his bowels overcame him, and he quickly turned to sit on the toilet, clutching his stomach as he moaned in pain. It had to be the antibiotics. Only two days ago, he had had a minor medical procedure without any complications. Feeling exposed and vulnerable, he noticed the bruising in his groin and recoiled at its ever-growing spread. Earlier consultations with both his personal physician and the local surgeon had reassured him that the procedure would be appropriate and safe for a man of his advanced age. The nurse had taken his temperature only this morning, said it was normal, and that he looked well.

President Khan crawled out of the bathroom,

desperate to reach the buzzer on his nightstand. Only inches away from the edge of his bed, his heart stopped. A soft thud rattled the carpet, and the wolfhound suddenly stood up and whined. She sniffed her master, pawed at his body, and finally settled with her head resting on the back of his thighs. Early the next morning, the housekeeper knocked, then opened the bedroom door. The president's faithful pet greeted her with a wagging tail and warm nose. Her master, however, was dead.

Chapter 2

Boston

I've done some terrible things in my life. Big lies splash in my wake and follow me until the water creeps into my lungs. I've murdered many people who deserved to die. I take the phrase "pick your poison" literally. My arsenal of natural toxins and poisons hidden deep within a freezer provide enough variety to mimic natural death. The cool salt air at my seaside cottage coaxes plants in my poisonous garden to yield the natural killers that I need. And I have collaborators around the world who can provide for me what my garden cannot.

Yes, it's true that I've spent much of my life taking care of patients as a physician, and I've taught a generation of medical students. But it was this very expertise in toxicology that captured the attention of the U.S. government. They seduced me and then orchestrated a transformation from consultant to assassin. Some say it's my jewel-green eyes, raven-colored hair, and even my stiletto heels that tend to disarm my victims. They are blinded to the truth. With eyes closed to the Hippocratic Oath, I travel the world, eliminating terrorists and traitors with poison, stealth in a bottle, in the name of preventing mass destruction on a global scale. Our small covert counter-terrorism team weeds out threats at home and abroad—sanctioned killing, the price of doing business. I'm told that "the good of the many outweighs the good of the one." It's become my guiding mantra, allowing me to rationalize this dual existence.

I hide my secret life beneath the cloak of justice, and I've discovered that others do, too. So I ask you if you're sure you know the truth about those around you. This last year of my life has been fraught with revelations that I didn't see coming. For more than twenty years, I thought my baby, my little girl, had died in the Colombian jungle. Not only did I learn that she's alive, but I discovered that she's attending the same medical school where I have my academic appointment—a life-changing disclosure. I tremble when I think that we may have brushed by each other not only at the university, but in my fleeting past. I look back and see momentary images of familiarity etched in my mind. Was my beautiful Rose right in front of me while I wore blinders of guilt and despair?

JP, my lover, and partner in our covert government band, grasps my turmoil. Desperate to soothe my soul, he promises that life's twists and turns can only make us more resilient and resolute. Facing the wind, my body stands tall and hard like a tree firmly rooted in the ground. Having no support on its own, a vine uses its tendrils to clutch to the broad trunk. My stories are like this vine, ever climbing, ever strangling—a complicated life that requires both intelligence and strength.

There's a knock at my office door. "Come in," I say. It's my fellow, Dr. Kelley. He's almost finished with his training as a toxicologist/pathologist, and when he does, I'd love to see him on staff here in Boston.

"Hey, Dr. Robinson, good to see you."

He's looking polished today—crisp white lab coat, his dark hair newly clipped close at the sides, and I can see he's looking at my shoes. It's become our little game. I wait for the comment.

"What shoes are you wearing today? Are those the black snakeskins? They're your favorites, right?" he asks, trying to peek around my desk.

"Yes, Kelley," I tell him. "So, what's our case for the day?"

"Okay. A 40-year-old woman was brought into the ED last night with convulsions and renal failure. She and her husband hosted a party at their house on Saturday night. She wasn't feeling well after the party, you know, she had nausea, vomiting, and she went to bed early with abdominal pain. Her daughter noticed her mother having a convulsion on Sunday and called 9-1-1. We ran a general tox screen, and it was negative."

"What were the results of the other lab tests?"

"Came in with a pH of 6.67, creatinine was 2.5 mg/dL. She also had cardiac dysrhythmias noted on her ECG."

"Wow, that's a very low pH, and clearly, she's in renal failure given the high creatinine. What was the serum osmolality?" I ask Kelley, knowing that there must be an osmotically active substance in the blood that we haven't measured that may be causing her symptoms.

"Yeah, we measured that. It was 437 mOsm/L, so you're right. I asked the lab to run an expanded volatile screen," Kelley says, clearly in command of the case.

"Great. If the ethanol was negative, my guess is our patient may have ingested one of the other toxic alcohols like methanol or ethylene glycol. Please, let me know when the results are in."

"Will do, doc," Kelley says, then adds, "Oh, I forgot to tell you, that first-year medical student is dropping by sometime in the next week or two. I'm hoping you'll have a chance to meet with her."

"Thanks for the update, Kelley. Keep me posted."

The medical student that Kelley is referring to is Rose Moreau. Yes, *that* Rose Moreau. My daughter—and the adopted daughter of Adrienne Moreau, my lover's first cousin. It's complicated. JP's cousin, Adrienne, raised Rose when, at only three, we were separated during the massacre of a research party I was part of in Colombia. At the time, I didn't know that Rose was brought back to the coffee plantation where Adrienne lived. I lost my memory, and my little girl, and didn't find out she was alive until recently. Nature has a way of fooling your brain when the facts don't add up, and you only see a fraction of life, like seeing the world through a prism. All the spectrum's bright colors dazzle you; maybe you only focus on one particular wavelength and therefore miss the fact that together, the colors form a single beam of white light illuminating a path forward.

I haven't felt the same since I returned from France a few months ago. Jean Paul and I took a short holiday after our mission in Asia. We were back and forth between Hong Kong and South Korea more times than I care to remember. Using a novel toxin, I eliminated a missile scientist from China whose design would have been a game-changer on how rockets could fly across continents, posing a threat to world peace. Oh, and I also killed a traitor, Aaron Stone, who happened to be someone I knew back in my college days. That was self-defense, but he was still a threat to our country. By the time I got to France, any hidden emotion left in my body had dissolved. I need time to recover from these missions of death, even if they do hide under the umbrella of righteousness.

The holiday in Reims lulled me into a false sense of normalcy—spectacular, romantic, even relaxing—until JP and I visited the Moreau Winery, his childhood home. There it became evident to JP that my Rose had thrived and was attending medical school in Boston. Breaking that news to me was probably one of the most difficult things he's had to do in our relationship. I was devastated, and the hardest part for me is keeping my promise that I will not tell Rose she is my biological daughter. It's for her own protection. No one likes collateral damage. I was asked to live with this promise and carry on. I thought I could handle it, but the more time I've had to think, the angrier I've become. Knowing that the Agency played at least some role in the cover-up of the massacre makes me furious. At the moment, JP and I aren't talking. There's been no communication between us since we said some things that we probably should have kept to ourselves.

I hear a knock on my office door. It's either Kelley or my assistant, Lisa. "Come on in," I say.

"Hi, Dr. Lily," Lisa says, "I'm dumping a whole lot of paperwork on your desk that needs your review. Some of it is from the medical school and some from the hospital. I'll leave it to you to sort out."

Lisa is very efficient and runs the office without question. Today, her cobalt-blue dress contrasts nicely with her dark hair, and I can see that her lips are pursed together, letting me know that she wants me to get this all done, and soon. It's true, I have been lax on getting down to the busywork, but the pull on the other side of the looking glass is just too strong. I concede to Lisa's stern voice.

"Thank you, Lisa. I promise I'll have all of these completed by the end of the week." I plead silently with her dark eyes to cut me a little slack. She abruptly turns, a smile on her face, and leaves the office.

Since I've returned, I never did get a one-on-one with Rose because the day she stopped by my office, the French hospital notified her that Adrienne, who had been in a coma, had regained consciousness. After that, Rose left for Reims to be with her mother, taking a leave of absence from medical school. According to Kelley, she should be returning within the next few weeks. It scares me when I think of being alone with her. I must guard against the truth, hide behind the mask, for fear that my danger could become her danger.

Another knock at the door. I probably should leave it wide open at this point. "Come on in," I say, but the door is already ajar, and it's Kelley, no doubt with news on our patient.

"Hey, Dr. Robinson. We got the results back on the woman with the toxic ingestion. It was ethylene glycol. Old-fashioned antifreeze. And unfortunately, she didn't make it. pH was too low; we found ethylene glycol crystals in her urine, too, and the ME has accepted the case. The DA's been alerted, and now he wants to talk with you."

"Thanks, Kelley. I'm sorry to hear that. Do we know what happened?"

"From what I understand, it looks like the husband added the ethylene glycol to her Midori Sours. That's a liquor that has the same greenish coloring as EG. And since EG has a sweet taste, our poor patient didn't realize her drink was poisoned."

"Interesting. Ethanol used to be the antidote for ethylene glycol and methanol poisoning since the same enzymes metabolize all three compounds. Most people don't realize that it's the metabolites of these alcohols that are toxic, not the primary compound. Methanol, or wood alcohol, is also found in windshield wiper fluid and is metabolized to formaldehyde and formic acid, while ethylene glycol is metabolized to oxalic acid, among others. The body can't handle all those acids, and the pH just drops." I stop after giving my short lecture.

"According to the police, who got this story from the daughter, the husband was having an affair with his wife's best friend. The party served as an innocent backdrop for the poisoning. Several of the couple's friends attended that evening, too. Damn," Kelley says with emphasis while he rearranges his ID badge hanging on the lanyard around his neck. I see the sadness in his eyes. None of us like to lose a patient.

"As you already know, Kelley, EG and methanol poisoning cases can occur any time of the year but tend to increase during the colder months. It's fairly common and easy enough to pick up through lab testing once the patient presents to the ED. It's a shame she didn't get to the hospital sooner. But then her husband would've had to take her, and he was in no rush." I shake my head. "I'll give the DA a call tomorrow. Anything else pending?"

"Just one case. One of our pathologists just finished an autopsy on a man who died yesterday. When they opened up his skull to expose the brain, the brain tissue was a greenish color. They asked me about it."

My secure phone is buzzing in my bag. It feels too soon to hear from the Agency after my last mission, but it must be important, or they wouldn't be contacting me. I look up at Kelley, who is poised and alert.

"Sorry, Kelley, will you please excuse me? I need to take this call." Kelley nods, lets himself out, and I answer the phone with pending anxiety. It's Chad, my case officer.

"Hi, Chad. What's going on?"

"Hello, Dr. Robinson. I'm sure you're surprised

to hear from me, but I need to speak with you right away. It's important." His voice sounds serious, not casual. I feel a few thumps in my chest.

"I've got a minute right now, between cases, if you'd like to chat," I say.

"No, not over the phone. In person. I can come over to the hospital this evening."

"Sure, I'll be in my office. Lisa will be gone, but I'll leave word at the check-in window so they can buzz you in. My door will be open; it's been that way all day," I say and hang up, feeling ever so queasy.

And so it begins. With a deep breath and a steady hand, I reach for the antacids sequestered in the cabinet drawer and feel myself carried away by the murky river of fate.

Chapter 3

Boston

The sun has set, and there is creeping darkness out my office window, disappearing red clouds, and a moon struggling to get up out of bed. I'm waiting for Chad. I remember when Chad first came to me. He had such a hard act to follow.

It had all begun with Pixie Dust. She had a pink streak in her hair, and that's how she got her nickname. I worked with her for almost ten years. Those were fresh years for me at the Agency. Sometimes she'd arrive at my office with flowers, and we'd enjoy them while we discussed the next assignment. Pixie had a vibrant laugh, sparkly eyes, and a keen mind—always looking for clues from the world of academic toxicology to understand what she and others in the organization heard as background terrorist chatter on the internet. The potential for chemical warfare exists now, as it did then.

I see I have a text from Chad. He's here.

"Knock, knock," he says, poking his head through my office door first, then pushing it open.

"Come on in, Chad."

He stands in the doorway, and I see him take

in every aspect of the room. He's like a cat—scanning systematically for anything new, noting any item out of place, missing, or disturbed in one way or another. When he feels comfortable, he enters the office and takes his usual seat.

"How are you, Dr. Robinson?" he asks. His voice is quiet.

I smile before I answer, giving him the once over, too. His medium frame fills out the shoulders of his sports coat, with a blue striped tie bold against his white shirt. Tonight he's wearing his khaki pants. The last of his remaining hair struggles to cover as much of his scalp as possible. I remember when he had much more of it, but then age and stress have taken their trophy over time.

"I'm fine, Chad, thank you. I was reminiscing about Pixie Dust right before you got here," I tell him. He had big shoes to fill after her death, but Chad and I have managed to forge a relationship for all the years that followed.

"Wow, Pixie. She was the best."

He pauses, and I can see that it's hard for him to continue, so I change the subject, for now.

"So, Chad. What's going on? Why the visit? It's not been that long since I got back from Asia. Any updates there, by the way?"

"Well, Robinson, let's leave that for the time being. I have something else for you to consider," he says, getting ready to tee up news that will no doubt prompt me to reach for another round of antacids. "You know, of course, that one of our senior senators recently passed away."

"Yes, so very sad. Senator Lawrence Steinman was a driving member of Congress. Very active in foreign relations. I heard that he died at home. What's going on, Chad?"

"Robinson, he was the Chair of one of the Foreign Relations subcommittees. There was no autopsy after he passed, although immediate family wanted one. Apparently, some government sources pushed the widow hard to have him cremated. Thankfully, she balked at the idea and had him interred with the rest of the family. He was laid to rest in a mausoleum just outside of D.C. only last night."

My eyebrows lift within my forehead. "Where'd you get that info about the autopsy?"

"After the senator was placed in the mausoleum, I was approached discretely by one of the staffers who worked directly with Steinman. She helped the widow make the final arrangements."

"Okay. So, Steinman was what, seventy-nine, or close to that? I thought I heard on the news that he had a cardiac procedure. They didn't specify. Was it a bypass or valve procedure?"

I can see Chad thinking about how he wants to phrase his next sentence. He's looking down at my desk, his forefinger trying to etch a design on the surface.

"That's right, Robinson. He had an aortic valve replaced. After he returned home, he was found dead in his bed the following morning by his housekeeper. His wife was asleep in another room. She reported that the senator appeared well the evening before, although he did complain about being nauseous. She brought him a bowl of chicken broth and dry crackers for dinner and didn't think any more about it. Both the wife and the senator attributed his queasiness to the antibiotics he had been taking after his procedure. And later, she did check with his doctor and confirmed that the nausea was most likely due to the medication. There was no need to worry."

"But there was a need to worry, or you wouldn't be here. Right, Chad?"

I can see his eyes now—hazel-colored irises circle his ever-widening pupils. Tension permeates the space between us, and I wait.

"It's possible he may have been poisoned," Chad says quietly and then stops.

This is not what I expected. Why would someone poison a senior member of the Senate? After slipping back into my high heels, I rise from my chair and come out from behind the table I use for a desk. Even though it's the end of the day, I now have renewed energy as my mind races. I can feel my heart pumping, too.

"Chad, what makes you think this was poisoning? It could've been natural causes even without the medical intervention. You know, true, true, unrelated, as we say in medicine," I explain.

In medicine, it's possible to have two true statements about a patient's condition, and yet they can be unrelated. Senator Steinman had a narrowed aortic valve, and he died in the middle of the night. Both are true but not necessarily related. I walk to one of the bookcases skirting the office perimeter and pick out a cardiology book while waiting for Chad's response.

"Why do I suspect foul play? This young staffer was scared, Robinson. She told me that the senator was very upset about a week before he had scheduled his medical procedure. He didn't say what, but he revealed to her that something big was about to explode. He wanted a little more time before he shared the details with her. Wanted to get his procedure over with so he could have his full attention on the issue."

"I'll buy that. So, the staffer thinks he might have been murdered to shut him up. But why poison?"

"Look, you know better than anyone. If we don't find bullet holes in the body or a knife in the back, and the guy's dead in his bed, isn't poison a likely suspect?" Chad squirms in the chair.

"Yes, of course. I suppose he could've been poisoned sometime after his medical procedure, so you'll need to find out who had access to the senator during his recovery. But let's just hope it was natural causes and not murder."

"Right, doctor. We're going to exhume the body and would like you to work with our forensic team. You know, put on your poison hat and take a fresh look at the case. I'll get you in touch with the lead on this. He's an independent contractor. Now remember, all these people are not aware of what we do or what you do for us. They're not assassins."

Wow. That stings. Of course, I get it, but it always hurts when it's said out loud.

"Yes, yes, Chad. I get it. Should I expect JP to contact me?" I'm still angry with him.

"Actually, no. He's overseas working on another case at the moment. So, I'll make arrangements for you to come down to D.C. and meet with the team I'm putting together. I've contacted a forensic pathologist who will be heading up the exhumation and conducting the autopsy. We want you to be present in the room when the body's opened. You can slide up to the table if you desire, that's up to you, but nothing should happen in that autopsy suite without your eyes on it. The senator deserves as much."

Chad finishes telling me what he needs to. He gets up without a sound, just a nod of the head, and walks out the door. He knows his way back to civilization. I'm now left to ponder. First, I want to review the various approaches for the repair of the aortic valve. I open up the cardiology text and study the anatomy of the heart. For an aortic valve replacement, there are several options. The most difficult for the patient is open-heart surgery. Here the chest is literally opened to expose the heart. Then the heart is stopped allowing the surgeon to remove the damaged valve and sew the new one in place. The downside to this type of surgery is the long recovery time. In a less invasive alternative, a smaller incision is made into the chest, and the surgery is conducted with the help of a robotic instrument—imagine the surgeon sitting at a console using a joystick to control a video game, only in this case, to perform the surgery. Lastly, in the least invasive procedure, a **T**ranscatheter **A**ortic **V**alve **R**eplacement, or TAVR, the interventional cardiologist can place a valve into the heart by threading a catheter through a large blood vessel. The catheter contains a collapsed mesh frame "valve" wrapped with either pig or cow tissue. The replacement valve is superimposed over the existing valve and functions immediately after it expands in place. Patients have a much shorter recovery time because they haven't had their chest cracked open. Given the time frame that Chad mentioned, I'm guessing this is the procedure Senator Steinman had, but I'll have to confirm.

    Tomorrow, I'll plead with Lisa to rearrange

my calendar, and I'll soften the blow with an arrangement of flowers. Ah, Pixie Dust. Then there's the creation of the new lie to explain the upcoming disappearance—much more challenging than buying flowers. I'll also tell Kelley that I'll be gone again—in radio contact only, so to speak. But he should be leaving the nest soon anyway. He's done his time, has turned into a competent toxicologist, and I would like to see him spread his wings and fly. We have one outstanding case to finalize before I go to Washington. What happened to the man with the pistachio-colored brain?

CHAPTER 4

Washington, D.C.

Logan Pelletier turned to the woman in bed next to him and scooped her up in his arms. There was still enough time for one more round of lovemaking before he got into his scrubs. The petite blond could feel the weight of his body on hers as she wrapped her legs tightly around his waist. The foreplay from the night before had been so deft that just the thought of it carried her into the morning. Their sweaty climax felt explosive, and after, the doctor held her in his arms, stroking her hair and leaving her eyelash kisses in his wake. The woman had never imagined that the man lying next to her could fulfill all her wishes. He checked every box: tall, dark hair, green eyes, and just a hint of a beard. She watched her date exit from the bed and took him all in—his sculpted rear and glorious six-pack mesmerized her. Logan was smart, too. A graduate of all the best universities and top-notch residency and fellowship programs that New York and Boston had to offer.

"Hey, I'm going to take a quick shower, and then I have to get to work," he said as he pulled his hair into a short ponytail. "You're welcome to stay awhile. No rush to get out of bed." He stopped for a moment, looked around the room, and then started speaking again. "Would you mind putting the champagne glasses and dishes in the dishwasher if you get a chance? I'll take care of the rest of the mess when I get home tonight."

He smiled at his date and watched her head fall back on the pillow. She returned his smile with a nod and pulled the covers up to her chin. Logan had enjoyed her company but was not interested in pursuing a relationship.

At the office, the morning meeting wrapped up a little earlier than expected. Fifteen dead bodies, less than the usual daily quota, were on the autopsy list for the day—homicides, suicides, and any suspicious deaths that might require forensic intervention. The cases had been thoroughly discussed and assigned. All would have toxicology testing. Logan Pelletier reviewed the contents of his clipboard and noted that he was expected at the cemetery for an exhumation later this morning. This was not unusual, as he was frequently consulted in those cases where the cause and manner of death were contested. However, the clipboard did not contain any information about a second exhumation that was to happen later that night, under cover of darkness, to reduce any possibility of media attention. For Logan, the intrigue was palpable.

After he finished the autopsy of the decomposed "floater," he felt particularly ripe and sought an additional shower before leaving the premises. He considered changing back into his street clothes but chose instead to don a fresh pair of scrubs. For the first exhumation of the day, arrangements had been made with a specific mortuary to obtain the casket. Barriers would be set around the grave site to ensure privacy for the deceased and reduce intrusion on others tending to their loved ones in the cemetery. The mortuary employees would be wearing the necessary personal protective equipment (PPE), so Logan didn't see the need for anything more than scrubs. He would observe from a distance.

Dr. Pelletier exited the building and headed to the adjacent garage to get the car. Before hopping in, he walked around the vehicle to make sure there were no dents or scratches. The new sports car had been a fortieth birthday present to himself, and he admitted to fully embracing his midlife crisis. And the money had never been a consideration. Satisfied that the red paint was intact, he started the engine, listened to the roar, and drove down the twisting ramp to the exit. He swiped his key card, waited for the gate to rise, and hit the gas. On the way out, he punched the button to retract the convertible hardtop so he could let the full heat of the sun fill the cockpit.

It was only a short drive to the cemetery, but he would purposefully take the back roads that would lead him to the countryside, even though it would take longer to reach the graveyard. The rich green scenery dotted with red, purple, and yellow flowers marked the way as he shifted through each challenging turn, making the most of his break in the day.

Logan Pelletier was well respected in the field for his independent thinking, unbiased approach, and his inability to be corrupted by the dollar. His father made his billions with hedge fund investments and could afford to send his sons to the best Ivy-League universities knowing each son had the academic fortitude to gain entry without a monetary donation. The senior Pelletier hoped that both sons would join him in business, but only Logan's older brother took that opportunity. As the younger sibling, Logan chose an independent path. Though his father disapproved of his son's chosen profession—why would anyone want to dissect dead bodies, he had asked—he left his son a sizable trust fund and the gift of independent wealth. The billionaire father appreciated Logan's exceptional mind and understood his youngest liked getting his hands dirty. Choosing to use his money in a venture that he thought would make a difference, Logan Pelletier opened an independent autopsy service that provided second opinions, unearthed what others missed, and championed those that could not speak for themselves.

When he reached the cemetery, Logan pulled his car in as close as possible to the grave site. He could already see that the backhoe had finished clearing away the topsoil and was poised to unearth the casket. With a disinterment, the preservation of the body—or how much decomposition had already taken place—could make the subsequent exhumation autopsy more or less difficult. Coffins made of metal—either bronze, copper, or steel—or grave sites that had a liner, or better yet, consisted of a concrete vault, went a long way in keeping the corpse intact. While those measures were expensive options, they were necessary to block the environment from creeping into the final resting place. Logan hoped for the best.

With the white tent now surrounding the open grave, Dr. Pelletier could see that the coffin was indeed metal and that there had been a grave liner present. He sighed, knowing that there was a better chance that the body would be undamaged by intruding soil or water. The funeral director noticed Dr. Pelletier and came over to greet him.

"Hi, doctor. I see we have another case going to your shop. Been quite a few these last couple of months. Anything special going on?" the funeral director asked.

"No, Frank, just the usual. This one skipped

the ME's scrutiny after the toxicology results indicated a drug overdose. However, the family requested a second look, given some suspicious behavior on the part of the boyfriend."

"All right. We won't open the casket until we get back to your place. Do you have any additional instructions for us?" he asked. His men were already loading the coffin into the hearse.

"Thanks, Frank. No, I'll just meet you back at the morgue," Logan said. He turned and headed for his car, left baking in the sun, with the others parked nearby in neat rows.

On the way back to the lot, he noticed a woman with raven-colored hair standing at a headstone near a grove of trees. She wore a black skirt with a peplum suit jacket buttoned neatly at the waist and a pair of stilettos. The silhouette of the shoes captured Logan's imagination, and he couldn't help but wonder who she was and why she was there. Rather than intrude on her solitary reflection, he passed her by, entered his vehicle, and created a story around the mysterious woman in black to keep him entertained on the drive back to the morgue. Fantasy filled his mind as he sped around the curves, downshifting only—no brakes—until he finally gave up her image and focused on the upcoming autopsy that was waiting for him.

Once back at the office, Dr. Pelletier first reviewed the paperwork associated with the case. A thorough investigation of the deceased's medical history, occupation, hobbies, and personal associations allowed the forensic pathologist to logically approach the autopsy. Logan combed through the medical record reviewing the toxicology results obtained during the initial postmortem examination. The cursory autopsy suggested a drug overdose. The death certificate listed intoxication with amitriptyline, an antidepressant, as the cause of death, and the manner of death was recorded as accidental. Dr. Pelletier was skeptical. He noted that the autopsy report stated that the postmortem blood used for the analysis had been collected from the heart and not from a peripheral vessel like the femoral artery. A knock at the door interrupted his thought.

"Yep," Logan said. It was his junior associate who had been prepping for the autopsy.

"Are you all set?" he asked. "The body's on the table, and we're just waiting for you. Where you going with this, man?" The associate was already dressed in fresh scrubs and would don the rest of the PPE once he got into the autopsy suite.

"Yeah, just finished looking over the material. I'm planning on a detailed neck dissection to look for a hyoid bone fracture, and I want to take a piece of the right lobe of the liver for tox. The liver might be a long shot given the embalming."

"I see where you're headed. You think this is

a strangulation that was overlooked. During the initial autopsy, they just assumed the elevated amitriptyline concentration indicated overdose when it was just an issue of postmortem redistribution."

"That's it. The detectives told me that the boyfriend liked rough sex—a little erotic asphyxia, but I think it was probably more. Had his hands around her throat so she would pass out, heightening the sexual buzz, but surprise, she never regained consciousness. If we can coax anything out of that liver, my guess is that we'll find a therapeutic ratio of antidepressant to its metabolite that is consistent with her prescribed dosing."

Both forensic pathologists knew that toxicology results obtained from heart blood could show deceptively elevated concentrations of some drugs more than others because, after death, drugs move down a concentration gradient as the body pH falls. That is, highly fat-soluble drugs move from the body's lipid stores and into the heart and great vessels—postmortem redistribution. When this occurs, the drug concentration found in heart blood reflects a greater amount of medication than was actually present in the systemic circulation at the time of death.

Logan and his colleague finished the autopsy and exited the stark white room, leaving the body on a cold stainless steel table.

"Looks like you called that right," his associate said, taking off his mask and PPE in the anteroom.

"Yeah, those bones in her neck spoke to us. The hyoid bone was fractured. I think everyone was distracted by the boyfriend's admission to liking erotic-asphyxia, a lack of external bruising around the neck, and by the original tox concentration of the antidepressant, which I'm sure will prove to be a deceptively high number. Turns out, the detectives later learned that she was sleeping with the boyfriend's best bud. Jealousy is always the dark killer in the room. Apparently, lover boy and our dead young lady argued, and his anger, still brewing, boiled over during make-up sex." Logan tossed his PPE in the biohazard bin and headed for the shower. It was his third one of the day.

Earlier in the week, a government official had called Logan requesting a second opinion autopsy. They wouldn't provide him with the deceased's name or any circumstances surrounding the death; however, the forensic pathologist was assured that the information would be available at a later time. The mystery piqued Logan's curiosity. Expectations were clearly outlined during the call: the autopsy was to be a low profile engagement— just a few men who would obtain the casket and bring it directly to Logan's building. Most importantly, it needed to be thorough yet nearly invisible. They also let him know that they would be sending another pathologist to work with him on the case. While Logan preferred working exclusively with his team, he was open to having another physician join him. The only other information he obtained was that the casket would be retrieved from a mausoleum and not a grave site. This would certainly make things easier.

Finally, out of scrubs, Dr. Pelletier dressed in a bright blue suit, a white button-down shirt and slipped into a pair of brown loafers without socks. He checked the mirror in his office bathroom and approved of his short ponytail curled into a bun and the small amount of beard stubble that remained after a cursory shave. He felt presentable for his government meeting. During the second drive of the day to the cemetery, Logan gunned the engine harder as the empty roads beckoned him. The hardtop remained retracted, so now starlight, rather than sunlight, could filter down from above. Cool night air tugged at his hair but without success.

Logan let his mind drift. He thought about the previous night's tryst, their marathon sex, and wondered if he would have a kitchen to clean up once he returned to his penthouse. It was unlikely that his date had rinsed the champagne glasses and plates from their dinner and put them in the dishwasher before she let herself out. Leaving reality behind, he turned on the radio, and guided by the loud music, fantasized about the woman he saw near the headstone during his earlier trip to the cemetery. Always one to engage in "what ifs," he created a story, the central character, his lady in black. The fantasy played in his brain like a streaming video, the soundtrack booming through his car's speakers, stoking his imagination. While Dr. Logan Pelletier could have almost any woman he wanted, he chose no one. He embraced his bachelorhood and had shunned committed relationships. With money and good looks, he only lacked the kind of power his father had. And yet, Dr. Pelletier wouldn't want to change a thing.

When he reached the cemetery, he parked where the official said to meet. He closed the hardtop, locked his car, and stood by the driver's side door, and waited. Within ten minutes, two large dark SUVs with tinted windows and a hearse pulled up. A middle-aged man with wisps of brown hair emerged from one of the SUVs and introduced himself.

"Dr. Pelletier? I'm Chad Jones, USG. Thank you for meeting us under rather mysterious circumstances."

"Mr. Jones. The pleasure's all mine. What's going on? What's this about?" Logan said, extending his hand for a firm shake.

"Um, why don't you get into the vehicle so

we can speak privately," Chad said, opening the back door so both of them could slide in. "Look, sorry for all the cloak and dagger stuff, but we need you to understand that no one can know about this meeting, the autopsy, or anything else I'm about to say. I'm to be your only contact. Is that understood?" Chad said, his lips pursed and the fold between his eyebrows evident.

"Sure, I get it. So, what are you, FBI or CIA?" Logan said, his mind now filled with curiosity over all the intrigue.

"Neither, really, but that's not the point. Look, Dr. Pelletier, as you know, Senator Lawrence Steinman was found dead in his bed, and we have reason to believe he was murdered. This information cannot become public knowledge, not even that it's suspected. If it's true, there's no telling who may be involved."

Logan felt his jaw drop. A short puff of breath fell out of his mouth. He was aware of the senator's passing and respected him as a senior member of Congress.

"Dr. Pelletier, I can see the shock on your face. Yes, it would be hard to believe if it were true. That's why I brought in my own team. However, your isolated facility could provide the required discretion, and we also know you to be an incorruptible front-runner in your field of forensics."

"I'm flattered," Logan said, still surprised. He turned away from the agent to catch his breath and glanced through the tinted window. The silhouette of the woman he had seen earlier in the day appeared in the distance. It was unmistakable. He recognized the peplum suit jacket and high heels in the moonlight.

"Dr. Pelletier, is everything all right? I lost you there for a second," Chad said.

"Oh no, sorry. No, please go ahead," Logan answered, still staring out the window.

"I want to introduce you to the other physician that we've asked to help. Dr. Robinson has some unique attributes, by training a toxicologist, and you know, one of those academic types. Scary smart, and knows poisons like nobody's business," Chad said with a slight laugh to lighten the tension.

"Sure, sure," Logan said, still distracted. "When can I meet with this pathologist?"

"Right now, as a matter of fact."

Chad got out his phone, sent a text, and waited. A few seconds later, the rear door of the car opened, and the woman in the black peplum suit jacket and pencil skirt slid in next to Logan, her stilettos careful not to step on his smooth brown loafers.

Chad leaned around Logan so he could address both of them. "Dr. Pelletier, I'd like to introduce you to Dr. Lily Robinson."

Green eyes and a simple smile greeted Logan while he sat in silence. He rewound his fantasy video in his mind, edited the story, and played it from the beginning.

CHAPTER 5

France

Rose had shed tears of joy and relief when she got the call that her mother had opened her eyes and come out of her coma. Arrangements were made to take a leave of absence from medical school and fly to Reims as soon as possible. All the interruptions meant that there would have to be a fresh start again next year, but she hoped that on her return to Boston, she could work in the lab with Dr. Kelley until she could resume her medical studies.

    The push-pull of her mother's condition had left Rose anxious and unsteady, and the guilt over having read her mother's letter prematurely lingered. Adrienne had been clear about that. The note to her daughter was only to be read after her death. Nevertheless, in an impulsive gesture while in the loneliness of her Boston apartment, Rose chose to study the missive stashed in her top dresser drawer. Shock ensued when she learned that Adrienne had been raped and Bella had been born as a result. Rose missed her sister and wished that Bella was still alive to help with the care of their mother. Sadness washed over her whenever she thought about Bella and the day they both got their tattoos. The vision of the kidnapping, Bella being dragged by her beautiful golden hair, was one that Rose would never forget. Now another tragedy enveloped Rose's life.

When Rose first returned to France, her initial visits to the rehabilitation hospital were both discouraging and rewarding. She was thrilled her mother had awakened against all odds only to find that Adrienne had no recollection of her name and her family, much less of her daughter. Initially, Adrienne was able to follow commands, but speaking was challenging. Confusion and disorientation prevailed, and Adrienne did not remember Rose and others around her, sometimes from day to day. Her mother's lack of memory was the most distressing of all, and Rose cried when she left Adrienne only to be later comforted by the village priest, Père Berger. She had never felt so alone.

The doctors explained that brain injuries were sometimes unpredictable and that Rose should not give up hope. Though Adrienne couldn't recall her devoted daughter, Rose still talked with her mother every day, retelling their life together on the coffee farm and Rose's own head injury during her horseback riding accident while attending a boarding school in Massachusetts.

"Mother, Père Berger says it was God's plan that you survived the car accident while driving back to Reims. We know you were disappointed that you couldn't find any of your Moreau relatives in Chalandry. I tried too. It seems that once your cousin Jean Paul emigrated to the United States, he disappeared," she said, letting out a big sigh and rubbing her mother's arm to comfort her.

Some days her mother would stare into the distance as if she were trying hard to remember something, while at other times, she would close her eyes and appear to doze off. Adrienne's doctors described how her sleep continued to be disrupted and how sudden noises could also startle her, and yet, they reassured Rose that her mother's brain, a remarkable plastic organ, continued to heal. Although a struggle, they were confident that in time Adrienne could regain much of her function. Patience was a virtue.

The doctors expected that Adrienne would need extensive rehabilitation. Some of this would occur at such a facility, and some of the retraining of Adrienne's brain could take place at home under medical supervision. Rose worked with the hospital caseworkers to make the arrangements for her mother's future care and also to hire a home health aide for when she would transition to home. Père Berger, the priest who had helped Rose when she first learned of her mother's car accident, continued to be involved in Rose's life and had organized some of the women from the parish to provide meals and comfort for the small Moreau family when the time came. Their kindness was overwhelming, and with gratitude, Rose accepted all they had to give.

When Rose wasn't at the rehab facility, she spent time at the Moreau estate with the men and women who worked in the vineyard and at the winery's business office. The property was one of the most beautiful estates in Reims, and the champagne from the vineyard was served at the finest restaurants and hotels in France. The imposing stone main house, its Gothic architecture a reminder of another era, was surrounded by outbuildings and acres of grapevines. The weather was on the verge of change—the anticipation of warm air chasing the cold out of the drafty house and encouraging the vines to burst forth with spring greens and new fruits. To some extent, it reminded Rose of her days at the coffee plantation. How ironic that each of her domains involved raising crops that became either a sparkling celebratory delight or an earthy dark liquid to kick-start the day. The demand for both remained high.

Although Rose had elected to postpone her first year of medical school, she was not about to give up her studies. Each evening she reviewed some of the online textbooks that were required for her initial classes. Forever an optimist, despite her creeping depression, Rose embraced this as an opportunity to get a head start for the following year. Both her roommates kept her spot in the Commonwealth Avenue apartment back in Boston, and even though they would eventually move into the second year without Rose, they could still study together and maintain their friendships.

Rose continued to correspond with Dr. Kelley. Her laptop stayed open on the ornate French Mazarin desk in the spacious living room of the main house in anticipation of his emails. Sometimes she took his phone calls while curled up on the peach-colored velvet couch she had grown to love. Kelley had taken a great interest in her, and she felt comfortable with his guidance. Hoping to keep Rose interested in pathology and lab medicine, Kelley started sending her teaser cases for her to solve. The initial case involved a middle-aged woman who was poisoned by her husband with ethylene glycol. Kelley sent much of the laboratory data and many pictures of beautiful crystals in the shape of an envelope found in the patient's urine for Rose to review. After she studied the case, they both discussed the results via email. Rose was currently working on the findings of another one of Dr. Kelley's cases—that of a pistachio-colored brain from an autopsy. She was excited to engage in new disciplines and looked forward to seeing Kelley when she returned to Boston.

Visits to the rehabilitation center to check on Adrienne's progress were a daily obligation, and when not studying for her first-year medical school classes, Rose read the literature on traumatic brain injuries. She was curious about an article she came across titled, "The Epidemiology and Impact of Traumatic Brain Injury," which she found online. Rose had not been aware that traumatic brain injury was a huge public health issue and that about fifty-seven million people worldwide have been hospitalized with one or more of these injuries. These injuries resulted from motor vehicle crashes, falls, assaults, and events that occurred during military conflicts. The consequences of these injuries could be long-term physical, emotional, or cognitive problems.

Rose read the statistics with concern and worried that Adrienne would never fully recover her memory and that once again, she would find herself all alone in the proverbial jungle. On some days, the sadness was so overwhelming that her visits with Adrienne were cut short. Emotion flooded Rose's mind, and focusing on her school studies became a pacifier that diverted her attention. While the village priest spent as much time with Rose as he could, there were some problems beyond the scope of his prayers. He encouraged her to keep her faith and spend time with her friends back in Boston—even if only over the phone or through a video call. Rose's connections with Dr. Kelley via a video internet link became more frequent. Seeing his face made her happy, and she found their conversations began to extend beyond medicine. These sessions boosted Rose's spirits as the dutiful daughter cared for her mother, just as her mother had cared for Rose as a lost child.

Chapter 6

Washington, D.C.

"Nice to meet you, Dr. Pelletier," I say to the man sitting next to me in the back of Chad's car. Is it just my imagination, or is he actually staring at me? "Dr. Pelletier?"

"Yes, sorry. Nice to meet you, Lily Robinson, Dr. Robinson. Sorry, I was expecting a man," he says, clearly caught off guard.

"Oh? And why is that? Surely you must know many women physicians," I respond in a very cool tone, not sure I like where this is going.

"Can we please start over again? Hi, I'm Logan Pelletier, and I run an independent autopsy service, mostly second opinions, or when asked, I also help our colleagues who get backed up. I'm very pleased to meet you, Lily Robinson," he says, extending his hand.

"Nice to meet you too," I say with a firm shake, his hand surprisingly warm. I can see Chad rolling his eyes, praying this is not going to somehow derail.

"Well, great. Now that we've got the introductions out of the way," Chad says with an um, clearing his throat, and another eye-roll, "let's outline our objectives here. Senator Steinman was in moderately good health, only complaining of some fatigue several weeks ago." Chad pulls out a few notes and continues, "On further examination, his doctor recommended an echocardiogram and ECG, and after reviewing the results, they discovered he needed a new aortic valve. Then came the CT scan."

"Chad, thank you," I say and take over the medical speak, getting Chad off the hook. "The CT was to determine what his vasculature looked like. Since they were considering a TAVR, his doctors had to be sure he had adequate access." I can see the look of relief on Chad's face letting me know he appreciates my finishing his presentation.

"So, what's your concern?" Logan asks, finally looking at Chad and not me.

"Dr. Pelletier, we're looking for anything suspicious. I have credible information from someone who worked closely with Steinman that right before his death, he was working on something that would have been critical with respect to foreign affairs. I'm waiting for more details. This same person also helped Steinman's widow with the funeral arrangements and heard from her that she was pressured out of getting an autopsy, which she expressly wanted. I confirmed this with the widow, and I agreed to look into this as it did send up a few red flags."

Logan focuses on Chad's words before he speaks. "Please, call me Logan," he says, then adds, "I understand. You're considering that the senator's death could have been the result of foul play."

"Exactly, Logan," I say. "Hopefully, the post-mortem can pinpoint the cause of death. The senator's body was placed in a mausoleum only a few days ago, so no grave to dig up. And, his wife chose not to have the body embalmed."

"I see; it's good news and bad news. No embalming will mean more decomposition, but we may find some residual blood for analysis. And, there's a better chance that any evidence of murder will be intact."

"Right," Chad says. "What I want is for you to do the autopsy tonight when no one is around. I have a few assistants here with me to help transport the body back to your place, Dr. Pelletier, and Dr. Robinson will be with you in the autopsy suite."

"Dr. Robinson, can I call you Lily? Do you want to belly up to the table and cut with me?" he asks, looking directly into my eyes. I see a maybe smile on his face. And now that I look at him more closely, he's attractive—dark hair and light-colored eyes. I guess that's my type.

"Sure," I tell him. "Chad, the guys have already left with the casket. We should get going."

"I'll meet you there," Logan says. "I've got my car here." Logan opens the door, and sticking his head back in before he shuts it, he says, "See you there. Park on the street at the back. You can avoid the garage cameras that way. Send me a text when you arrive, and I'll let you in." He gives Chad his cell phone number and closes the car door.

"Well, Robinson. What do you think?" Chad asks.

"About what?"

"About Dr. Pelletier. He's smart, you know, and very good at what he does."

"Chad, that's true for all the people you engage. Yes?"

"Yes, of course. Look, he may be a bit of a highflier, but please try to get along with him. I know this is not our usual ask of you, but we need every brain on this that we can get."

"I could use a change from your usual ask of me—*Lily, eliminate so and so,*" I say with a small laugh. "But seriously, Chad, who knows about this autopsy?"

"Well, for one, we have permission from Senator Steinman's widow, and she didn't want to let anyone in government know. Then, of course, there's the senator's staffer who brought her suspicions to me. She also pleaded with me to keep this under wraps. I think she's a little scared too. But, like I said, it may turn out to be nothing, and the last thing we need is a huge political scandal."

"Let's go, Chad. The magnificent forensic guy is probably already there waiting for us."

• • •

"This is an impressive setup you have here, Logan," I say, looking at the bright white tiled walls and the meticulous stainless steel tables. Everything appears freshly scrubbed.

"Thank you. We're going to use this room; it's for decomps, so there's a high rate of air exchange. You'll find the dressing room just outside. There are fresh scrubs, hooded Tyvek jumpsuits, booties, masks, face shields—the works. When's the last time you performed an autopsy, Lily?"

"I can't remember. Let's just say it's been a while."

"Okay, meet you back here in ten–fifteen minutes."

Yes, it has been a while, but doing an autopsy should be like riding a bicycle. I hope. Put the scalpel in my hand and start with the initial Y incision. We'll see where it goes from there. I have questions about what we can learn from this autopsy. It's my hope that in the end, we find nothing and succeed in putting the widow's mind to rest—that her husband died of natural causes. Chad was wise to keep this a secret operation to avoid any embarrassment or political scandal.

I'm ready. I brought with me a little eucalyptus ointment to put in my nostrils—a cheat for the sensitive. It'll help mask the smell of decaying flesh. I admire those forensic pathologists who perform these autopsies every day. They're underpaid and overworked. And Dr. Pelletier? I'm trying to get a read on him. The man has an abundance of enthusiasm, a winning smile, and Chad says he's the best in his field. I leave the comfort of the dressing room and face the steel door that'll lead me to the path of discovery.

As I enter the room. I can see the body's already on the metal table. And despite the eucalyptus, I still smell decaying flesh.

"Come on in. I hope you found everything you needed," Logan says.

"Yes, thank you."

"Dr. Robinson, in addition to you, we have one other person with us at the body—my assistant Dennis—and if you turn your head around to the right, there's Chad sitting in the corner, presumably keeping an eye on all of us."

I turn around, and Chad's giving me a little wave. He has on some PPE and looks very uncomfortable. I'm surprised he hasn't vomited by now, although I did give him a little bit of the eucalyptus ointment to block the cadaverine and putrescine odors.

The body is out on the stainless steel, and despite this being several days since the Senator's passing, it's well preserved. The cooler temperature in the mausoleum has slowed some of the decay, so we have a better chance of finding intact organs and less autolysis. Deterioration of the organs makes it hard to find anything pathological.

"Dr. Robinson, let's do an external examination of the body and see if there's anything notable," Dr. Pelletier says.

"Senator Steinman had a TAVR procedure, so we should focus on the aortic valve and where the device was threaded into the heart. What I'm already struck by is the large hematoma in the left groin area. I would expect some bruising, but this seems to be out of proportion to his procedure," I say, finding the amount of blue, green, and yellow discolored skin large and streaking down his leg.

"I agree. Let's do a careful dissection of the hematoma to see if there was any perforation of the femoral artery where the catheter was inserted. But if that'd been the case, he would've bounced back to the hospital."

"That's true. Frank bleeding would've been picked up early while he was still in recovery." Then I point to a scar below the belly button and above the right hip.

"Yes, I see it, too," Logan says. He takes a ruler and measures the defect. "Dennis, please note the scar is approximately eight centimeters long and located between the umbilicus and the anterior superior iliac spine."

"McBurney's point, probably the result of an appendectomy he had while he was much younger. We can confirm that when we explore the bowel," I add. "Let's turn the body over and examine the dorsal surface."

Dennis helps turn the body over so we can look for any obvious signs of trauma or any clue as to the body's condition perimortem.

"There's nothing apparent here," I say.

"Right. Let's turn him back over and begin," Logan says.

"Before we start, I want to make sure we collect hair, nails, and, if possible, vitreous for toxicology. I realize vitreous humor may be a long shot," I say as I look at the eyes after retracting the lids—they appear sunken.

"Dr. Robinson, I don't think you're going to get anything from those eyeballs. You're way past the time interval for collecting vitreous," Logan says. I know he's right, but I figure I can give it a try and only fail. So, I ask Dennis to hand me an 18-gauge needle attached to a syringe.

"Yes, you're right. But I thought even if we could get one drop, it could be helpful. As you both know, the intraocular fluid is considered a protected site—protected from microbial contamination or the degradation of toxins by enzymes found in the blood. Electrolyte chemistry can be telling, and from a toxicology perspective, vitreous humor's a good place to start. Normally we can usually extract around 4 or 5 mL from each eye."

Logan's amused that I'm telling him his business—I can see it in his eyes. Eyes can be expressive, even when one has a mask on. Of course, he and Dennis know all this, but I have this habit of "teaching" as I work. It helps me think.

"Go ahead, Dr. Robinson, you can do what you want, but I think if you're concerned about poisoning, we should focus on the hair, nails, and whatever we can collect once we open him up," Logan says, his eyes reflecting annoyance. I ignore him and forge ahead.

Getting the needle inserted at the lateral canthus, the outer corner of the eye, with sunken eyes, proves tricky; am I in the center of the globe? After several attempts, I acquiesce. Logan is right.

"Well, I tried. There's nothing there." I say, feeling a little foolish. Logan's look above the mask is one of "I told you so."

We get a clean nail clipper and cut the nails on both hands and then take hair from the back of the scalp. There's not much there, but we take what we can get.

"Please make sure you note which part is the root end of the hair, Dennis."

"Yes, of course, Dr. Robinson," now shooting his boss, Dr. Pelletier, a knowing look.

"I'll take over from here, thank you," Logan says. He clearly doesn't like being second.

"Please," I quickly add as I'm prompted by Chad giving me the evil eye. Logan begins.

"All right. I'm starting with the standard Y incision," he says as he cuts from shoulder to shoulder and then down the midline to the pubic area.

Dennis then hands Logan the rib cutters so he can cut away the sternum and ribs, allowing us access to the thoracic cavity. The heart's our primary area of focus. Now, seeing the organs in situ, nothing looks out of place. However, there's a considerable amount of hemorrhaging when I look at the intact organs.

"Let's get the block out into the pan so we can make a careful dissection and collect specimens for microscopic review," Logan says.

The block of organs, still in their correct anatomical proximity to each other, is now sitting in a pan so that we can review each organ. Logan begins a beautiful dissection of the heart, paying particular attention to the valves.

"There looks like a little necrosis in the area around the artificial valve. That's a bit unusual. However, the valve appears undamaged," he says, probing the dead tissue.

"I'd like to have that valve intact, please," I say to the two men at the table. Logan looks up directly at me.

"The valve looks fairly normal, Lily. I don't see any issues."

"Perhaps, but I'd still like to check it out," I

tell him picking up the valve and placing it into a small specimen container. "Could you also take a piece of the heart tissue you think looks a little necrotic? Right there," I say, pointing to some damaged heart muscle near the artificial valve.

I can see Chad feels uncomfortable with the growing tension in the room. He's squirming in his chair. This is Dr. Pelletier's domain, and I'm irritating him.

"Doctors, maybe we can take as many specimens as possible since this is the only chance we have with this body," Chad says.

Logan nods his head in agreement, shoots me a look that I can only assume includes a smile behind the mask, and proceeds to take several specimens that he'll fix in formalin for histologic review later, and some tissue, the liver, and spleen, unfixed for toxicology. To appease me, he's collected as many clots as possible for toxicologic analysis. He moves on, does a careful dissection around the groin area, and finishes by examining the bowel, noting that the senator's missing his appendix. Logan also points out what looks like small areas in the kidney and lungs that appear necrotic, as well as some gross hemorrhaging.

"Yes, I see it. Do you think we should also look at the brain?" I ask, deferring to his experience. I probably have what's necessary for toxicology without it.

"We should. Even if it's putrefied, we could still collect some tissue for analysis."

Logan makes an incision at the back of the skull from one ear to the other and pulls the scalp forward. He uses a high-speed oscillating saw to cut into the skull cap, and once the bone is removed, we see the exposed brain. Gently removing the brain from the cranium, we can see that it appears normal. Logan takes a few samples of tissue for toxicology and deposits them in a specimen jar.

"All right, from a poisoning perspective, I've got what I need," I say.

Logan steps back from the table and looks at Chad, who's now standing. "Here's what I think. My preliminary anatomic diagnosis is disseminated intravascular coagulation, DIC, based on the gross findings."

"DIC. Incredible. The senator used all his clotting factors and then just bled out." I feel disheartened.

"Right. The mystery's to determine the precipitating trigger. There are so many causes of this: inflammation, microbiological sepsis, blunt force trauma, and in women, pregnancy complications like an amniotic fluid embolism. It'll have to be confirmed with the microscopics, but as you can see, there was a fair amount of bleeding in the major organs," Logan says.

"I agree. "DIC is tricky. If this is what killed

him, we need to identify the underlying root cause that brought this on. Something activated Steinman's entire clotting system, and once all the clotting factors were consumed, he hemorrhaged. This can happen after surgery, but he had only a minor procedure, something relatively insignificant from a surgical perspective to have caused this. And there were no signs of infection either. But certain toxins can produce DIC."

"Lily, we'll know more when the microscopics come out, and I did collect some tissue for the culture of any microorganisms, but I agree, what we saw wasn't a picture of infection. As for toxins, well, I'm told that's your department," Logan says.

Dennis now takes over, putting the remaining organs back into the body cavity and after, suturing the skin back together. Logan, Chad, and I leave the autopsy room. Once in the women's locker room, I doff my PPE, throw it in the biohazard bin, and decide to take a quick shower. There seems to be everything I need right here—body wash, shampoo, fresh towels. Dr. Pelletier's operation is exceptional.

When I finally emerge, Chad and the others have left with the body to return the senator to the mausoleum before daylight, with the hope that no one's the wiser. Logan's waiting for me and having a cup of coffee in the break room. With his mask off, the stubble on his face makes him appear rugged. It gives shape to his face, and I find it attractive.

"Sorry for the wait," I say, "I just thought it would be a good idea to take a shower before I get back to the hotel."

"Yes, I did too. That was my fourth shower of the day," he says with a chuckle. "Hey, you want a cup of coffee or something? It's been a while since I've had to pull an all-nighter," he says with a broad grin, completely sucking me in with his savoir-faire.

"Listen, I'm sorry if I was a little too direct in there. Coffee? I'd like it light." I let him know. He nods his head, again smiles, and hands me a cup of coffee with skim milk.

"Hey, no worries. This is a highly unusual case, and I guess there's a lot at stake. How did they drag you into this mess?"

"Oh, you know, think outside the box. Let's ask an academic what her thoughts might be. Yes, I was just as surprised as you to find myself in the middle of all this intrigue." I'm so good at lying at this point in my life, I hardly notice it anymore.

"Do you want to review the microscopics with me when they're ready? We should have them in a day or two."

"Yes, absolutely. In the meantime, I'd like to make arrangements to have the unfixed specimens sent to a toxicology colleague of mine. I can stop by in the morning, well, I guess it's already morning, you know, later today, so I can give you the information as to where to send them."

"You're aware that we've some great tox labs here on the east coast, right?"

"I do; there's a terrific lab close by in Pennsylvania, and if we head out west, there're ones in Minnesota and Utah, but the lab I need's in Hong Kong. There's a toxicologist there I work with regularly, and well, he's used to the beyond strange," I say with a bit of a laugh. My hair's still wet from the shower, and I only had a lipstick and an eyeliner pencil in my bag for makeup. Why do I suddenly feel self-conscious about how I look?

Logan is staring at me. "I better be getting back now," I say.

"Sure, can I give you a lift?"

"No thanks, I'm certain Chad left a car and driver for me out the back. Can you please ring Chad when you're ready for the microscopic review?"

"What, you don't want to give me your cell phone number," he says with a wink. "Are you afraid I might abuse it?"

So arrogant! I'm not going to get sucked into this. I breathe out a heavy sigh, and I can see that he regrets his comment. His smile fades.

"Thank you, Dr. Pelletier. I'm happy to have

met you," I say, coolly, and extend my hand. "I'll reconnect with you when the slides are ready." My back now toward him, I head toward the stairs.

"Dr. Robinson, don't forget that you need to leave me the name and address of the toxicologist where the specimens are to be sent."

"I'll have Chad get you that information," I tell him and leave. I'm abrupt, and I'm sure he got the message.

Why, then, do I feel some excitement, even titillation, after performing an autopsy with a man I just met? It's simply business, after all. A case. Only now, I'm going back to my hotel, and once I arrive, there'll be no connecting rooms, no knock on the heavy door that hangs in between, and no lover to find me in the darkness.

Chapter 7

Hong Kong

John Chi Leigh received the call from his colleague, Lily Robinson. Once again, she asked for his help in analyzing specimens for poison. The fact that she suspected that the death of a senior U.S. senator was the result of foul play gave him pause. Dr. Robinson's suspicions were good enough for him to get his mind on the task.

Dr. Leigh and Dr. Robinson had worked together ever since their surprise meeting in California. It was there, in Hollywood, years ago, that the pathologist from Boston had been an assassination target—a job assigned to him. However, after Leigh learned the true nature of their intersecting past, the chemist turned, and killed the man who hired him, sparing Lily. He never shared the details with her of that day until their meeting in Seoul, South Korea, where the truth spilled forth like a confession.

Their love of poisons and their dedication to suppressing inevitable evil in the world created a bond of friendship and respect. Together they were greater than the sum of their parts and enjoyed designing novel toxins for the cause. John Chi Leigh and Lily Robinson became close colleagues, co-conspirators, and worked together unraveling—or creating—the mysteries of deaths that appeared natural—but were not.

John Chi Leigh returned to the quiet of his private laboratory the next morning. This was one section within the larger facility that he could call his own. Here, the black epoxy resin countertops were covered with instruments used to analyze and detect various drugs and toxins. Small windows let in diffuse light, and a large chemical fume hood provided a safe haven from the most toxic compounds. A Mettler analytic balance occupied the corner of the benchtop near a series of manual single channel pipettes. Leigh appreciated precision in his work, and in this small wet-lab, he had free rein to analyze and create.

The rest of the laboratory was a bustling venture with ten-foot-high windows providing natural illumination while the ceiling exposed elements usually hidden. Large rectangular lights hung from the rafters, and HVAC and other systems were readily apparent and accessible. Multiple laboratory benches held chromatographic/mass spectrometric equipment and specialized flasks and beakers for extractions, while large analytical instruments stood independently on the floor. Much of the toxicology work was accomplished by many bright scientists and technologists examining specimens sent from all over the world.

First, sealed specimens were received, usually under chain of custody, preserving each sample's integrity and the evidence, in a central holding area. With the paperwork completed at each step—recording where the samples were and who handled them—they were then stored in massive freezers or refrigerators until analyzed. When the technologist was ready for routine specimen analysis, they were initially screened by an immunoassay procedure that used specific antibodies to detect a drug or a class of drugs. After the routine screens, any positive result would be confirmed later by a more definitive assay using chromatographic techniques followed by mass spectrometry.

The separation of drugs found in urine, blood, vitreous, or stomach fluid occurred following the extraction with acids or bases, first using either gas chromatography or liquid chromatography before entering a final run through the mass spectrometer. Different mass spectrometers were capable of detecting ions indicative of a signature for a specific analyte. Sometimes, new and unidentified peaks or ion fragments showed up in the results, prompting Leigh to investigate further. But it was these square and rectangular instruments coupled with computers that formed the bulk of the analyses in this exceptional reference laboratory.

Having delegated the routine work of analyzing

the urine from the racehorse stake winners to the other chemists in his lab, Leigh could now focus on the specimens sent to him by Lily Robinson. Not every day did he have the chance to examine part of the remains of a senator from the United States. Using his skill to tease out chemical compounds hidden in the body fluids from innocent victims was the kind of work he enjoyed more than anything. But this case had broader implications.

Leigh had recently heard some rumors about the resurgence of a formidable Russian political assassin who had disappeared into the background years ago. He couldn't remember precisely when this man dropped out of sight, but it was before Grigory Markovic came into play. If there was poison in the senator's remains, could it be the work of this man? Leigh chafed at the thought. Identifying the type of poison and how it entered the body could establish a link between his old nemesis and this death—if there was one. Leigh made plans to resurrect his hidden journal on old hits, review his handwritten notes, and search for cold information on the internet—a tool that wasn't fully developed before 1983.

John Chi Leigh sat at the bench, pushed his dark frames up the bridge of his nose, and prepared his specimens for extraction. Lily Robinson once told him that it was his rare ability to find an obscure molecule in a sea of chemical signals that was his gift. But his real genius was the art of making a toxin that no one in the world had ever seen. And that brilliance was only surpassed by the most gifted chemist in the world—Mother Nature.

Chapter 8

Russia

With her lover Scottie gone and her subsequent capture by the Russians, Alexis Popov feared that death would soon find her. Her handlers had allowed her to keep her Moscow bookstore job as a convenient cover, but they would only spare her life as long as she could be of use. Alexis moved robotically through her daily routine, stocking and restocking shelves, one book at a time, hoping that no one could see her pain beneath the thin veneer of humanity. Careful not to shake loose her innermost thoughts, she buried her longing for her mother's comforting embrace. It had been so long since she had lived as Bella, along with her mother Adrienne and her adopted sister Rose, in isolation from much of the world on the coffee plantation in Colombia. But like a ghost, that existence ended abruptly after a Russian terrorist named Grigory Markovic kidnapped her.

Forced to serve a cruel and demanding master, Bella, who had been rechristened Alexis Popov by Markovic, became part of his Russian terrorist faction and helped with his plans for mass poisoning, which started in New York City more than a year ago. However, after learning that Maxim Petrikov, Markovic's second in command, had been killed by the Americans, Alexis escaped, fleeing to Russia and dissolving into the gray world around her. When no one came looking for her, she had emerged from the underground basement apartments and took a job at a Moscow bookstore, hiding instead among the floor-to-ceiling English-language books of recent fiction and the nonfiction hardcovers of art and travel. Her life percolated with bitterness until, through a friend, she had met Scottie—a man who cared for her and she for him—and for whose death she felt responsible.

For the first time in Alexis's life, she had felt hope and a renewed sense of purpose after meeting Jackson Scott—her Scottie, her Sasha. They had fallen in love, but on the evening of their planned declaration of love, American operatives had picked up Alexis, coercing her into helping them find information on Markovic's plans in South Korea, and had taken Scottie into custody too.

However, the elegant blond was unaware that Scottie worked under deep cover for United States Intelligence. Although guilt had plagued him, and his love for Alexis was true, Scottie's duty to his country took precedence. His superiors had proposed that Alexis be given a new identity and life in the United States in return for her cooperation; this had prompted Scottie to reexamine his own life. When his assignment gathering sensitive information from Alexis Popov was completed, he requested duty back in his homeland to be closer to his lover. But the ill-fated pair never got their chance for happiness—after a harrowing shoot-out, Scottie's bloodied body had been recovered by the Americans while Alexis fell into the hands of the Russians. Unknown to Alexis, Markovic finally met his end in Seoul, South Korea, with a poisonous dart wielded by an unlikely source.

One cloudy morning, while Alexis was unpacking some boxes, she was approached by a familiar-looking man. On several previous occasions, the lanky bookstore clerk had noticed him watching her. He was direct with his request and asked her to meet him at a local café later that same day. Alexis understood this was not optional and took her lunch break early to meet the stranger. The café was around the corner from the bookshop.

"*Dobryy vecher*. Alexis, we have not formally met—I was assigned to keep an eye on you. But you already know that. My name is Sergei Petrikov. I am Maxim's brother," said the man in the navy pea coat. He stared directly into her gray-blue eyes, admiring her graceful swan-like neck as he spoke.

The waitress stopped by the table, and Sergei

ordered two cups of black coffee. Alexis remained quiet, now seeing through fresh eyes Sergei's physical resemblance to Maxim. His salt and pepper hair complemented a strong jawline, but she convinced herself that there was more softness behind his hazel eyes than there had ever been with Maxim. Only time would tell.

"*Dobryy vecher*, Sergei. Nice to meet you," she said, not sure that she meant it. "Who do you work for?" Alexis felt uneasy and waited for an answer.

"I work with a group that knew Grigory Markovic. You remember him, do you not?"

Sergei was purposefully vague, and Alexis knew it. She felt a stomach cramp and a chill climbed up her spine at the mention of Markovic's name. Sergei continued.

"We have an interest in controlling some aspects of world politics for our own gain. The less you know, the better, *da*?" Sergei's grin revealed worn-down yellowish incisors.

Alexis shifted her weight in the chair and dropped a spoon into her coffee mug, giving it a mindless stir.

"We have a mission for you. You are to meet us at the following place for details," he said, handing her a piece of paper with an address.

Alexis couldn't understand why he couldn't have given her this bit of information while she was at the bookstore. How easy it would have been to slip her a note between the pages of one of the books. Then she understood. "We have been asked to travel to the Middle East. More will be revealed later. Importantly, I have asked to meet you here so we can establish an arrangement," he said.

"What do you mean, an arrangement?" Alexis said, feeling herself slide further into the pit. Her heart started racing, and she felt a drip emerging from her right nostril. Grabbing a napkin, Alexis blotted her face. She had worked hard to rid herself of her cocaine habit, but times of stress pushed the cravings into a corner she could not always escape.

"My superiors want us to appear as a couple to reduce any suspicion of our time together. There may be others watching us and what we do. This afternoon's meeting in a café, out in the open, will look more like a social encounter," Sergei said, reaching across the table to take her hand. "The details of what is expected of us will be discussed later this evening."

Alexis remained frozen. She could feel his hand touching hers, and her fingers blanched, squeezing any remaining warmth out the tips. Physical abuse, such as she had sustained with Markovic, was something she would not, could not, go through again. Alexis had endured so much trauma in her life already and knew that either way, her only true escape would be through death.

Leaning into her, Sergei said, "Alexis, you will

do this." His voice sounded less soft now, even a little forceful. A darkness came over his eyes, and she shuddered.

Alexis's mind pushed through the clouds until a vision of her home on the coffee plantation stood before her. She regretted those days of petty jealousies and wished she could be little Bella—a time before Markovic stole her, changed her name, and her life.

Alexis always felt her existence moved in a sinusoidal wave pattern, one alternating peak, followed by one precipitous fall to the bottom of the pit. She had only given herself freely to one man, Scottie. They had shared so much in their short time together, and after she was yanked from Scottie's bullet-ridden body, she never saw or heard from her lover again. The memory of his death proved raw, and she vowed never to love another. How far was she expected to go in this new arrangement with Sergei?

Sergei got up from the table, having drunk his cup of coffee, and paid the tab. Alexis had barely touched hers.

"So, I will see you later, *da*, Alexis?" he said to her.

"*Da*," she said with eyes looking down. She swallowed hard, dreading this masquerade.

After the sun had disappeared from the sky, Alexis drove to the outskirts of town, weaving in and out of side streets hoping that she would not be followed. When she reached the desired address, she parked the car around the corner and walked back to the house. It seemed ordinary—wood and stone with a small yard surrounded by a metal fence. Alexis took a deep breath and walked to the front door. It opened after only a minute. The extent of her mission was about to be revealed.

"Popov, come in. Take a seat," the burly man said, first standing in front of her, then leading her to the inside of the house. She trailed behind his medium frame into a bland room filled with worn chairs and an old tan sofa. Threads could be seen dangling underneath where the material had worn through.

Alexis scanned her surroundings and saw Sergei sitting on the couch at the end of the room. She walked over to join him, her eyes darting from side to side. The burly man with the thick beard and black-framed eyeglasses was the only other person she could see. His glasses were tinted and blocked any expression from his eyes. Even so, there was something vaguely familiar about him, but Alexis dismissed the feeling. Ever since she escaped from Markovic, she was suspicious of anyone who reminded her of either him or Maxim. The burly man could see Alexis's mind tossing about and interrupted her thought by looming above her and Sergei.

The burly man stroked his beard before he spoke. "You two are going on a little trip together. We are sending you to the Middle East to pick up a package and deliver it to this address in Moscow," he said, handing Sergei a slip of paper. "I will be waiting. Sergei has the rest of the details. That is all."

Alexis felt the blood surge through her heart, saturating every cell in her body. The pull into the black hole was too strong to escape and a single tear balanced on the edge of her blue-gray eyes. Shoulders drooped, she followed Sergei out the door and looked to the stars for an answer.

Chapter 9

Washington, D.C.

The microscopics are ready, and I'm about to go to Dr. Pelletier's lab. Specimens of liver, spleen, some blood clots, and the implanted aortic valve have already been sent to Hong Kong for toxicological analysis. Other slices of tissue were taken from each organ to observe the histology under the microscope, looking for any abnormal findings.

The white silk blouse I'm wearing this morning is paired with a black fine wool pencil skirt and black suede stilettos. I grab my leather jacket and leave the hotel for Logan's facility. While in D.C. I admit to a little bit of window shopping, but mostly I worked on my laptop answering emails from Kelley and checking out Dr. Pelletier on the internet. Chad was right. The forensic pathologist is well regarded in his field as an expert witness, having testified in some recent high-profile cases. What I found more interesting were the several pictures of him at charity functions with impressive eye candy on his right arm. The doctor looks dashing in a tux, and I wonder if he has women falling all over him. Is he a player or just scared of commitment? Strangely, I find myself engaging in my own fantasy about him.

And I don't feel guilty. My anger toward JP persists even now. Maybe we needed a break.

Chad had let me know earlier that he still hasn't heard from JP and doesn't know where he is. Fine with me. Apparently, JP is helping out another government official with a confidential problem overseas. Even though Chad gave his permission, the specifics weren't shared with him. Highly unusual, but then I don't know everything that goes on in our little organization and exactly where we fit into the big picture. I have a limited scope of responsibilities and only provide, well, consultation when asked.

The taxi drops me in front of Logan's building located on the outskirts of the city. Now, seeing it in the light of day, it's a formidable structure with an interesting facade. Two stories of large glass panels dominate one side of the building, hold a covered entryway, while cement slabs line the left half of the building, with only a ribbon of windows above. Bright blue blocks wrap around the tops and sides, creating an envelope or outline. The architectural design's modern and inviting, and there's not a lot of traffic around the building, reducing the unexpected prying eyes. I hit the buzzer on the outdoor camera and give my name. They are expecting me. When I reach the front reception area, I'm handed a badge and buzzed in through another door to wait for my host.

Dr. Pelletier descends the stairs multiple steps at a time. His trim body is apparent to me even though he is wearing scrubs—not exactly fashionable but practical. I bet he's the kind of man who goes to the gym or jogs several miles every day.

"Good morning, Dr. Robinson. Have you already had your coffee this morning, or would you like to grab a cup before we start?" he asks. I didn't realize that his voice had an almost husky quality to it.

"I'm fine, thanks. I can sit with you at the scope now if you're ready."

"Great. Is it okay to take the stairs up to my office?" he asks, looking at my heels.

"The stairs will be fine. Let's go." I may have done a little eye roll; I can't be sure.

Logan Pelletier shows me into his office, which sits in the corner of the building. Windows drench the room in light, and his desk is rich wood flanked by a soft beige chenille couch. I would have expected leather. Maybe he has a soft side. The double-headed microscope rests on a pneumatic table made to adjust to the height of the pathologist as they sit in their chair. His scope also has ergonomic heads so the eyepieces can be moved into position easily, and each chair allows for individual comfort settings. This is a sweet setup that not every laboratory can enjoy.

"Why don't you take a seat there, and I'll

drive." He opens up a gray cardboard slide tray, and I can see all the glass slides forming two neat columns. "I previewed the slides before you got here and dotted a few important areas. If you don't mind, I'll just jump ahead."

I sit down and glance across the table at the man sitting opposite me. He's staring at me. Yes, looking intently at me with his lips closed but forming a smile. What's he thinking? And what is it about him that I find, so, so, attractive? I take a deep breath. It's his eyes—green with a brightness that captures the light. I quickly look away to avoid his gaze, put my face up to the objective lenses, and start twisting the right lens to bring the field into focus. Concentrate, Lily. He's just trying to rattle you.

"Take a look at this clot. What do you see?"

"Broken red blood cells—schistocytes. I see it. Lots of fibrin strands choked with fragmented red cells. If we could have had a peripheral smear with antemortem blood, we could better appreciate this feature. Normal red blood cells trying to squeeze through a sieve-like net of fibrin leaves them damaged," I say, shaking my head. Logan removes the slide and replaces it with another.

"Lily, look at the kidney. Showers of tiny clots—microthrombi throughout the tissue, and if you check the spot where I've dotted the slide . . ." He moves the glass slide to an area with a green ink dot. "You can see damaged kidney tubules—acute tubular necrosis. It's consistent with what we saw grossly. Let me show you the lungs," he says, swiftly replacing one slide with another. His large hands turn the coarse focus on the microscope and then twist the fine focus until another area dotted with ink clearly comes into view.

"I see it. All that fibrin deposited in the blood vessels. So, in addition to hemorrhage, he had evidence of disseminated microthrombi. A classic finding in DIC. Logan, what was the unknown trigger that set the senator's clotting cascade in motion?"

"That's the key, Lily. Isn't it?"

I shake my head in disgust. "This showering of clots throughout the body reduced the blood flow to each organ and essentially set up multi-organ failure. This is horrible, and yet he might have had a chance if someone knew this was happening the night he became ill."

"True. I'm not sure why he was alone. So, cause of death is disseminated intravascular coagulation, which is what we thought. Once his body consumed all these clotting factors, he bled out. That would explain the large hematoma we saw in the groin area. It would've been where they threaded the catheter to get access to the femoral artery," Logan says.

"Agree, COD is DIC, but secondary to what?

We don't see any signs of infection, there was no trauma, and he only had a minor procedure, the TAVR."

I say this aloud to Logan, while in my mind, I know there are many different ways to introduce poison into a patient during surgery. Obviously, I can't share this with my colleague, but it does make me want to dig further into this case.

"Logan, I did send the specimens we collected to that lab in Hong Kong. It's going to take a while to get the results back. You know how it goes with toxicology. We won't know if a toxin was the precipitating event, but given what we see here, I wouldn't be surprised."

"Jesus, if that's the case, then Lawrence Steinman was murdered. Who would do such a thing?"

Logan's face is pale, his eyes close as he takes a deep breath. I can see him holding it in. He juggles with death every day, and he's no stranger to murder. But this? This was different—an assassination. And it's right up my alley. Someone who knows the art of secret poisoning. I need to think about this some more.

"Look, Logan, I find this upsetting too. Let me speak with Chad. I'll take that on. We need to keep this very quiet. I mean, share with no one, not even with your staff."

"I don't get it, Lily. What's your role in all this? Look, I trained with the best of the bullet pullers and then decided to become a second opinion guy. I do autopsies all day long. But you. You're a doc with some style in academics. What the hell?"

"Logan, I've been tapped because I know poisons, and well, they must have suspected something, or I guess they wouldn't have called me."

"It sounds like maybe you've been here before since you said you would handle Chad. I think we've got what we need," he says, pushing himself away from the table.

"I just thought, as it's probably poison, I should be the one to talk with him."

"If you say so. Let's grab a cup of coffee if you've got time."

"Sounds good. Let me just make a quick call."

"Fine. I'll step out, leave you to your call and get us some coffee. Light, right?"

"Yes, that's right. Thanks."

Logan leaves his office and shuts the door. I make a call to Chad on my secure phone. It's ringing. "Hello, Chad. Yeah, it's me. Where can I meet you this afternoon? I want to talk about the case. Okay. I'll be by a little later." I hear a bump at the door, and Logan pops his head in.

"All set?"

I sweep him in. "You bet."

Logan hands me the coffee. My hand goes to take it, but he doesn't let go. His fingers creep up slightly and touch mine. A small tingle fans through my body. I don't think his touch is accidental. He's flirting while watching me with those eyes—for a reaction? I don't think I'm misreading the signs.

"Thanks," I tell him as I back away and take a seat at the circular table by the window. I'm not sure what to think. I feel the chemistry and spin the platinum bracelet on my wrist.

"So Lily, what do you like to do in your downtime? What's your sport?

What's your music?"

"Geez, Logan. This sounds like a date. Tell me ten things about yourself." I'm squirming a bit in the chair. If it wasn't for the nature of this meeting, I might think this is cute. The man does have a certain charm about him.

"Not a date. Just trying to shift the conversation to something lighter than, you know, murder. Me? When I take time off, I really want off. Not connected. Know what I mean?" I nod my head. "I like sailing around those little islands off Maine during the summer, tear-assing down the black diamond slopes in the winter, tinkering with my cars, so they're in shape for some speed, and well, listening to some good old rock-n-roll."

"I see," is all I manage to say. I usually don't share so much of myself.

"Now, there's a little bookstore in Brunswick, Maine called *The Coffee Dog Bookstore*. I sometimes stop there on my drive up the coast. I think you'd like it, Lily. You know, chill. Run by a guy who's a real character. Goff Langdon. Does some private detective work on the side. I'm telling you all about me. Come on. What about you? You're all closed up."

"Okay, okay. I did most of my training in Boston, including a fellowship—"

"Stop right there, doctor. I don't want your goddamn resume; I want to know about you. What do you like, what do you do for relaxation? Tell me about *you*." His voice changes as he makes his point.

Now, what am I supposed to do? Tell him that I cultivate a poison garden, work with a couple of assassins on the side, and have friends who can synthesize death in a bottle?

"Sorry, Logan. When I get the time, I like kayaking, gardening, and biking. I also enjoy reading novels to help me relax," I tell him, knowing this sounds pretty boring.

"See, I knew there was more to you than meets the eye," he says with a wink. "I've got a couple of bikes too. I like the road bikes but have to admit that I have a few mountain bikes as well."

Logan is truly charming; it's just that this can't go anywhere.

"Hey, Logan," I start while looking at my watch. "I've really got to get going. Thanks for everything. I'll be in touch."

"Another brush off, Lily Robinson? You're a tough nut to crack."

And with that, I pick up my pocketbook and head for the door to meet with Chad.

As planned, Chad and I meet back at the hotel later that afternoon. Our rooms overlook the Marina and are close to downtown Washington. Chad is waiting for me in his room, which has a stunning view of the Thomas Jefferson Memorial from his window.

"Well, what did you find out?" Chad asks, eager for information.

"Quite a lot, actually. I agree with your suspicions; I think Senator Steinman was murdered with poison."

"Oh shit, I hate being right. So, what's the poison?"

"Chad, you and I both know that this is not going to be some easy find. I've got my genius colleague Dr. John Chi Leigh on the tox. If anyone can find the poison, he can. That's why I've worked with him exclusively over the last several years. Anyway, it's got to be something that causes both clotting and hemorrhaging. But more importantly, why would anyone want to kill Steinman? I don't see him as a particularly controversial figure." I find myself thinking of the current political climate, here and abroad.

"I know, I know. Maybe the poison will give

us a hint. Certain groups or factions favor certain poisons."

"You mean like Novichok, the nerve agent? Yes, we encountered that when we were on Markovic's tail. He liked that and was happy to sell it to the North Koreans for their missile warheads. But Markovic's dead, and we've got to look elsewhere. Speaking of which, where the hell is JP on this?" Despite my feelings, he would be the one I would be working with.

"Lily, I told you I don't know, and I don't. He's on a loaner to another director. Something very top secret, no doubt."

"Well, if this really is murder and we're going to have to track down an assassin, I'm going to need his help. Parker too. Is Parker around?" JP's right-hand man is part of the team and probably his best friend.

"No, Parker's gone with JP."

"So it's just you and me? That's not right."

"Okay, I'll track JP down, but in the meantime, get the information on the toxicology from Dr. Leigh. Whoever did this is still out there, and we have no idea about the who or why."

"Will do."

"Oh, and how was it working with Pelletier? He seems like a good guy. I think we can depend on him to be discreet."

"Pelletier? He's interesting. Does his involvement end here, or do I see him again?"

"I guess that's up to you, Robinson." The grin on Chad's face is telling.

"In that case, I'm going to go back to Boston. If you need me, just call. And when I find out something from Leigh, I'll contact you."

"Robinson, you do know that Pelletier is a very wealthy man, don't you? And I might add that he's single."

I feel overtaken by a full blush. Hot cheeks and all.

"Chad, whatever do you mean?" I say as I walk out the door.

Chapter 10

Boston

The trip to D.C. was unsettling. If Senator Steinman was murdered, then there's a killer on the loose. But why would someone want to kill him? What's the motive? I'm anxiously waiting to hear from Dr. Leigh. If John Chi can identify a toxin in the samples I sent him, it might give us a clue. Chad's quietly looking into the senator's assignments. That's his job. And there's still no word from JP. On reflection, our time in France several months ago was bittersweet. The more we learn about each other, the more challenging our lives become.

"Hey, ready for this case?" Kelley's at the door of my office, interrupting my reverie. He's always bubbly, but when there's a lot to do, he gets overwhelmed. I can tell by his pressured voice. Today's one of those days.

"Kelley, are you okay? Lots of cases?"

"Yeah, just busy." The brightness disappears from his face.

We walk toward the pediatric floor, and he begins to relax.

"Tell me what you know about the patient."

"He's a 15-year-old boy who presented to

the ED with a generalized tonic-clonic seizure. On ECG, he had ventricular tachycardia. The preliminary drug screen was positive for antidepressants. The only medication he was taking was imipramine."

"So the imipramine is the antidepressant that we picked up. I assume we got a quantification of the drug."

"Yup, the imipramine concentration was 2010 ng/mL, and its metabolite desipramine was 400 ng/mL."

"Add those two numbers together, and you have a fatal dose. It's a win that he got immediate medical help. Was he depressed? Could this have been an intentional overdose?"

"I don't know. We'll have to ask him."

We stop outside the room and let the house staff looking after our patient know we're here. Then we pump hand sanitizer before we enter the room.

"Good morning. Are you James Mulligan?" I ask the teenager who's casually sitting in his bed. He's dressed in sweatpants and a T-shirt, appears well, and is in no apparent distress. He nods, looking up from his phone.

"I'm Dr. Robinson, and this is Dr. Kelley. We're from the toxicology service. Can you tell us what happened?"

"Sure, yeah. I was at school, didn't feel well, so I went down to see the nurse. I felt hot, my heart was racing. I felt like crap. After a little while, I just fell back on the cot. The nurse said I had a convulsion, so she called an ambulance."

"James, I understand you're taking imipramine for depression. Did you take more of your intended dose that day?"

"No, but my psychiatrist was slowly increasing my dose."

"Had you ever felt warm and like your heart was racing before when you've taken this medication?"

"Yeah, and it was getting more frequent, but I never had a convulsion before."

"James, we're going to order additional blood work and see if we can find out what made you sick. You take care now."

We leave the room, pump the hand sanitizer and head back down to my office.

"So, what do you think, Dr. Robinson? And by the way, I like your brown print heels today."

"Thank you, Kelley. As for our patient, the total concentration of imipramine plus desipramine was 2410 ng/mL—that's toxic. And if we look at the concentration ratio of the parent compound, imipramine, to the metabolite desipramine, that's 5. Consistent with an overdose. So we have several possibilities. One is that our patient took more than his allotted dose and doesn't want to tell us based on the implications; another's that he could've taken additional medication unintentionally if he didn't remember he'd taken pills earlier. Or, if we're to assume our patient's telling the truth, and he seemed reliable and not at all like he was trying to hide something, there's another possibility."

"Which is? I'm sorry, I know I should have that right here," Kelley says, tapping his forehead, "but I just haven't had a chance to look further into the case with all the other work I have."

"That's fine, Kelley. I certainly know what it's like to be distracted by other things. I think we both could agree that his initial presentation to the ED was classic for an anticholinergic toxidrome. He displayed all of the effects: mydriasis, hyperpyrexia, tachycardia, seizures, and cardiac abnormalities."

"Right, the ED notes said he had very dilated pupils, elevated temperature, and fast heart rate in addition to his seizures and the heart rhythm abnormalities."

"Assuming he took the correct dose, it's possible that his body didn't metabolize the drug properly. As you know, the liver contains enzymes, the cytochrome P450 system, that converts drugs into substances that the body can easily eliminate."

"Of course, depending on a patient's genes, they can either metabolize drugs very fast, very slow, or something in between. So I'll order a genotype analysis." Kelley's brightness returns, knowing we are both on the same page.

"You got it. Great. Let me know when the results come back. Oh, and any word on our medical student Rose?"

"No, she and I have been corresponding, but she's still in France looking after her mother."

"Thanks. Have a great weekend."

"You too, Dr. Robinson."

I'm anxious to spend more time with Rose and get to know her. It makes me feel good to think that she's so responsible. Her dedication to Adrienne shows true devotion. JP called it when he said that she'd been raised right. I didn't have a hand in that, and who knows what Rose would be like today if I did.

Finally, some alone time in my Boston condo. I'm looking forward to a weekend to catch up on my writing and think more about the Steinman case. The morning sun reminds me that I need another cup of coffee before I get down to work.

I hear a knock at the door and look at my watch. It's still early. Maybe the doorman has a package for me? Looking through the peephole, I see it's Logan. Oh, Lord!

"What're you doing here?" I say with such surprise that Logan takes a step back.

"A simple hello would suffice," he replies. Logan's fixed to the spot waiting for me.

"How did you find me?"

"Oh, come on, Lily. It wasn't so hard. I just

asked the guys we're working with. Told them I was coming up to Boston this week for some consulting at the OCME. And by the way, the Chief Medical Examiner says hello. She wonders when you're coming back to give another toxicology lecture." The smile on Logan's face is warm and melts me.

"Logan, come in. You don't have to keep standing in the hallway." Frankly, I'm stunned that he's stopped by the apartment.

"Now that's more like it," he says, looking around the place and spying the gray chenille sofa; he heads right to it and runs his hands over the surface.

"You didn't think to call?"

"I did send you an email saying I was going to be up in Boston the end of the week, but you didn't respond. And I didn't have your cell phone number, remember? And even if I did, I thought you either wouldn't pick up the phone or would just blow me off. There's nothing like the element of surprise."

"You got that right." I must have missed that email with so much going on. "Would you like something to drink? Maybe some coffee? It's too early in the day for anything else." I feel a big sigh escape my chest. I'm settling.

"No, I'm good. How long have you lived in Boston?" he asks.

Logan's very direct; he comes right out and

asks what's on his mind. Most of our previous conversations have revolved around the autopsy. He's such an attractive man—those green eyes stand out against an expressive face. I wonder if the stubbly beard's out of laziness, or if he is trying to be sexy.

"A while," I tell him. I'm not very comfortable giving him too much information. Logan's wearing navy shorts and a sky-blue lightweight cotton pullover sweater. He's got on some fancy flip-flops, and he looks like he's ready for an early summer adventure.

"So I was thinking, Lily, maybe we could discuss some aspects of the case."

"You mean, now, here?"

"Not exactly. I'm taking a few days off and headed up to Maine to go sailing. How'd you like to come along with me? It's just for the day. I'll get you back by nightfall," he says, staring at me with those eyes, begging me to come. I'm tempted.

"I, I don't know Logan. I'm not so sure that's a good idea," I answer. He's overly confident that I'll say yes. Damn him. Can he see right through me?

"Trust me, it's a good idea," he says in a persuasive tone.

His hand lightly touches my arm. I feel that familiar tingle spread through my body. Why do I sound so hesitant? Is it because I'm interested? JP crosses my mind.

"It's just sailing?"

"Just sailing. I'll drive us up, we can pick up a few lobsters on the way, and I'll have you back safe in Boston by night. Come on. You're not going to spend this Saturday working on whatever it was in your apartment in Boston."

"Oh, all right, Logan. You twisted my arm. Now, what do I need to bring with me? I imagine it will be cool on the water." I'm hoping I won't regret this.

"Yes, it's still early in the season, so make sure you have some long pants and a sweater or a light jacket."

I tell him to give me a little time, and I change into slim jeans and a tank top. I know I have flip-flops, but unfortunately, they're at the cottage. Instead, there's a pair of white low canvas sneakers in the back of my closet, buried behind boxes containing my lovely heels. I pack a small bag with a jacket, sunglasses, a wide brim hat, scarf, suntan lotion, and a water bottle. I peek out of the bedroom and see Logan walking around the apartment, no doubt looking for clues to my existence. I emerge from the bedroom to find him looking out the window over the Boston skyline, trim and fit, his calf muscles thick from exercise. He has his hair pulled back into a short ponytail, making me wonder if I should do the same. He catches me watching him.

"Okay, you ready? Let's go."

And with that, I lock the door behind us and push down that trickle of guilt that I feel in my belly.

CHAPTER 11

Maine

I don't think I've ever had such an exhilarating ride up to Maine. Logan's turbo-charged sports car roared along the highway, defying the speed of sound. With the top down, I did have to pull my hair up into a ponytail. Now I understand where Logan's coming from. It's amusing that his car is bright red, like mine. As pathologists, do we see a pool of blood in the image of our cars, a color that reminds us of the heart filled to the brim?

The ride up Interstate 95 was filled with conversation. Logan and I shared stories from our medical training days, who we knew from what university or hospital, and who we admire in the field. Turns out he knew the Chief Medical Examiner from New York City, Marie Washington, too, and gave her a wide berth. It's a small world.

"Lily, now that we're off the highway, we're going to take the back roads to get to South Bristol. That's where I have the boat."

"Why, if you live in the D.C. area, do you have a boat up here in Maine?"

"Sailing off the Maine coast is golden. I already

told you this. There are so many little islands to explore. The rest of the east coast can be boring, you know."

After about thirty minutes, we pull into a small parking lot just above the dock. I can see many sailboats in the water. The inlet is calm, and the sun feels warm on my back as we get out of the car.

"Why this spot?" I ask Logan.

"Turns out that my old college roommate, Tom, lives up here. We actually share the boat. He does all the maintenance, and I pay all the bills. It works. He's always after me to sail to the Bahamas. Maybe one day we will."

Logan has an excited look on his face. A broad smile reveals perfect white teeth that I'm sure he had straightened as a boy. He stops by the small shed, orders two steamed lobsters for lunch that we'll enjoy later, and then lets me know that we should head toward the dock.

"It's stunning here," I tell him as we walk down the ramp to the water's edge. Tall trees surround the harbor, and large puffy clouds fill the spaces in between. "Where's the boat?" I ask.

"Right in front of you," he says, pointing to a thirty-seven-foot vessel with a single mast. I can see a teal Bimini top covering the stern while teak trim defines the outline. "She's a sloop; sails like a dream in light air. I've got a couple of spinnakers and even a Code Zero sail."

"A Code Zero sail? What's that?" My smile beams.

"It's a cross between an asymmetrical spinnaker and a genoa; a genoa is a large jib that stretches past the mast. It's not a type of salami," he says with a laugh.

"Ha, ha. I know that. It's not like I've never been sailing before." He's already on the boat and now extends his hand to help pull me aboard.

"Welcome aboard. Let me show you around."

"Aye-aye, Captain," I say. By now, he's removed his sweater and is only wearing a white T-shirt with his shorts. Those muscular arms are bursting at the edges of the cotton sleeves and probably are well acquainted with lifting weights.

"Okay, Lily. There's some seating here in the stern, and if you take these steps down, come on, follow me, right, careful now you don't hit your head."

"I'm okay; I've got this, Logan," I say, holding onto the sleek mahogany sides climbing down the ladder.

"Now, on the left is the galley, and on your right is the head." Then he pulls out a sideboard from the wall and secures it. "This is the table that can be extended when needed, and up near the bow are the sleeping quarters. Very compact and comfortable for two or even more."

It feels cozy in here. I see netting strung over the galley sink and filled with fresh fruit.

"Let's go topside and start heading out to open waters," Logan says, taking the stairs in one bound.

He starts the motor and weaves his way with skill between moored boats and endless lobster pots until we reach a stretch of water that's not so cluttered. The sail goes up, taut against the fifty-foot tall mast, a huge white triangle with the call letters 002. I feel the breeze in my hair and turn my face into the sun, absorbing the heat so I can tap into it later when the chill moves in.

"Lily, do you want to take the helm?"

"What me? You're the captain. I'm just the first mate." I see his smile light up his face as he takes my hand and leads me to the wheel. The wind blows my hair into my mouth, and Logan rescues the wayward strand pushing it behind my ear. My heart picks up the pace feeling his fingers brush my lips and linger at my cheek. Soon he's back, giving commands.

"Now, just keep both hands on the helm. Look, you can see where we are on my GPS," he says, pointing to a virtual marine map. "Just keep heading straight and try and avoid those lobster pots. Last thing we need is to get tangled in those lines."

Logan is standing at my back, his arms around me, his hands on mine guiding the large wheel in front of me. I feel his breath on my cheek as he leans in with instructions. How is it that I feel guilty? This man is attractive, and I've seen him staring at me when he thinks I'm not looking.

"I've got it, Logan, no, really, I do," I let him know, thinking I should shake him off.

He points out the Pemaquid Point lighthouse and several of the smaller islands along the way. Soon we see Atlantic puffins perched on rocky outcroppings, their bright orange bills a beacon from a stony shore. Off in the distance is Old Hump Ledge protruding from the Gulf of Maine, and Logan lets the jib sheet out to run with the wind.

"Lily, any word from your toxicology colleague on the senator's specimens we collected? I know you said it would be a long shot," he says, finally settling down to business.

"There's something there, but my friend's not sure what it is. Toxicology results can take some time, particularly if the toxin we're looking for is not common. And that's his specialty—the uncommon."

The wind's picking up now, and I reach in my bag to tie a scarf around my head—pirate style. I've been snacking on chunks of sugar-coated ginger to ease the queasiness I feel growing in my stomach. It's been hours since we left the dock.

"You do think he was poisoned, right?" he asks as he sails toward the edge of a small island. I can see pine trees high above rocky ledges and a small pebbly beach hidden between large impenetrable boulders.

"Yes, I do think Steinman was murdered, and I believe it was poison. It's like we said when we looked at the microscopics. But right now, I'm at a loss for how it was done. I'm still waiting for the tox results to confirm my suspicions, but I think we can rule out that he was poisoned by food or drink, given that he shared his meal with his wife. So there has to have been another way."

Logan nods his head and works on setting the anchor. We stop for a simple lunch near this jewel in the ocean—a gorgeous backdrop of stubby pines, gulls floating in the air and water, and a marine breeze kicking up whitecaps in the sea. A splash heralds the plunk of the anchor.

"While you're thinking about this, Lily, I'm going to get those lobsters ready. Do you want some corn on the cob as well? Tom left me some fresh groceries," he says, handing me some corn to shuck.

"Sure. I've asked to have the senator's medications analyzed. The most obvious possibility, don't you agree?"

I've started peeling back the layers of the corn husks while angel-like silk escapes into the wind, white-gold strands taking flight over the sea. What will we uncover when we peel back the layers on our mystery?

"I think it's a good possibility. Something I

would check," he says, melting butter and heating up the lobster.

I feel relaxed. I'm in the company of a man who's at ease with himself, unencumbered by having been seduced to commit murder like the rest of Chad's team—Logan's only job to identify its telltale signs.

We sit in the cockpit under the Bimini, its function to keep the sun at bay, and eat a messy meal, butter dripping down the corners of our mouths. The lobster crackers break open the succulent claws allowing us to handpick the warm meat from the shells. I find myself caught up in Logan's story about his falling off the boat.

"So, I asked this rookie sailor I took out for the day to push the throttle forward and inch up to the mooring so I could grab it with the boat hook. Next thing I know, we're going backwards, bump into another boat, and I fall overboard. I was pissed," he says, laughing. I find myself laughing too and put my hand on his arm. It's warm from the heat of the sun.

Logan's hand reaches toward my face. "You have a little butter on your chin," he says as his fingers gently wipe away the mess.

"I do?" Feeling slightly embarrassed, I pick up a napkin and blot my mouth. Yet, his touch sends tingles through my body. He sees it too and leans in for a kiss. I freeze for a moment, then blurt out, "What an absolutely gorgeous spot. Can't believe

I'm out here working on a case." Logan gives me a surprised look wondering if he misread the signals. He hasn't; I'm just conflicted.

The lunch consumed, residual lobster shells spill over the boat's edges, feeding the fish below and the gulls soaring overhead. Logan gets the sail in place so we can make it back before the light slips away.

"Logan, have you always been a sailor?" I ask, the wind picking up and the boat heeling to one side. I can feel the water running by me at a steady pace, my hand dipped into the sea below while watching the swells in the distance getting larger. The clouds have now turned dark and could herald rain tonight.

"Yes, I learned to sail off the North Shore of Long Island. Then I spent a lot of time sailing with my roommate up in Maine and got to know the islands pretty well. Lily, you have that PFD on? It's getting a little rough," he says as he furls in the jib.

I check my inflatable life vest, pulling the strap a little tighter around my waist. My stomach's churning, and I wish I'd taken some motion sickness medication before we started up again. The black clouds that seemed so distant have suddenly caught up with us, and rain is pelting my face. I didn't bring any rain gear since the sun had had command of the sky for most of the day.

"Logan, is everything all right?" I ask, the

boat rocking from side to side as the wind blows harder, pushing dark clouds on top of us. This is a sudden storm. I feel vulnerable out in the middle of a murky and churning sea. "Do you have an extra rain jacket I can wear? It's freezing." He throws me a windbreaker that's large enough to fit over my life vest.

Logan's now focused on the lines; one has gotten wrapped around the forward hatch. He crawls out on the deck toward the bow, exposed to the elements, trying to manually free up the line. He can see that I'm anxious.

"Lily, take up the slack in the jib sheet," Logan shouts. "Take three wraps on the winch. It'll be okay. Hold on to the boat's wheel and try and keep us on course," he yells, fighting the drowning storm.

"Logan, I'm having trouble keeping the boat straight," I shout back, our vessel rocking fiercely with each hit of a swell.

"Can you turn on the automatic pilot?" he asks, still struggling with the line.

"I don't know how," I answer, wrestling to keep us upright.

Logan jumps down off the deck into the cockpit, gently but firmly nudges me aside, and reaches for the switch to the automatic pilot.

"Goddamn. That last gust of wind just blew the hatch open again. I guess I didn't secure it when I was trying to free the line."

"I'll get it," I say and quickly move up on the forward deck, inching my way to the open hatch while Logan steadies the boat.

"No, Lily, it's too dangerous, come back."

I ignore Logan's plea and push the hatch down as hard as I can. "Logan, I got it!" I call out over the wind. "I was able to close the hatch."

"Careful coming back aft," he says, heading the boat into the wind.

I'm about to return to the cockpit when I see an enormous wave heading for us as a gust of wind jibes the sail. *Rogue Angel* suddenly shifts, the boom swings across the deck, strikes me, and I feel myself go overboard with one last shout, "Logan!" The water encompasses me like an arctic winter, and then there's nothing but blackness.

"Lily, Lily. Wake up, Lily. Come on, open your eyes."

I hear a muffled voice call out my name. I'm having some trouble focusing. There's a lump on my head, and I find myself wrapped in a blanket and nothing else. I'm down below deck; there's a heater blasting, warming up the cabin.

"Logan? Logan, what happened?" I ask, remembering how cold the water was.

"Thank God, Lily. You had me scared. We got hit by a rogue wave, the wind shifted, the boom hit you in the head and knocked you overboard. Jesus, I had all to do to get the boat turned around.

Thank God, this boat's got a step-up transom; I was able to get next to you and haul you out of the water pretty fast. That water's cold, and you dropped your body temp. Probably became a little hypothermic. There's no surviving in Maine waters this time of year. Ah, look, sorry about the clothes. I had to rip every stitch off you quick, so you wouldn't freeze to death. I promise I didn't look," he says, looking down at the floor, trying to hide his face.

By now, I'm alert, mortified that I'm only in a blanket, my hair clearly towel dried by a man I hardly know. I pull the fleece wrap in close around me.

"Logan, are we heading back now?" My voice has a note of concern. I can hear the wind howling.

"No, we can't. The weather's made it too dangerous—surprise storm with elevated seas. Now, I've made it into this little harbor off Damariscove Island. It's protected, so we'll be safe here for the time being. Also, when the boom hit you, the boat veered, and the prop got tangled in the lines from a lobster pot; Goddamn things, I hate steering around them."

"What do you mean, the lines got tangled?" I stop and rub my head.

"I mean, for now, we're stuck here for the night. Tomorrow, I'll have to see what I can do about the lines."

"I don't understand," I say, my pitch elevated and with a sense of panic in my voice, "can't you call the Coast Guard or something?"

"Lily, there's no cell phone coverage out here, and my antenna at the top of the mast isn't working. Tom told me earlier that there were some problems with the solar panels keeping the batteries charged, and he was going to fix it next week. You're going to have to trust me. We're safe in this cove and just have to wait out the storm until morning. I've made some hot soup to help warm you up, and I have some clothes for you to put on. Let me get them for you. You'll feel better."

I can't believe this is happening. Why didn't I just stay in my safe apartment?

"Logan, please let me have the clothes." I can hear my teeth chattering, and I'm sure Logan can too.

"Sure, Lily. Right here. They're men's pajamas, but they should keep you warm. You're shivering."

He wraps his arms around me and vigorously rubs my back, trying to chase out the chill. I feel weak, the cold overtaking my senses. He pushes my head back and looks into my eyes. I take in his gaze and hold it, knowing full well what is to come.

"Lily, you're a beautiful woman," he says, stroking my damp mane, "and from the moment

I saw you, before I even knew who you were, I fantasized about being with you. I know it's crazy, but it's true."

"Logan, I . . ."

"Damn, woman, you knock me off my sea legs," he says, pulling me in tight.

I close my eyes and remind myself that I have a soul mate—one true love in my life. That's what I always told myself. But he's not here now, and our angry exchange flashes across my mind. I should pull out of this tailspin, and I can't. Or maybe I just don't want to. I'm Alice, falling down the rabbit hole. I feel Logan's lips touch mine, I feel his hardness up against me, and all the emotions I try to block from my brain seep in through the cracks, the fissures wrought by time, loneliness, and anger—the blanket slipping from my shoulders.

Our lips meet, and I find myself kissing Logan back. He breathes warm air into my ear, and I feel his tongue lick my lips before gently parting them. His kiss is smooth, not intrusive, wet, and yet warm. I pull his T-shirt over his head and run my hands along his tanned chest. He slips out of his shorts, bracing himself against the cabin as the boat rocks. The chill leaves me as his warm body lays on top of mine. I gently bite his ears, and he makes a sound of approval. At this moment, I want him and guide him inside me.

Don't look back, Lily. Don't focus. Just let

go. And Logan and I make love like the sun will never rise again.

The next morning the air is still, my head still aches, and Logan's nowhere to be found. I find myself in silky men's pajamas and pretend not to remember all the details from the night before. Hot states cause us to do things we wouldn't normally do. Science has shown this to be true—the hot-cold empathy gap. I manage to climb up from below, inhale fresh air and see sunlight once again grace the sky, just as Logan climbs up the transom in a wet suit.

"What are you doing?" I ask, trying to ignore how I really feel. I'll stay on safe ground.

"Good morning, Lily. I hope you're feeling a little better. I was down under the propeller trying to cut the lines that got tangled there last night. I think I was successful. I can make us some coffee, and then we can head back."

I'm silent.

"Look, Lily. About last night. I didn't mean for any of that to happen. I mean, I wanted it to happen, but I don't want you to think that was my plan all along. Neither one of us is married and, as far as I know, isn't with anyone. Isn't that the case? So, I'd like to see you again and not just professionally."

Here I stand, on the deck of a thirty-seven-foot sloop in sterling gray silk pajamas twisting the platinum bracelet on my wrist, desperately trying to find my sea legs while wrestling with my conscience. Another crossroad, another choice between life real or imagined. Pixie Dust, where are you now?

CHAPTER 12

Boston

No time to think, no time to feel—my head buried in my work. What've I done? Have I betrayed the man I call my soulmate? There's been no word from JP since we parted on less than happy terms.

I haven't spoken to Logan since he dropped me off in Boston. It was a long quiet drive back. He apologized to me if I thought that he hurt me. He said it really wasn't an ambush, but I'm not so sure. Am I just another conquest to him? People can change under the right circumstances or once they meet the right person. I've heard of couples claiming love at first sight. Maybe I thought JP was my soul mate when I first saw him in Cambridge all those years ago. I don't know. I take a long time to warm up to a person, play it close to the vest, and don't give freely of my emotions. But Logan? I'm still trying to understand him.

I have to go to the hospital this morning, then I have a video call with Dr. John Chi Leigh much later since we're twelve hours apart. He's been working on the specimens I sent him from the autopsy and said he may have preliminary results for me.

• • •

"Morning, Lisa," I say with a smile on my face.

Lisa is sitting at her desk, rifling through paperwork. It looks like those damn TEFRA reports she hands out every quarter. None of us like filling out time sheets that ask doctors at a teaching hospital to document the amount of time in a week they spend on teaching, administration, supervision, direct patient care, and research. The weeks for review are predesignated, and as of late, I have to say I may not have been at the hospital on the weeks I have to account for. Lisa knows this.

"Lisa, you're too cruel making me fill out these forms again," I tell her with sarcasm in my voice.

"Come on, Dr. Lily. You can do this. I know you can," she says, pushing herself away from her workstation and standing up. She's wearing sneakers again, so there must be a lot of running around between buildings today. She's really a very accomplished woman. She only does this job so she can have more time for herself.

"Lisa, I'll have to pick two alternate weeks. You know that, right?"

"Isn't that what you always say when you have to fill out these reports?" Now she's smiling, her broad grin lighting up her face. "Oh, and you have a message from a medical examiner in Washington, D.C. He would like you to call him about a case he's working on. Here is his name and phone number. He gave his cell phone number too, just in case."

"Thanks, Lisa." I'll have to deal with this.

When I get into my office, I see a note on my desk from Dr. Kelley. He has some lab results for me. I page him. Best get my clinical obligations out of the way before I talk to Leigh. I'm sure that conversation will have me heading down my alternate life's path.

"Hey, Dr. Robinson. I have the results on the teenager who overdosed on the antidepressant. You called it," Kelley says.

"So, what were the results?"

"Here you go," he says, handing me the report. "In a nutshell, he couldn't metabolize the drug properly, so the blood concentration was just building to toxic levels."

"Thanks, Kelley. We solved the mystery, and the answer was something that could've easily been overlooked. Others may have assumed the child was lying about attempting suicide with pills. We discovered that his body can't make all the enzymes he needs to break down and eliminate this drug. This will help him and his family tremendously. Please notify his psychiatrist so she can adjust his dose accordingly."

He's pleased with the case and will follow up with the family. Sometimes the toxicology service is more than endless deaths from opioid addic-tion. Sometimes we have an opportunity to track down a metabolic error and save someone from an overdose not of their making. Before Kelley leaves, he also lets me know that he's heard from Rose. She's still on leave from the medical school but will be coming by the lab this afternoon to meet with him. He wants to know if I can spend some time with her. Kelley's so excited that he's found a medical student interested in going into pathology that he wants to do everything he can to keep her close. I'm excited too, but worry about the feelings I bury, causing turbulence in my heart. I need a moment to reflect.

Is my life about to crash before me? There, dashing up against the rocks outlining the rugged coast, a sailboat struggling against the swells. I have to face Rose, my daughter, only to disguise my feelings and my true relationship to her. Honestly, I just want to hold her again, love her, and be part of her life. Then there's Logan. What a mess. Yes, I'm not married to JP, and as far as anyone knows, I'm not with JP or anyone for that matter. I've had colleagues ask me why I'm not in a relationship. "Lily," they say, "You're the total package. Looks, brains, a successful doctor, and you don't have a man?" What can I say? The truth? That some women don't need or want a man in their life, or that I have a man in my life, I just can't say who or anything about him. It leaves a lot of room for loneliness, contemplation, and speculation.

And, not to forget about Senator Steinman. I'm sure he's been murdered. When I speak with Leigh later, I will know if it's poison. But if so, how was he poisoned? We've ruled out the food. The medications were legitimate, so there had to be another way to get the poison into him. I'm the impatient type. I want to speak with Leigh, now. I've said it before, pathologists like solving puzzles, and this one has my name written all over it.

There's a knock at the door. Probably Lisa telling me I missed something on her to-do list. I do love that woman—keeper of the order.

"Come in, come in."

"Hi Dr. Robinson, sorry to barge in on you right now, but Lisa said you had a few minutes open on your calendar, and since I will be having lunch with Dr. Kelley later, I was wondering if I could speak with you now. If that's okay," Rose says. She's dressed casually in jeans and a short sleeve pink blouse. Her backpack is slung over her right shoulder.

"Rose, please come in. Yes, I didn't expect you until a little later, but it's okay. Have a seat." My heart is pumping, and my mind is racing. My daughter! "How are you doing?"

"I'm all right, I guess. You remember when I last saw you that my mother had just awoken from a coma after a terrible car accident. I flew back to France to see her. She's in rehab now, but her traumatic brain injury is severe. She doesn't really remember much," Rose said. I can see her emerald eyes swelling with tears, and I try hard not to let my own spill forth.

"Rose, I'm so sorry. You know that the brain's a remarkable organ. But TBI can sometimes lead to long-term deficits. I'm sure Adrienne's, your mother's, doctors have discussed this with you." I find it hard to acknowledge she has a mother other than me.

"Yes, they have. There's hope, I have hope, that she'll recover most of her function. But I feel so alone. There's a nice priest back in Reims who is helping me, Père Berger, but I don't have any family," Rose tells me, wiping the tears away with a tissue. I have a box on my desk just for this purpose. Sometimes my colleagues and doctors in training sit here, a safe place between these walls, and allow me to talk them off the ledge. Yes, doctors, too, sometimes look to jump when the job gets unbearable. Fighting death is a challenge.

"Père Berger, you say?" I know full well who he is, having met him in Reims on the Moreau estate when Jean Paul and I were on a short holiday in France. A lovely cleric who alerted JP and me to my Rose's existence and shares those rare green eyes with us. He couldn't help but notice the similarity in coloring between

Rose and me—dark hair, light complexion, and emerald green eyes.

"Yes, he knows my mother and helped me when she was in the hospital. He's been such a gift," she says, a tear spilling over her pink cheek. I'm aching inside for her.

"I'm so sorry, Rose. How can I help you?" I hate to sound so clinical, but what else can I say?

"No, I'm the one who should be sorry, Dr. Robinson, coming in here and babbling about my personal life. I apologize," she says, managing a large sniff. "What I wanted to ask you, what I wanted to say, is it okay with you if I shadow Dr. Kelley for the next few months? He says it's okay with him if it's okay with you. The medical school will give me a pass as a medical observer, so I'll be officially cleared. I plan to resume my studies the following academic year. I do have to return to France to see my mother, but then I should have more free time for shadowing Dr. Kelley." She twists the ring on her right hand to quell her anxiety. I've seen that ring before—a gold band with a heart-shaped red stone in the center.

"Yes, Rose, it's all right with me. Would it be helpful to you if we meet on a regular basis? I could function, as perhaps your advisor? What do you think?" My God, am I that transparent? I just want to be as close as I can. My heart is still racing. Bruised and torn as it is, it still beats.

"Dr. Robinson, that would be so great!" she tells me finally with some brightness in her voice.

"I'll have Lisa set something up for us. However, I'm sure she's told you that I travel quite a bit, so I apologize in advance if I cancel any of our meetings." I sound under control. I may have found a path forward.

"Rose, one more thing. What about the man with the pistachio brain?"

"I'm sorry, what?"

"The man with the pistachio brain. Kelley told me that he was going to discuss the autopsy case with you."

"Oh, yes. I remember. Well, I did a little research on that. There are several conditions that could cause the brain to turn that color. I've seen autopsy pictures, too, and it's really striking how the flat gray folds become this soft blue-green."

"So, what do you think?

"Well, I read that methylene blue can cause this. And our patient got this drug because he was in refractory shock. The medical team thought the methylene blue could improve his low blood pressure. Unfortunately, he didn't make it."

"Impressive, Rose. Your reading's paying off. I know Kelley still has to finalize the case, so I'll be interested to see his report."

"Thank you," she says, now standing and looking a bit more upbeat than when she came in.

As she makes her way to the door, I feel like

I can breathe again. I hope over time that I'll be able to keep my part of the bargain.

"Rose," I call out just before she slips out into the main office, trying to prolong the meeting just a few seconds more. "Where are you and Kelley going for lunch?"

"Oh, he's taking me to a sushi place near the hospital. I've never tried raw fish before."

"I know the place, Rose. You're a risk-taker. Watch out for parasites."

She laughs, and I see the delight on her face, her long dark hair falling below her shoulders, and her sparkly green eyes. She looks good in those form-fitting pants. I'm sure Kelley will appreciate that too.

"So, John Chi, what've you got for me?"

"Ah, Dr. Robinson. You do have the most interesting cases," he says.

We're on an internet call so we can see each other. My closest toxicology colleague lives on Hong Kong Island, yet we regularly cross paths on one continent or another.

"I do have some findings for you," he says, his short dark hair now grayer than when I first met him. An intelligent look peers from behind the simple black glasses that frame his brown eyes.

John Chi Leigh is beyond brilliant, and recently, I was stunned to learn that he also works in a small global consortium helping keep world order and peace. He's not beyond killing to make it happen, either. He's done it several times that I'm aware of, and twice he's saved me from inevitable death. I watched this superb chemist take out one of the worst terrorists on the planet, and afterward, calmly tell me a story about his grandfather and my grandmother—how they were once lovers. I'm wearing the ring—a gold snake coiled in diamonds with a ruby head—his ancestor gave mine to seal their bond of love all those years ago. However, the relationship was never meant to be, and each went on to marry someone else.

"Curiosity's killing me. Were you able to get anything from the specimens I sent you? What did you find, John?" I'm sitting on the edge of my chair, waiting for an answer.

"I found evidence of a venom that produces hemolytic, proteolytic, and cytotoxic properties. A potent combination."

"God, I knew it was poison," I say, jumping up from my chair like a loose spring from a mattress. "So a venom that causes bleeding and breaks down tissues and cells. Sounds like the properties of some snake venoms."

"Yes, it does. But it is not. I did an extraction process for acids and bases on the material you sent. The properties of this venom were interesting. It destroys tissue. Did you see evidence of necrosis around the aortic valve implant?"

"We did. And also both bleeding and microthrombi in several organs."

"There is more, Lily Robinson. The venom was microencapsulated, and these minute beads degraded over time, finally releasing the venom into the system."

"Microencapsulation? We saw that over a year ago in New York with the ricin mass poisoning. You remember, John—that was courtesy of the Russians. So, how in God's name did this poison get into the senator?" I ask, my mind going a hundred miles an hour and thinking of our encounter with Markovic and his men.

"This is where it gets fascinating. You sent me the implanted aortic valve from your patient collected during the autopsy. The tissue that overlies the metal alloy mesh was porcine. From what I could tell, there appeared to be a high concentration of venom in that tissue. I believe the artificial valve was the source of the poison."

"Oh my God! So a simple medical procedure produced a ticking time bomb. I cannot believe it. This sounds like a Russian hit job."

"I agree, Lily Robinson. Do you remember an assignment where you soaked corneal lens implants in toxin to assassinate a terrorist during his cataract surgery?"

"Of course, I do. I used toxin from *Leiurus quinquestriatus*, the deathstalker scorpion."

"And from where did you obtain that toxin?

"I have a contact in the Middle East that I've used in the past who specializes in scorpion venom and toxins."

"Lily Robinson, you need to travel and see that man again. What I found appears to be consistent with venom from the scorpion *Hemiscorpius lepturis*."

And a single word floods my brain. Omair.

CHAPTER 13

The Middle East

Omair opened the lid on the plastic container. Inside, the multi-legged creatures scurried as their hiding places were uncovered by the light. The collection was housed in a darkened room containing multiple shelves with plastic boxes—cages—filled with scorpions. Omair's basement was a secretive venom factory, where he could carry out his work undisturbed.

Using forceps attached to an electrically charged wire, he grabbed the scorpion by the tail and held it in the air. The scorpion's pincers opened and closed, trying to catch its aggressive prey readying its tail to strike if it could get free. Omair knew that as long as he held the scorpion's tail in the tweezers, he would not get stung. He was more than familiar with their anatomy: the metosoma, the tail; and the telson, the stinger, ending in a barb or aculeus. That was the business end that Omair was interested in.

On the table sat a homemade apparatus that he had constructed using electrical wires, a battery, and a small metal strainer originally utilized for catching tea leaves. Using the battery, he was able to pass a mild electrical current through the strainer. While holding the scorpion in one hand and a glass capillary tube in the other, Omair could provoke the scorpion into assuming a battle pose by flicking the small tube at its pincers, thus kicking up the amount of poison concentrated at the barb. Next, he gave the scorpion a mild shock as he dropped it onto the electrified strainer completing the circuit between the forceps and the metal sieve. The tip of the tail pulsated, pushing out a tiny bead of fluid, which Omair captured with the capillary tube. He would milk his scorpions daily, collecting each precious drop of venom until he had the desired amount and concentration.

The scorpion wrangler traveled the Middle East, collecting various specimens from underneath rocks and sequestered crevices where they hid by day. When he returned to his home, he separated the scorpions by species, keeping only those that yielded the most potent venom and with whom he had success in milking. A schoolteacher by day, Omair spent years studying the nature of his captives and was an expert on their behavior and the extent of their toxicity.

Bottled up, his venoms were for sale to the highest bidder. For the most part, he sold his venom primarily for use in medical research. Since he needed to keep his operation secretive, he worked with a single intermediary, who only contacted him by email. Once he received an email, he would send off the venom to the middleman, who, in turn, would forward it to the researcher. There was only one exception to this rule due to a long-standing arrangement with a military operation that had been in place for many years. The contact, whose name he did not know, arranged to see him in person on the rare occasion to collect their poison for purposes unknown. Omair never asked questions, and his client never ventured any information. It was their business.

Today Omair let his worries invade his mind. His sunbaked hands had been shaky during this morning's milking process. He tried to push these thoughts out of his head, but they kept creeping back. It was something unusual that had happened several months ago. Two travelers had shown up unexpectedly at his school and watched him while he was teaching his students. They had remained quiet at the back of the classroom but focused their gaze on Omair while he laid out his lesson plans that morning. Not wanting to alarm his students, Omair continued with his work, allowing the children's eager faces to rest their attention on him and not the strangers. When he was done for the day, he locked up the classroom and kept his eyes forward, not engaging the visitors while they followed him home. Unable to escape, Omair feared the worst.

When they reached his house, Omair stopped at

the door before going inside and finally looked into the faces of those who trailed him. His voice and his body shook. He clasped both hands together in an attempt to quiet their movement.

"What is it that you want from me?" he asked, shuffling nervously and speaking in English. The two travelers were dressed similarly—long white robes over light-colored pants and heads and faces wrapped with long gauze-like material. Omair had a sense they were not from the Middle East.

"Inside, and we will talk," the man said, lowering the wrap below his chin. His voice was forceful yet quiet.

Omair recognized the accent as Russian. He had no dealings with the Russians, and as far as he knew, his middleman only sold his product to scientists in Europe and the United States. The door closed behind the three of them, and Omair waited until the traveler spoke. He wasn't sure, but he suspected that the man's companion was a woman, having a slighter build and smaller hands. He or she didn't speak—just watched with blue-gray eyes above the gauze.

"The children are lovely, are they not?" the man asked. He wiped some of the red dust off his pants while speaking to Omair.

"What do you want from me?" Omair shuddered.

The children were a bright spot in the village. Sons, and even some daughters, of his neighbors, attended the small classroom. He felt the hair stand up on the back of his neck, and sweat dampened his tan robe and turban. Overt violence repelled him.

"I asked you what business you have with me. What do you want?" Omair said boldly.

"We require a particular venom," the Russian said, reaching deep into his pocket and pulling out a scrap of paper. He handed it to Omair.

Omair read the words scratched on the paper and looked back at the two.

"I am a schoolteacher; I do not understand what it is you want."

The man stepped closer to the scorpion wrangler and pushed him up against the wall. Hard metal poked into Omair's ribcage, causing him to wince. Unable to push the Russian away, he spoke.

"I, I do not deal directly with those requesting my harvests. I go through a middleman who distributes my products to scientists. How did you find me?"

"No middleman. Just us," the Russian said, sweeping his hand wide to include his traveling companion.

"I, I am sorry. I cannot help you," Omair said.

The person who looked as though they could be a female circled the room, stopped by a table, and picked up some children's books sitting in a neat stack. She flipped through the pages and then purposely dropped the books onto the floor. Then spotting a picture of the schoolchildren, the companion removed a knife from her pack, broke the glass in the frame, and slashed the photograph. Omair cried out. This was the signal for her companion to resume speaking.

"What a shame for the children. Just give us what we want." The voice was menacing, and Omair, breaking away from his grip, scrambled to pick up the books and the marred picture.

Omair recognized that this was not an idle threat. It would be one thing to give up his own life, but not the children's. His work as a quiet schoolteacher, helping his community using the education he'd earned, provided a practical cover for his scorpion business. He wanted to stay in the background—under the radar—while the world raced by. If he gave them what they wanted, Omair hoped they would leave the children alone. He had agreed to cooperate. Leaving the two upstairs, he padded down to his basement and opened the door to the ultracold freezer chest. Donning protective gloves, he pushed aside the dry ice he used for shipping and pulled out a vial from a marked box. That day, he gave them what they wanted, and he never heard from them again.

Worried though he was, this morning Omair dressed—as he would for school five days a week. A clean cotton garment to reflect the sunlight. When he opened his top drawer, he saw the small box given to him by the Russians at the end of their encounter. Their instructions had been clear. If ever there was a choice to be made between the lives of the schoolchildren, or the truth, this box would hold the answer. Omair knew what he had to do. He placed the gift on top of the small, worn wooden piece of furniture and left his room, ready for school.

Omair made his way to a small clay-colored building with two front-facing windows divided into nine small panes of glass. Inside the building, there were six rows of twelve tables, a center aisle in between—each table big enough for two students to sit next to each other. He stood at the front of the room, ready to begin his lessons of the day for his middle school learners. Teaching natural science and mathematics to his pupils paid little money, yet Omair was thankful that he had been given the opportunity to receive a good education when he was younger. The teaching had been his true passion, and the scorpion business only provided the means to keep it all going.

After several hours in the classroom, Omair left the building and returned to his home, still feeling anxious about his meeting later this evening. The modest abode, also clay-colored with few windows, would be ready to receive the single client he had worked with directly for years. This particular patron always knew precisely what they wanted and knew specific details of the species of scorpions they required. He expected the arrival tonight and in the presence of an escort entourage. This was always the safest way to travel to Omair's abode. He again fretted over the visit by the Russians months ago, but nothing had come of it, and he begged his mind to let it go. He had taken the money from that sale, hidden it in a secret foreign account with the rest of the money garnered from his covert business. Instructions, left with his middleman, described his plans for the money—just in case. Now he waited until nightfall.

Chapter 14

The Middle East

I've been here several times over the years under an assumed name. It's a treacherous journey, but I travel with a small military escort. The men from these special forces are unsure of my purpose, but they understand that it's part of an intelligence operation, so accommodations are made. If I don't harvest my own poison garden or work with Dr. John Chi Leigh creating novel toxins, I travel around the world, collecting what I need.

It feels like I've lived on a military plane for the last few days. I've slept in my clothes—sand-colored pants paired with an army brown T-shirt and sturdy boots. My head is completely covered, hair tucked under a hat, a large white scarf wrapped around my neck, while a tan camouflage jacket completes the getup. I have to admit that I'm never comfortable coming here.

It's dark with few people on the dirt roads. No one gives us a second look. We approach the house that I've gone to before—modest clay-colored stone with few windows. I knock on the door. A tall man with dark hair and a grizzled beard answers and invites me in while the few men traveling with me wait outside.

"Omair, thank you for seeing me," I say while unraveling the scarf. He speaks English, having attended some schooling in Britain, so we can converse freely.

"Very surprised to hear from you," Omair replies. "I thought you had collected enough of what you wanted the last time you traveled through the Middle East." I can see him divert his dark eyes away from mine. He shifts his weight while he shows me into a central room and offers me a chair. Do I detect a sense of hesitation, even a wobble, in his voice?

"How's business?" I ask him, taking a seat and not letting on that I feel his discomfort. His house is modest, sparsely furnished, clean, and I assume he has enough to meet his needs. I say that because I'm told he's paid handsomely for what he does for us. Where the money goes and for what purposes, I cannot say; it's a mystery.

Omair's quiet. Usually a little more conversive, he must know why I am here. I'm sure of it.

"Business has been good," he finally answers. His white robe reaches to the floor, and there's orange dust that stains its edges.

"Omair," I start cautiously, "we agreed that you would only sell your venoms to specific research institutions and to no individual other than me. Yes? I believe it was made clear to you that if you didn't follow the rules, well, you would be out of business." I'm not here to make threats, just tell it like it is and get the information we need. But his body language says there's more. So, I continue.

"May I ask you what is it that you do with all the money you make? I mean money from your venom business. Frankly, I don't see you putting it into your home," I say as I sweep my hand in the air indicating his modest dwelling. What he does with the money we give him and the discretion he affords us in return is not usually up for discussion. He and I don't talk about such things. But he knows that I'm on to him.

"Yes, we agreed," is all he offers.

"When I was here last time, you easily met my request and gave me toxin from the deathstalker scorpion. Most of the venoms or toxins you trade-in, Omair, contain neurotoxins from the genera *Leiurus*, *Androctonus*, and *Hottentotta*. I'm sure there are others. But toxin from *Hemiscorpius lepturus*—that's unusual for you. Who's interested in using venom from this scorpion, Omair?"

His discomfort grows. He stands directly in front of me, hands clutching one another to occupy his worry, and a look of fright on his face. I can see his eyes grow wide, and his chin scrunch his beard up and down as if he's grinding his teeth. I think he realizes that this could be his undoing. Not so much from me, but possibly from the men standing guard at the entrance and exit of his home. Or perhaps from those who bought the precious drops milked from *Hemiscorpius*. I'm reasonably sure I know whom I would choose to kill me.

"Omair, I found residual venom in the body of someone important—a United States government official. It's irrefutable—I've had it confirmed. Who'd you sell the *Hemiscorpius* venom to? I need to know now." My voice sounds stern, and the scorpion wrangler backs off.

A bead of sweat runs down his forehead, and I see his body sway. "Wait here. Let me get that for you," he says. Get what?

Omair turns and leaves the room. Yet, I can smell the adrenaline that permeates his body and spills into the air. It stimulates my heart, which begins to race, a signal molecule suspended in space, and then I hear the thud in the adjacent room. Now my mind also races, trying to keep pace with my heart. I know. Goddamn it, I know. I run to his room. It's Omair—on the floor. A final twitch seals his death, and a trickle of spittle escapes his mouth—no words for me. As I kneel down at his side, I smell the bitter almond odor on his breath and see the lifeless eyes before me.

"Help, me," I shout out to the men surrounding this house. There will be nothing they can do, but I need them here now.

My companions will come rushing in and surround Omair's body. They will ask me what's happened in a flurry of words. What do I tell them? Within seconds, I pull the disposable gloves out of my pack—necessary for the unexpected. Leaning over the body, I pry Omair's mouth open and find the remnants of glass. He had an L-pill. God, the man had a kill-pill. A small capsule of cyanide. A quick death, leaving us with many unanswered questions.

Poor Omair. Whoever took the *Hemiscorpius* toxin must have threatened him. What that threat was, I don't know. Other than milk scorpions and sell their venom, I have no idea what Omair did with his time. I should know, but I never asked.

"Fuck, what the hell happened here?" says one of the soldiers accompanying me. Danny, his nickname, is native to the area and speaks the language as well. But he works for us.

He puts his rifle down and bends over the body. "Shit, now what are we supposed to do?"

"Don't get too close," I tell him. "It's cyanide. He crushed a cyanide pill in his back teeth. Quick death. Nothing I could do to save him."

Mike, a big man wearing military fatigues, casts a shadow over us as he peers down. "Jesus, what the fuck?" he says, eyeing the dead man on the floor. Then he adds, "I'm going to sweep the place. I'll grab his laptop, phone, and anything else that looks like it could be connected to us." He's usually quiet and acts more like a bodyguard.

Now a thought just pops into my head. This would be where JP comes in, but he's not here, so it's up to me to doctor the scene. I kneel down next to the body and, with my gloved hand, sweep all the tiny pieces of glass from Omair's mouth.

"Danny, get me a wet washcloth. Now," I bark.

Danny scrambles and finds something in the kitchen that will do. I rinse out Omair's mouth. Look, this plan would not work if we were in Boston, but it might work in the middle of the desert, in the middle of almost nowhere.

I head toward the basement, where I've seen Omair disappear on my previous visits. Stone stairs lead me to a dusty dark place. It's just as I imagined. Racks of plastic containers that hold the scorpions and the insects used to feed them stand in rows. Omair was meticulous. He clearly labeled the creatures' cages, so I don't have to guess the species. There are about a dozen containers down here, most containing one or two scorpions. Some scorpions can live communally, others not so much. Fights to the death and cannibalism will ensue. Yet, if we leave them all here, someone may be able to connect the dots. I scan through the racks. Ah, this is what I'm looking for—*Leiurus quinquestriatus*, the deathstalker. I remove the cover and peek inside the container as several fat yellow scorpions scurry for shelter. These will do.

Next, I go to the small chest freezer. Again, Omair meticulously labeled each box and each vial with the date and each scorpion's genus and species. I use the dry ice in the freezer to surround the ampoules, and then stuff all of it into my backpack. There should be enough ice to keep things cold until we get back. Keeping *L. quinquestriatus* separate, I pour all the scorpions and their insect food source, mealworms, into one large plastic container. Within minutes, many of the species start fighting each other.

What to do about his milking apparatus? I pull it apart. The tea strainer will go in the kitchen. The wires and battery will remain here. Perhaps Omair would be thought to have an electronics hobby of some kind. I've asked Danny to find any kind of food that we could stick in the chest freezer down here. He finds something we think could be meat in the kitchen fridge, and I throw that in the basement freezer and close the lid.

Mike has grabbed as much paperwork as he thinks could be related to business, the small laptop, and Omair's phone. Lastly, I return to Omair's bedroom for one last-minute look-see and notice a little box on the top of the wooden dresser. Turning it over, it appears to have writing, in Russian, on the underside, so I throw the box into my pack, which is now getting filled. One more thing catches my eye. A slashed photograph of Omair and several children sit in a broken picture frame on his dresser. Did they threaten to kill these schoolchildren? Oh, God. I don't want to know. I absolutely do not want to know.

As we are about to leave, I bend over Omair and, using forceps that I found downstairs, pick up one of the fat yellow scorpions by the tail and provoke it. Then I place the agitated beast under Omair's robe observing the stinger prick the flesh, and repeat the process with a second scorpion. There's one more scorpion in the container, and I place it into a slipper I find near the bed.

We leave the modest dwelling, stacked plastic cages in hand, and flee into the night. Danny drives while Mike is riding shotgun. I'm in the backseat, holding on to the single container filled with dozens of nature's poison soldiers. When we reach the outskirts of the small village, we stop, and Danny takes the box with all the remaining scorpions and dumps them near some rubble. And we watch them scurry—some still locked in battle, others half-eaten by their enemies—to the darkest crevices of the underworld.

Chapter 15

Russia

Alexis had done what the burly man had asked months ago. She and Sergei had traveled to the dusty corners of the Middle East to pick up a "package" and bring it back to Moscow. Sergei had done all the talking and made all the threats that Alexis had no doubt he would keep. Her only role had been as a cover for Sergei and to create some drama while visiting the schoolteacher. Once back in Moscow, Alexis had tried again to slip into the wings, appearing only as a stagehand in black, moving the scenery undetected. She was unsuccessful.

Sergei regularly came to visit Alexis at the bookstore as he continued their charade of a romantic couple. Occasionally he'd take Alexis out to lunch to improve the optics, and Alexis did her best to keep up pretenses. In time, she came to accept her relationship with Sergei. Yet, they were not lovers—she was only an assistant doing his bidding.

When Alexis approached Sergei about the organization he represented, he explained that this was not Grigory Markovic's terrorist faction. Markovic had been a renegade. The stakes were different now, and after several drinks to loosen his tongue, Sergei told her about Global Tectonics. This company was working on a more subtle strategy for world dominance. He described the plan as both insidious and ingenious. While Alexis was curious to learn more, Sergei kept his cards close to his chest.

It became clear to Alexis that she would never have a normal life and that this life, one punctuated with intermittent episodes of Sergei's bidding, was what she could expect going forward. Yet despite living under the watchful eye of the new organization, Alexis still dreamed of an escape to the United States that had been promised her for helping the Americans corner Markovic. Her only regret was that Scottie could not share in the dream. A flash of his face—his thick blond hair and blue eyes—brought tears to her eyes, and she could see him in his three-piece suit, which at first she found stuffy, but later found charming and quirky.

Scottie wasn't the only vision that haunted her. Her mind had never fully left Colombia. While Alexis had felt frustrated as a child living on the coffee farm, there remained a small part of her that wanted to roll time back and be Bella before the kidnapping—a time when she and her sister had gotten their tattoos—Rose, her namesake, and Bella, a spider. This desire propelled Alexis to find out anything she could about the

Compound where she was born, but it proved more difficult than she expected. Alexis had no idea if her great uncle Alberto, her mother, or her sister were still alive and where they lived. She used the internet at the bookstore as often as she could to find information on her family but always came up without an answer.

Alexis remembered the small village where she'd gotten her tattoo and tried to reason where the plantation was relative to the town. While she was continuing her research, Sergei found her at the back of the bookstore and surprised her. He pressed her for information, and after resisting, Alexis finally relented. She took a chance and asked Sergei for his help in tracking down her mother. Markovic had abducted her from the Colombian plantation, and she knew he'd visited it several times after. He told her so. There was a chance Markovic had shared this information with Sergei's brother Maxim or that someone who knew Markovic would remember. It was risky, but Sergei had not pressed Alexis for anything more than a business relationship, so she felt she could ask him to check on her family's whereabouts. Alexis assumed Sergei considered his options before agreeing to help her. If he possessed this information, he would have something he could use to make her more compliant or threaten her when the time came. It was a chance Alexis would have to take. After a period of time, he located the coffee plantation in Colombia and obtained evidence that Adrienne had gone back to France long ago. There was no trace of a sister or even proof that a sister ever existed.

While at one of their lunches, Sergei received a phone call and proceeded to step away from the table to take it. Alexis overheard him acknowledge that Alexis's mother had regained consciousness but had not reclaimed her memory. She was sequestered in a rehabilitation facility in Reims, France, but other than a curiosity, she was no bother to Sergei and his comrades. Alexis was shocked. Why was her mother in a rehabilitation hospital?

This information sent a bolt of energy through Alexis and prompted her to entertain sneaking off to France to see Adrienne. How to accomplish this would be difficult, but perhaps if Sergei would accompany her, she could avoid trouble. That became her plan. Once in France, she could plead for asylum and escape the clutches of this Russian organization. But Sergei would not budge, and she sat at the bookstore dreaming about her family. Then something changed.

Those pulling the strings saw the need for a new plan. From Sergei, they were made aware of Alexis's longing to see her mother and used this lead to solidify the ruse of Sergei and Alexis's relationship. They were to go on holiday, first to France, then on to the United States, as a seemingly innocent couple. Their final destination would be Washington, D.C., to finish a job they had already started.

CHAPTER 16

The Republic of Jokovikstan

Jean Paul Moreau Marchand entered the bathroom and removed his clothes. He turned on the shower allowing the water to get good and hot before he took the plunge. Catching a glimpse of himself in the mirror, he thought his eyes looked tired, and he noticed increasingly dark circles beneath the lower lids. Stress from the job had created more wrinkles on his rugged face, and yet he tried to imagine what he would do if he didn't do this job. A position like Chad's would undoubtedly be less risky but, then again, also more boring. No, JP enjoyed the chase, the danger, and to some extent, the uncertainty of the outcome.

Jean Paul stepped into the shower and let the water wash over him. He closed his eyes and inhaled the steam. He turned his face toward the rainshower, ran his fingers through his hair, and recounted the past several months. What about his relationship with Lily Robinson? Had it run its course? He didn't want to think so, but he thought she seemed more restless and dissatisfied. A perceptible change had come over Lily after she discovered that her Rose was alive. It was subtle but clear to JP. He thought she'd grown tired of this unpredictable life and demanded more accounting from him. Their last meeting had resulted in angry words, some of which he regretted. And though he had no chains on Lily, he felt strongly that they were linked through a bond of love. The vision of another man with his lover was not something he could entertain. He pushed the thought out of his mind.

JP shook the water from his ears hoping to dislodge any lingering thoughts of his relationship with Lily, and stepped out of the shower. He wrapped the towel around his toned body after rubbing it vigorously over his crown of dark hair, now increasingly speckled with silver. He dragged the razor over his cheeks and under his chin, and his fingers reassured him when they swept his face that it was a close shave. He put on a white dress shirt and charcoal slacks and reviewed his notes while waiting for Parker.

JP had been sent to the small country of Jokovikstan after their president's recent demise. Although considered a territory of its own, both Russia and China had recently reinitiated their dispute of sovereignty over the tiny nation. The untimely death provided each of the two bordering countries an opportunity to instate a leader of their choice, a puppet government head, catering to either Mother Russia or mainland China.

JP had been tasked with discreetly looking into the Jokovikstan's leader's death. At the time, the United States had been finalizing a deal with the small nation. After the president was found dead in his bedroom, the U.S. government received a rather unusual call, sent through quiet diplomatic channels, from the deceased's wife asking for help. JP arrived a few days later, followed by Agent Parker the next day. They connected with each other at the hotel.

"So, boss, what's the deal here?" Parker asked, first smoothing out his wrinkled navy blazer before pushing his wavy brown hair into place. The agent's dark shade of khaki pants defined his trim body and offset his light brown eyes.

"The information I received was vague. Not like working with Chad. *Mais*, President Khan's widow was particularly close to one of our diplomats, and she asked him for help in investigating her husband's death." After seeing Parker fussing with his jacket, JP looked down at his own attire and checked for unnecessary creases.

"Are we going to meet with him or what?" Parker asked, now reassessing his ensemble.

"*Oui, mais*, first we should speak with the wife. We have an appointment with her in an hour. She has requested to meet with us privately in the presidential residence."

"And after that?"

"Then we will meet with the diplomatic connection between our two countries, Ambassador Thomas Thornton. He has an apartment in the downtown area."

"What do we know about this ambassador? Is he a straight shooter?"

"*Oui*, as far as we know. In fact, he is the one who communicated the message from the president's widow, asking for our help. He felt that it was not necessary but wanted to be supportive nonetheless," JP said, gathering some of the papers he had brought with him. "We should probably get organized to go over. I have a car."

JP and Parker left the hotel and headed for the presidential residence for the meeting. The information they had on the president's wife Marina, was that she was considerably younger than her husband, and had recently celebrated their seventh wedding anniversary. Marina had been educated in the United States and worked with her husband on his plan to sell rare earth elements, or REEs, to America. Now, with her husband's demise, uncertainty loomed in her future.

The quiet drive to the president's residence was punctuated with continued speculation about their meeting with Marina Khan and with Thomas Thornton. It was also sprinkled with gossip about other government agents.

"Hey, did you hear what happened to Kolya? I

heard he got the shit kicked out of him," Parker said.

"*Oui*, the circumstances surrounding his departure were not clear."

"Poor bastard. You never know what the fuck can happen in this job."

The all-wheel-drive SUV easily handled the slick roads, and the majesty of the surrounding mountains proved unmistakable. Jokovikstan, bordering on mountain crests that reached over twenty thousand feet, also encompassed deserts and plains, in addition to its snowcapped mountains. Woodlands sprung up in the valleys under the watchful eye of gray wolves and lynx while mountain goats and snow leopards peered down from the mountaintops. Yet amidst the natural beauty, man-made habitats of cement and marble flourished. While newer buildings exhibited construction representative of a modern Western style, the capital city still contained remnants of Russian architecture. The government was housed in a gleaming rectangular white building covered in marble and notched with multiple window indentations reminiscent of the older Soviet buildings.

JP and Parker found their way to the personal residence of the first family, showed their credentials to the guards, and were escorted to the president's widow, Marina. She requested that her meeting be held in private.

"Please, please come in," she said to JP and Parker. "No, it's all right; you can go now," she added, turning to the bodyguard. She was confident that her safety was not in jeopardy.

"Madame, we are pleased to make your acquaintance," JP said after introducing himself and Parker. "How can we help you?"

"I know you must find this very strange. I'm the recent widow of the president of a foreign nation, and yet here I am asking for help from the United States."

"No, madame, it is quite all right. Please go on," JP said. Parker remained silent, standing behind and observing the surroundings.

"You see, my husband was very committed to making a specific arrangement with America. He felt that he needed to do something for our country that could release us from the shadows of Russia and China. My husband was aware that these rare earth minerals, recently discovered in our mountains, are necessary for the future of technology. Don't misunderstand; we all know that these elements are used in military weapons, but the greatest advances will be in communications: computers, phones, and satellite technology. The President of Jokovikstan, my husband, wanted to give back to the world while making money for our country."

"*Oui*, madame," JP said, "*mais*, but why bring us here to Jokovikstan?"

"Because I believe my husband was murdered."

Marina's blond hair fell gently on her shoulders, and the simple bob collected in a bright red velvet headband outlined her blue eyes. She let her hands drop to her sides as she exhaled after releasing her secret burden. Feeling only slightly less anxious, she scanned her surroundings, eyeing for a landing place. Her red dress, surprising for one in mourning, picked up single rays from the sun spilling through the ten-foot-tall windows in the sitting room as she walked to the center of the room. She sat down.

"Please, I apologize. Have a seat so we may talk," Marina said, pointing to several settees encircling a large marble coffee table.

JP and Parker were intrigued. They sat on separate settees, each dark blue velveteen and at right angles to one another. JP responded, troubled that too much time had passed since she expressed her concern over the president's death.

"Madame, why—" JP began before he was interrupted.

"Please, please call me Marina."

"Marina, why do you think your husband was murdered?" JP's tone appeared soft and non-threatening.

"There were many men in the Cabinet who disagreed with my husband's decisions. They resented what they thought was my interference. I'm not sure if you're aware that once, Jokovikstan was a political ball tossed back and forth between China and Russia. There are still some here who wish us to be with one side or the other," she said, now pouring each of them a glass of seltzer.

"We were informed that your husband had some surgery," Parker said, now feeling as if he could speak. "Do you have any concerns regarding the procedure?"

Marina looked at both agents, tears in her eyes.

"I know you are asking me for some hard proof, and I have none. Call it a woman's intuition. But I know my husband. He may have been eighty, but he had both a strong body and spirit."

"So you have no evidence. No calls or notes indicating a plot to remove your husband from office, and nothing unusual about the circumstances surrounding his death," Parker said.

"There is one thing. After his procedure, I had a prescription filled for his antibiotic. I left that with him for the evening. You should know that I loved my husband, but we no longer shared the same bed, and I wanted him to have complete rest after his surgery. It wasn't until the next morning that I realized the wrong prescription had been left by his bedside. It was my prescription." Marina paused, catching her breath and searching JP's and Parker's eyes for feedback.

"So you think your prescription is what killed him?" JP asked. He was surprised at her methodical approach. Almost without emotion as she continued her story.

"No, I don't. I only discovered my mistake when I went to take my medication the next morning. It was shortly after that that the housekeeper came running into my room with the news. You see, the doctor and the others believe that it was a reaction to his antibiotic that made him so ill. But he never took that antibiotic; he took my antihistamine pill."

"So, what do you believe was the cause of death?" Parker asked.

"I think there was something in the soup that they gave him. Of course, that's all been cleaned up and taken away, but I think someone got to him with the soup. I think he was poisoned."

Both JP and Parker sat for a minute without saying anything. They didn't want to appear rude, but it was clear to the president's wife that they didn't believe her from the looks on their faces. JP made an effort to move through the awkward silence.

"Madame, does anyone else know about the medication switch?"

"No, I collected all his medications after his death. I have them with me," she said, getting up and walking over to an ornate desk in the corner of the room. JP could see the elaborate scrolls carved in the woodwork.

Parker stood up and followed her to the desk.

Marina opened a zippered tote and pulled out two prescription bottles, which she handed to Parker. The agent reviewed the names of the patient and drug on each bottle. The labels were not as sophisticated as those from pharmacies in the U.S. but clearly listed the necessary information. The bottle with the president's name identified cefuroxime, an antibiotic, while the one with his wife's name recorded cetirizine, an antihistamine. Parker understood that, at first glance, how the confusion could occur. He walked back to the settee and handed the medication bottles to JP.

"Madame, may we keep these?" JP asked, putting the bottles into a small plastic bag he was carrying in his jacket pocket before Marina answered. Parker raised a single eyebrow.

"Yes, of course."

"Who prepares and brings meals to you if you and your husband are not eating in the dining room?"

"Cook has been here for many years. If my husband is taking his meal in his room, it would come from his valet. Josef has been with my husband for the last three years," she said, having made her way back to her own settee. She puffed up one of the pillows tucked between the back and the arm of the love seat before sitting down.

"Excuse my bluntness, but did you consider having your husband autopsied?" Parker asked. He squirmed in his chair. The heat crept under his collar, signaling his reluctance to question the widow. The agent recalled the drive down to the shipyard in South Korea with JP, Sam, and his favorite doctor, Lily Robinson. Chasing down Markovic had been the kind of fun he liked. This questioning was not his usual line of work, but he had to follow orders.

"I wanted an autopsy, but his doctor said no. He wanted a cremation, but I emphatically turned them down. We were at a stalemate. It's not like the United States. Here, the government is very strong-willed. Agent Marchand, is it possible to get an autopsy in the U.S.? Or could we not bring some of your doctors here? I'm not sure how it would work." Marina's face looked worn at this point. Attractive and well put together for a woman of fifty, the creeping wrinkles around the corners of her eyes and mouth revealed her inner emotions.

"Madame, I am not certain that we could ship your husband's body back to the United States for an autopsy. There would be too many diplomatic hurdles, and I think it would be difficult to remain inconspicuous. However, there may be a way, with your permission, to have one of our specialists fly here and perform a discreet medical procedure," JP said, not quite sure he could pull this off.

"Yes, anything you could do to help me," she said. Parker saw her eyes fill up and felt sorry for her.

"Where's your husband's body now?" Parker asked.

"The body's in the family mausoleum. It's not far from here."

"Madame, thank you, and again, sorry for your loss," JP said. "We will be in touch."

JP and Parker left the presidential rooms and returned to the SUV.

"So what do you think of it, boss? Pretty lady. She seems genuinely sad."

"*Oui*, Parker. I agree. *Mais*, I am not sure what to think. It is a bit of a stretch, and it would be surprising if we found anything in the body at this point."

"Well, do you think we should have Robinson check this out? She's our queen of all poisons, you know," Parker said, laughing. He saw the look on JP's face and quickly added, "Come on, ol' man, you know we all love her to death if you can take that clinical demeanor."

The senior agent gritted his teeth beneath the frown and chose not to remind Parker that he didn't like being referred to as ol' man. He wasn't old at all, just older than Parker, who was in the prime of his manhood. And JP hadn't spoken to Lily Robinson since their disagreement over Rose.

"Sorry, JP," said Parker. Jean Paul ignored his friend and partner.

"Let us talk to the ambassador, Thomas Thornton. He may know more about the president and his wife. If he thinks she is credible, then I will break from our secrecy here and call Chad. He will know if it is possible to get Dr. Robinson here under special circumstances."

Driving through a dense area of the city populated with more modern architecture, JP focused on the road letting Parker champion the map and provide directions for a change. A few minutes later, they pulled up near the U.S. Embassy, a concrete building studded with multiple windows and surrounded by a fence with a guardhouse located outside. Ambassador Thornton kept a small office here and lived in a modern apartment complex not too far away. They left their vehicle out front and, after showing some identification, were led into the compound.

"Thank you. I'll take it from here," Thornton said to the man dressed in a crisp military uniform. "Gentlemen, please follow me," he continued, leading JP and Parker to an inconspicuous set of offices in the back.

"Please, have a seat," he said to them, pointing to some comfortable leather chairs in his office. Thornton stood behind a bulky wooden desk, his large frame blocking the American flag behind him. One side of the desk had paperwork stacked in a neat pile, while the other side contained some photographs. The larger picture was presumably of his two grown children, a girl with a beaming smile and shoulder-length light brown hair, and a son in his cap and gown at his college graduation flanked by the ambassador and his wife. The smaller photograph showed Thornton with his dirty-blond hair shorter than in the previous picture and his body looking trim. He had his arm around the waist of his wife, an attractive woman, wearing her tennis outfit. They looked like an athletic couple in their early sixties, having an outing on the tennis court.

"*Merci*, Mr. Ambassador," JP said. "Thank you for contacting the Agency regarding the president's death. We just met with his widow and wanted to discuss some aspects of the case with you."

"Yes. Marina, the president's widow, was distraught over her husband's death and begged me to discreetly ask the U.S. for help. I tried to discourage her, but she can be very persistent when she wants to." Thornton's body stiffened, and his hands rearranged some of the paperwork on his desk.

"So, you do not suspect foul play?" JP asked. Parker cast his eyes wide around the room while JP continued with the questioning.

"Not at all. I think she's a hysterical woman who lost her husband suddenly. That's all there is to it. Now I only asked you folks over here, so we could put this conspiracy theory to bed and get on with business," Thornton said while drumming his fingers on the desk. "Look, I don't mean to sound harsh, but I've been close to these people for the last several years, and understand them. I'm sure you know what I'm talking about." His mouth assumed a crooked shape indicating annoyance.

JP sat quietly, contemplative, while Parker had gotten up and walked to the window.

"Frankly, Mr. Thornton, I am not certain I understand you," JP finally said, raising an eyebrow. The creases in his right cheek looked more pronounced as he leaned forward in his chair.

"Marina's gotten herself involved in government business and sees shadows on the wall. Her husband didn't need her interference. Yes, we all agree it was unfortunate that the president died so soon after his medical procedure, but his doctor found it to be quite coincidental; after all, President Khan was a man of eighty, and he might've died anyway."

"Whose idea was it to have the body cremated?" Parker asked, who, up until now, had been unable to sit in one place. He planted himself back onto the leather cushions.

"Oh, no mystery there," Thornton said, "it was the president's personal physician."

Parker ran his fingers through his brown hair and looked at JP, trying to get a read on what to do next. "Excuse me, Mr. Thornton, would it be all right if I used your restroom? One too many cups of coffee today." Parker tried to garner an embarrassed look staring directly at the other two men.

The ambassador and JP looked a little surprised, but then Thornton directed Parker to a private restroom inside the office.

"Training a young operative?" Thornton said to JP, half laughing. "I know how this goes. We don't like to admit we're getting any older. The truth is that work will keep you young." There was the sound of a flush, and Parker emerged from the bathroom. JP stood up to meet Parker and make their way to the exit.

"Thank you for your time, Mr. Ambassador. It seems there are no problems here for us. If we have any further questions, or you have any additional information, please, contact us through embassy channels," JP said.

Both Parker and JP shook the ambassador's hand and left the building. They waited for their car to be brought around, and only when they got inside did Parker start to speak.

"*Attends*," JP said, putting his hand up. He removed a small device from his briefcase and swept it over the interior of the vehicle. "It is safe," he said to Parker.

"Jesus, boss. No bugs. Well, I was going to ask you what you thought, but I guess I already know," Parker said, rubbing his brow. "So, listen, I'm with you on this. Something doesn't add up."

"I did not find the ambassador convincing. He is hiding something. So I suggest we stick around and do a little more investigating," JP said.

"I agree."

"I will have to check in with Chad at this point."

"Of course. Listen, the leak I took in the bathroom was bogus. I just wanted to poke around. Know what I found? I found a comb with long blond hair in it. From the pictures on his desk, his wife looks to be a brunette, and his dirty-blond hair is short. But you know who's got long blond hair, don't you?"

"Marina."

"You bet. And I got a little plastic bag here in my pocket with the golden strands if we want to go the DNA route," Parker said, giving himself a pat on the back.

"*Eh*, not bad, *mon ami*."

Chapter 17

Washington, D.C.

I'm more terrified of meeting Logan today than I've ever been facing death on a mission. When I'm trying to save the world, I don't overthink the possibility of dying; no, I bury my emotions and focus on the clinical, the task at hand, and only after, the reality of what's happened seeps in. But with Logan—I've had too much time to think about what I did, what I want, maybe even need, as I go forward with my life.

Chad should be here any minute.

"Chad, thanks for picking me up," I say. He's parked the rental car out in front of the hotel. We're planning on meeting Logan at his office. There's safety in numbers.

"No problem, Robinson. Nice heels. What are they anyway?" he says, eyeing my stilettos.

"Oh, these?" I say with a raised eyebrow. "I picked up these shoes in Hong Kong. A rainbow suede print." After I bought them, I was kidnapped and had to fight for my life. That seems like a lifetime ago.

"So Lily, I'd like to wrap up this case with Dr. Pelletier today. He's done his part. No point in dragging him into this any deeper unless it's necessary. But good to know we've got him in our back pocket if we've got the need. You agree?"

"I do. But why bother even meeting with him now?"

"I want some semblance of normalcy. He's provided his expertise, and that's been useful. Let's tell him so."

I pull the car door shut and study Chad's face. He's worried. This is homegrown murder. It's really out of our scope, but since we work with fuzzy edges, who's to say we're dipping our fingers into a forbidden pie. He changes the subject.

"So, guess who called me last night? My man, JP," Chad says before I have a chance to answer.

"Oh?" I just listen.

"Seems he was sent to Jokovikstan. I had no idea. As I told you already, it was all very top secret."

"Jokovikstan? What's he doing there?"

"Well, here's where it gets strange. The President of Jokovikstan was found dead in his bed after some surgery. Now the guy was eighty, so it could be a coincidence, but JP's gut told him there's more to it. So he and Parker are digging a little deeper," Chad says, keeping his eyes on the traffic as we work our way to Logan's building.

"Why would we be involved in something like that over in Jokovikstan? Wouldn't the officials there take charge of that investigation?"

"You're right, but you know how things don't always go the way they're supposed to. Pissed me off, really. Pulling my guys." Chad hits the gas hard.

I'm curious. "Did JP have anything else to say?"

"Robinson, I knew you'd be all over this. But we're going to have to delay this conversation until after we meet with Pelletier. Yeah, and I know you've got more information about your little sortie in the Middle East, too. Heard things got messy. We've got a lot of catching up to do," Chad says.

The car abruptly slows down and takes a sharp right into a parking lot. I jerk in my seat, shoot the driver a look for unnecessary roughness and let out a sigh. We park under a beautiful hardwood, all leafed out in its early summer glory, and walk to Logan's building.

"Logan, so nice to see you again," I say, trying hard to keep my emotions under control. I've been avoiding his calls.

"Dr. Pelletier," Chad says, shaking Logan's hand, "thank you for taking the time to meet with us."

"Dr. Robinson, Chad. Let's go up to my office. Stairs okay?" Logan asks, looking at my stilettos.

"The stairs will be fine, Logan. Lead the way." I'm sure my tone sounds a little annoyed.

Logan shows us to our seats around the circular table so we can start putting the pieces of the puzzle together as only pathologists can. Chad kicks it off.

"First, I want to thank both of you doctors for helping your government. I know this has been a very unusual ask, but I needed the best experts in their field. Now Dr. Robinson, could you please review the toxicology findings in the case."

"Thank you, Chad. I'm afraid that your concerns regarding the possible murder of Senator Steinman have been confirmed." Chad, of course, already knows this, but I'm keeping up some pretenses. "And please, Dr. Pelletier, feel free to jump in at any time." Wearing my clinical hat, I feel myself in total control. Emotions are buried.

"Of course."

"We found poison was administered to the senator via his implanted aortic valve. Seems that the porcine portion of the valve was immersed in encapsulated scorpion toxin from *Hemiscorpius lepturus*. I'm sure you know that scorpions are in the class *Arachnida*, which also contain spiders, mites, and ticks, all having eight legs and no wings or antennae." I can see Chad squirming a bit in his chair, a slight eye-roll, and if I'm not mistaken, I think he just whispered into Logan's ear, "just let her lecture; that's what she always does." They think I can't hear them. Logan catches my critical look.

"Sorry, Lily," he says. "Shit. We, you thought it was poison, and you've confirmed it."

I can see the color drain from his face with the realization that someone deliberately meant to kill the senator.

"And, how in the fuck, excuse me, did he get a valve that was tampered with? Are we looking at the surgeon here as a possible suspect, or was he in the dark over this?" Logan asks.

"Now, Dr. Pelletier, it'll be my responsibility to unravel those details. Your and Dr. Robinson's role is to determine the manner and cause of death. And from what I'm hearing, you have."

"So, Lily, all the bleeding and the microthrombi—DIC caused by scorpion toxin?"

"Exactly. Once Senator Steinman's clotting cascade started, it couldn't be stopped."

"Jesus Christ. Yes, I see poisonings at my shop. Usually, it's someone killing a spouse or business partner with mundane things like methanol, ethylene glycol, or rat poison. You know, just household stuff. But scorpion venom? That's a first for me."

"Well, doctors, I'll take it from here," Chad says, looking at me, knowing that we'll be putting our heads together on this.

"Listen," Logan says, "if I can be of any more help, please don't hesitate to ask. Just like you, I want to know what happened to Senator Steinman. The deliberate murder of a government official is outrageous."

"Thank you, Dr. Pelletier," Chad says, rising

from his chair and nodding his head in agreement with Logan.

Logan takes a step back. He's thinking. I can see his forehead scrunch, and the glabella crease between his eyebrows deepen.

"Chad, and Lily, please, while you're in D.C., come over to my place for dinner tonight. You can avoid the restaurant scene, and we can discuss more of the case. I won't take no for an answer. Here, let me write down the address for you," Logan says, giving us his business card with his home address and cell phone number on the back. "I'll see you both at seven."

"Dr. Pelletier—"

"Please, it's Logan."

"Thank you, Logan. I'll be there. Robinson?" Chad asks, turning to look at me.

"Um, sure. Thank you, Logan."

"Then it's settled. Anybody have allergies or special diets concerning food? Gluten-free, vegetarian, that sort of thing."

"I don't eat any red meat," I tell him. "Haven't for years."

"Good heart-healthy diet, doctor," he says with a smile lighting up his face.

"I'm okay with anything," Chad says.

Chad and I walk out together and wait until we get into the car before we speak.

"Shit, Robinson. This is a hell of a case. I'm

not sure who to trust or who to bring this to."

"I know. We're going to need more information. And by the way, why did you accept that dinner invitation? I've got a ton of work to do."

"Oh, come on. We've got to eat, and I like this guy, anyway. I think we may just use him again. Come on, Robinson, I can tell you like him. Just a tiny bit," he says with more of a chuckle than a laugh.

What is Chad playing at?

"Seriously though, what the hell happened in the Middle East?" Chad asks, looking to pull out onto the main road and head back to the hotel.

I fill Chad in on what happened at Omair's house. I tell him that I assumed the scorpion wrangler faced a choice when I confronted him and chose suicide rather than have those children harmed by whoever threatened him.

"Shame. But I did hear that you did a pretty good job of cleaning up the scene. Not bad, Robinson. Want a full-time job?"

"Chad, I thought you'd never ask," I say, sticking my finger into his right arm hard enough to make him flinch.

"So, where does this leave us?" he asks, holding on course despite the jab.

"While I was in his house, I found a small box on his bedroom dresser that presumably contained the kill-pill. The box had Russian writing on it, so it may be a clue. And given that Leigh thinks that the microencapsulation of the poison looks similar to the technology used previously by the Russians, well, fill in the blanks."

"What the hell. Why would the Russians want to murder the Chair of one of the subcommittees on Foreign Relations? Shit, I'm sure there's a connection."

"I agree, but before we go there, tell me more about Jokovikstan. You said the president died after surgery. Do you know what kind of surgery it was?"

"What? Oh, the medical procedure," he says after a slight pause. "No, I don't, but I've held off telling you about the big ask. JP wants you to come over to Jokovikstan and have a look at the body. I guess something similar to what we've just done in our own backyard."

Finally. Now JP wants my help. Bastard.

"That was an exhumation autopsy, Chad. Not just a quick look at the body," I say.

"Well, exactly. Now that I think more about it, what if I quietly send you, and Logan, over to Jokovikstan? You could do a discreet autopsy, and we could put this baby to rest," he says with a big grin on his face.

Again, what is he playing at? "I don't know if that's such a good idea, Chad."

"Look, think about it, Robinson. This would be just a short diversion for you. And the sooner I get my team back together, the sooner we can figure out what happened to Senator Steinman," he says, pulling up to the front of the hotel.

I open the car door and turn back to Chad, his baldness looking shinier through those brown hair strands. "Why don't you pick me up around 6:45, and then we can drive over."

"Sorry, Robinson. I'll meet you there. I've some errands to run while I'm in D.C. I'll bring the wine. You go spend a couple of hours working on your whatever."

He pulls the door closed and disappears into the streets of the district. Once again, I'm at my own crossroads—headed for parts unknown.

"Knock, knock," I say into the speaker after pressing the buzzer for Logan's place. Looks like he lives in the penthouse, so I'm expecting posh.

"Hey," the voice from the speaker starts. "I'll let you in. Go left in the lobby and take the far elevator labeled Penthouse. It's a direct access elevator, so it'll let you right off at my place."

"Got it. Thanks."

I wonder if Chad's already here? He's in charge of drinks, so I stopped by a bakery and bought some French macarons. I'm not sure what Logan would like, but at least I won't show up empty-handed. I'm arriving slightly fashionably late, so there's less chance of my being alone with Logan. Speaking of fashion. Tonight, I'm wearing a dress for a change. Most of the time, I have on a suit of some kind, unless I have to go to an elegant affair. I may be overdressed for dinner, but I'd rather overdress than underdress. Guess I should've asked Logan if he meant this to be a jeans casual dinner or what. *C'est la vie.* So, I chose a dress with cap sleeves and lace over a blush pink satin lining. It's quite sophisticated. And I've got on black velveteen stilettos. My trick for compromise? I'm wearing a jean jacket over the dress. That should do it.

The elevator takes me directly to the 20th floor. When the door opens, Logan's there to greet me.

"Lily, I'm so glad you could make it," he says as he gives me a quick kiss on the cheek. I feel the electricity between us. It's still there. Of course, he's dressed in jeans and a white button-down shirt, with only the front tucked into the waistband. He's wearing brown loafers with no socks.

"This is for you," I tell him, handing over the box of macarons. The box is neatly tied with ribbon instead of plain bakery string.

"Thanks, Lily. Come on in and have a seat."

He points me in the direction of his living room. There's a large sofa of buttery brown leather and a sizable area rug that has small raised squares in neutral colors planted on a pale beige background giving texture. I can see the gas fireplace surrounded by marble that climbs to the ceiling. It's probably too warm for a fire tonight, but the overall appearance of his apartment is stunning. I look around for Chad, and he's nowhere in sight.

"Logan, where's Chad? I thought he would be here already. His job was to bring the wine. I brought dessert." I take a seat under a large sweeping floor lamp that looms up toward the tall ceiling with two off-white shades, one telescoped within the other.

"Hasn't shown up yet. I'm sure he'll be here shortly. What can I get you for a drink? Something hard or soft?"

"You know, if you've got some sparkling wine, I'll take a glass of that," I say, living on the edge.

"Champagne? I have some brands, any in particular?"

"Champagne's perfect. Whatever you have will do." I'm not about to tell him that I now have a thing for the Moreau winery in Reims. Which makes me think about JP. Chad and I still have to finalize the arrangements if I'm to go to Jokovikstan. I'm not sure that Logan should be part of that equation. Better to start with small talk.

"So Logan, how long have you lived here?"

"Oh, maybe five, six years. I had a place in the country but decided I wanted something closer to the city. Here you go," he says, handing me my glass of bubbly.

"Thank you. Your place is pretty spectacular with a wonderful view of downtown. Did you furnish it yourself or have a decorator?"

"I did have some help," he says, laughing. "Why, do you think it's too masculine and needs more of a feminine touch?" His smile is broad, and his cheeks prominent even behind the stubble.

"No. I think it's you." Not that I exactly know what "you" means. Best to change the subject. "Did you always know you wanted to go into forensics?" I ask between sips. Hmm, this is the good stuff. I can taste the difference— there is a freshness and vivacity that sweeps the palate.

"I did. It's the standard line of giving a voice to the dead, providing closure for families, getting evidence from the body to nail the bad guys. You know, the usual suspects. After working at the medical examiner's office for several years, I decided to open my own business for second opinions and closer looks. Like what we're doing with Steinman. Still can't wrap my head around that. Who'd want to murder a senator? This was deliberate. Not some random shit."

"I know. It is shit. He stood up for this country." Logan genuinely seems to care about finding out the truth, not only in this case but for all his cases. A perfect medical examiner. I look at my watch. "Logan, I'm surprised Chad's not here yet. I think I'll send him a text."

Just as I say that, Logan's phone rings. Although I can only hear one side of the conversation, I know what's going on.

"Sure, sure. Next time. You got it. A rain check," Logan says, and he hangs up the phone and turns to me. "Well, Lily, it looks like it's just the two of us for dinner. Chad got stuck at some meeting and sends his apologies. Why don't we go into the dining room, and I'll get our meal," he says, pointing me into a well-appointed dining area. There are three place settings on a sizable Parson's table anchored in a dark steel base and a polished quartz top with veining. The chairs are black leather wrapped around what I presume to be a metal frame. This man has good taste.

I'm feeling very overdressed and vulnerable now, but I can't just get up and leave. "Thanks, Logan," I tell him and try and take control of my situation.

Logan has prepared a lovely dinner. We start with a Caprese salad, followed by broiled arctic char topped with a citrus sauce, fingerling potatoes on the side, and spinach sautéed in olive oil. He refills my glass with champagne.

"Logan, this all looks amazing. I didn't know you were such an accomplished chef."

"Okay, you caught me. I had my catering service send over three dinners for tonight. I'll keep Chad's in the fridge for tomorrow."

We talk more about the case, politics, and science, and I begin to relax. My shoulders drop, and I listen to Logan tell me a bit about his family. Then he changes the subject.

"So tell me, Dr. Robinson, you've been avoiding me ever since we went sailing. Why?"

"Come on, Logan. You know it wasn't the sailing. It's just that I . . ."

"It's just that you what? You're single, interesting, and I know you feel the same chemistry that I do. So what's the problem?"

"It's not you. It's . . ."

"Oh fuck, excuse me, not the it's not you, it's me thing. Is that what you're saying?" I can tell he's annoyed. He's put his fork down, and now he's staring at me across the table.

"No, I, it's just that I can't be in a relationship with you." I find myself wrestling with my conscience.

"Did I ask you for a relationship? I just want to see you. Look, no strings attached, okay?" he says. I'm drawn in by his magnetism. His voice is softer now, and the burn in his eyes has subsided. "If it's the distance thing, we're not that far apart geographically. We can work this out. Come on, Lily."

"You know, Logan. Maybe it's better if I just go," I say, pushing my chair away with some force and getting up from the table. I feel myself boiling over and my control in flux.

"So, what. So, now you're going to leave? What's it that you can't face? For a smart lady, you don't make any sense to me." Logan's standing now and headed over to me.

He puts both his arms around me and pulls me in close, looking directly into my eyes. I can see the flecks of light reflected in his, and I feel my heart beating madly. I push him away and yet stand there about to burst. The champagne's given me a buzz. His fingers reach out and touch my face, and that undeniable tingle explodes. He sees it. His chest swells, and his nostrils flare as he takes me in his arms.

"Lily," he says, kissing my neck. "I'll stop if you want to. Do you want me to stop?"

"No," I say softly. I'm not resisting. I should, but I'm not. It's Logan's cue to carry on.

"I told you, I fantasized about us being together the first time I saw you. I find you extraordinary, exciting, not like other women I know," he says, now unzipping my dress.

I take in several deep breaths and inhale him. His mouth near mine, I gently nibble his lower lip, and my hand takes hold of his hardness. He moans, bites my shoulder in response, lifts me up into his arms, and sweeps me into his bedroom, fully charged on the mounting electricity between us.

The next morning I wake up in my hotel room with a bitter taste in my mouth and guilt in my heart. I know Chad should be knocking on my door any minute.

"Sorry about last night, Robinson. I just

couldn't get away from that meeting to make it to dinner. How was it? Logan's place nice?" Chad asks.

"It was fine. I didn't stay all that long," I lie, looking down through my deceit.

We're having coffee in my hotel room. The morning light beams through the window, lighting up the silverware on the surface. A sunray bounces off the cutlery and strikes Chad in the face. He moves slightly to the right to escape the shaft.

"Just fine, Robinson? Okay, never mind, let's move on. I'm going to send you to Jokovikstan to link up with JP and Parker. Now, I can get Dr. Pelletier to sign a non-disclosure agreement and send him along with you. You two can do the autopsy, and when you're finished, you can tell him to go home. I'm sure JP and Parker would like you to stay with them. Can you get away from the hospital?"

I have to laugh at this. I finally changed my status at the hospital and medical school to a consultant since too much time off was creating a problem for me—and for them. I can do most of my work from home anyway, unless of course, I have to see patients. I haven't told Chad this.

"I can get the time. Do we really need Logan on this trip? It makes it much more complicated, and how do we explain JP and Parker?"

"I feel we can trust this guy, Robinson. You

disagree? He seems like a straight shooter, and our background check didn't turn up anything unusual about him. Like I told you earlier, the sooner you get back here with JP, the sooner we can figure out who killed the Senator. Of course, I'll be working on that while you're gone, but I don't want this other fucking director hanging over my head on the Jokovikstan thing. Excuse my French." His tone deepens.

"All right, I'll go back to Boston and collect a few things, just in case. You go and tell Logan what the deal is. And if he doesn't want to come? What's your plan?"

"Oh, he'll want to come if he knows you're going. I'm still a man first, Robinson, and I know when Mercury's been smitten by Venus," Chad says with a smirk on his face and tapping his pointer finger on the table. He takes the last sip of his coffee and shakes his head, giving me a long look as if he knows something I don't.

The reality is that Chad, observant as he is about male behavior, hasn't spent much time in the field with JP and me. He usually gives us our instructions, and we do the dirty work. As far as he knows, JP and I only work together—doesn't know we also play together. Parker may be a different story. It's possible that as JP's partner, he's observed the chemistry between his boss and me as much as we try to conceal it. Romantic entanglements in this line of work can jeopardize a mission, so we're careful when in the company of other team members. But, sometimes, you're blind to your own behavior. Your feelings can trip you up in the most innocent of places. A touch on the arm, a glance across the room, an endearing word. You forget where you are, who's around you. I think JP and I have done well over the years. The irregularity of our time together and careful orchestrating of our encounters have provided the camouflage we need. But if Chad sends Logan to Jokovikstan, well, as they say, all bets are off.

Chapter 18

The Republic of Jokovikstan

The trip to Jokovikstan was long but uneventful. Logan signed up for the mission as Chad had predicted, and I made it clear we cannot see each other socially anymore. Our relationship must be purely professional, and we need to keep our distance. He promised he would, although he disagreed with me intensely. For the sake of the mission, Logan accepted these conditions. I only hope he can keep our affair a secret. How will I feel when I see Jean Paul? Will my face betray me?

Logan and I have cleared customs using my diplomatic passport and work our way down to baggage claim.

"The plan is to meet at the luggage carousel," I tell Logan looking around for our contacts.

I push down my rumpled suit. The plane flight felt endless with a stopover in Istanbul, and flying coach only allowed me to sleep in my seat—so uncomfortable.

"Doc, over here," a voice calls out. I recognize Parker's enthusiastic words and turn to see him with JP. It's going to be an interesting car ride to the hotel. Butterflies bounce off the walls of my insides.

"*Bonjour*, Dr. Robinson," JP says, clasping my one hand while Parker grabs the other. JP and I resort to our roles as colleagues using appropriate business greetings.

I can barely look JP in the eye. I swallow my guilt, and the anger that's consumed me these last months needs to be handled. The acid in my stomach churns and reaches the back of my throat with a burn.

"Doc, so glad you're here. We need your input," Parker says. I try and give him a look that will tamp down the enthusiasm. Pelletier shouldn't know that JP, Parker, and I are very used to working with one another. The less history he knows, the better.

"Agent Parker, Agent Marchand, I'd like to introduce you to Dr. Logan Pelletier. Chad has arranged for him to work with us on this exhumation autopsy." I've made it through the introductions without cracking.

"Gentlemen, very nice to meet you," Logan says, extending his hand to shake both JP's and Parker's. I can see JP's and Parker's eyes assessing Logan in a first impression.

Logan still has on his jeans and a button-down blue oxford. Parker's in his khakis with a tattersall shirt while JP is dressed in charcoal slacks and a crisp white shirt. He looks good. I see a discreet smile on his craggy face as he tries to catch my eye.

We collect our bags and drive to the hotel. Parker's in the driver's seat while JP is sitting next to him. That's our standard procedure when we're together. Only now, I'm in the back seat with Logan. The view out the window's a breath of fresh air—the scenery, different—exciting. Mountains surround the city in the distance and provide a closed-in feel.

After we reach the hotel and check-in at the front desk, each of us goes to our respective room to freshen up before we formally meet to discuss the case. JP has arranged for me to have a connecting room with him—our routine arrangement when we are on a mission together. Finally settled, I take the opportunity to shower and rest before we meet. I need to get my head in the right place. It's the pangs of guilt that are plaguing me.

There's a knock at the adjoining door.

"My Lily," JP says, making my name into two syllables as he walks through the door and takes me in his arms for a giant bear hug.

A big sigh escapes my chest, and an undeniable sense of security surrounds me. I don't want to let go. I don't want to lose him.

"JP, you've no idea how much I've missed you," I tell him, letting my anger go, my head still resting on his chest. I have missed him. More so, since I felt our connection had changed since our time together in France. Did I have unrealistic expectations of the relationship? Maybe I thought there wouldn't be such long periods of separation in our future. I don't know what he thought.

"*Ma chérie*, I have missed you too," he says. His voice is quiet. "About our quarrel over Rose." We're now sitting on the bed next to each other.

I don't let JP finish his thought. "I don't think you realize how hard this has been for me. I've carried guilt about Rose all my life." I slump back on the bed, fighting tears and fatigue, wishing I could undo many things about the past.

JP strokes my hair and whispers something in French in my ear. We kiss—his soft lips greet mine, and his tongue finds its way into my mouth, gently exploring. I feel a mixture of chemistry and guilt. We break the moment as he takes off his shoes and then pulls the bed covers back, revealing jacquard print sheets.

I watch him remove his shirt and can't help but think that it was Logan the last time I saw a man naked. Now, my emotions, spinning ever faster, ambush my mind like the enemy. My flirtation with Logan had been purely sexual. But doubts creep in like water in an unlined grave. Is it possible that JP has sexual liaisons when he's not with me? He's a man. I've never dwelled on this before we visited his childhood home. I can't bear to think of him in another woman's arms.

Perhaps I thought his sharing part of his other life with me gave me some entitlement.

"Ah, Lily, once more, you are not in the moment," he says, unbuttoning my silk blouse.

He's right; I'm not in the moment. I feel his warm breath on my neck, my head now resting on the pillow. Gentle kisses work their way to my shoulder, and he hesitates for just a moment. In response, I cup my hands around his face and pull him into me. Our lips and tongues meet, and our breathing grows faster as his engaging fingers massage my nipples.

My lover nuzzles his way down to the center of my core, and I throw my head back with a delicious moan. Taking the cue, he moves my arms over my head, pinning me with his hand and the weight of his mass, his frame covering mine. I feel the heat of his body and smell the pungent odor of our chemistry. Now, my mind only sees him. Only him. I take the lead and move my body on top of his, riding him hard while his mouth teases my breasts and his hands drive my hips. In the end, we explode like a rocket, fueled by longing, passion, and our past feelings of anger. We hold each other tightly, our hearts still racing and our chests heaving. I do love this man. He is the love of my life.

The tension now at bay, we catch up on our work, at home and abroad.

"Lily, Chad said that you and Dr. Pelletier were working on a case that involved Senator Steinman. We heard that he passed away in his sleep. Does Chad suspect something different?" JP slips back into his slacks while I watch him dress.

"Yes, JP; it was murder. Logan, Dr. Pelletier, and I found evidence of poisoning. But Chad sent us over to you before we could finalize everything in D.C. I'm anxious to get back home to see it through."

"Murder? You suspect that the senator was murdered? How did this happen?"

"I can tell you more about it later. First, I'd like to get to the business in Jokovikstan. What's the timeline, JP?"

"*Mais oui*. I hope to wrap this up in a day or two. The president's widow needs some reassurance that her husband died of natural causes. He had a minor medical procedure shortly before he died. He was elderly *et* nothing was found to be suspicious. *Mais*, my gut says something different."

"Where's the body now?" I ask, buttoning my blouse and searching for my shoes.

"In a mausoleum. I know it has been maybe a few weeks, *mais* we have hope that you and your colleague can put this to rest."

"So, what's the plan?" I ask.

"Marina, the president's widow, will take us to

the mausoleum tonight. I am sorry to say that you and Dr. Pelletier will need to do your examination there. *Oui*, not ideal. Perhaps you can find what you are looking for with a superficial PM."

"All right. Pelletier and I've brought over some basic gear. We've some PPE, rudimentary autopsy tools, and containers for the collection of specimens. It's not perfect, but considering that we shouldn't even be here and are probably breaking who knows how many laws, it'll have to do."

The drive this night to the mausoleum is quiet. The four of us sit without talking while Parker focuses on the dark roads to the cemetery. The president's widow's going to meet us there. I've brought with me the necessary equipment. Since I came in using a diplomatic passport, I put as many items as possible into a diplomatic pouch, in this case, a crate, hoping the inviolability would protect us from detection. It's not ideal, but I believe Logan and I can make it work with what we have.

There's no activity at the cemetery. The darkness covers our presence, and we go into the burial chamber. We are greeted by Marina Khan and a few of her trusted attendants.

"Madame, I would like you to meet Dr. Robinson and Dr. Pelletier. They are here to perform an abbreviated autopsy on your husband.

Et, when they do, I think it would be best if you waited in your car," JP says.

"Madame," I say, looking into her eyes. Dark circles are under the lower lids, and her crow's feet cling delicately in their place. "I'm so sorry for your loss. I hope that my colleague and I can ease your mind and put your fears behind you." My words bring forth tears and a nod of her head.

Logan also shakes her hand and reassures her that we'll do our best.

Marina leaves the chamber, and the casket is opened, releasing the stench of decay. We're told that the president was not embalmed. I can see a slight patina of mold on his face. Logan and I, dressed in PPE, undress the president who's wearing his official uniform for the Republic of Jokovikstan. Once his clothes are removed, we do a more complete external examination of the body. Decomposition has begun, but considering the circumstances, I'm struck by how well preserved the body is.

"JP, did you find out what medical procedure the president had before he died and what medications he was taking?" I'm usually much more prepared before I engage. It's a little late to be asking these kinds of questions now, but with so much going on . . .

"*Oui*, Dr. Robinson. He had a procedure called a TAVR. This is where an artificial valve is placed—"

"JP, we know," I say, looking at Logan with my eyebrows raised and my voice intense. Logan looks at me, and we are both thinking the same thing. Oh God, this is too much of a coincidence. So we get to work.

"Mr. Parker, can you hold that light a little higher so we can get a better view," Logan asks. The conditions consist of dim light and damp air.

The external exam is revealing for hemorrhaging and extensive bruising. We quickly cut into the chest and isolate the implanted valve, which we remove with great care and place into a container. We also take some samples of liver, spleen, kidney, and anything else that might help us unravel the death. We keep the postmortem short and focused based on what we saw during Senator Steinman's autopsy. Logan and I work as a trained team, even though we've been through this only once, using few words and knowing precisely where we need to look.

The *in situ* autopsy's complete. No diener has removed the organs *en block*, so all we need to do is replace the sternum and approximate the edges of the now decaying skin. We dress President Khan in his uniform, and JP and Parker alert the men standing by the entrance that we have finished our work. The casket's ready to be resealed and put back in place. One of the men leaves us to find Marina in her car. Her entrance into the chamber is in small steps, and her hands clasp one another in support. Her face, now taut, seems pale like her husband's.

"Please, doctors, what have you found?" she asks. I can see the anguish on her face.

Logan and I have not said a word. Not even to JP and Parker, who watched us work. So I speak up.

"Madame, I'm not a hundred percent certain, but I'm not so sure this is a natural death. I'll know more in a few weeks. I'm so sorry."

"Oh God, I thought so. Someone poisoned the soup; it had to be the soup," Marina says.

Jean Paul and Parker have eyebrows raised, and their lips are parted. I can tell that they wished I had spoken to them before saying anything. And yet, the distress on Marina's face compelled me to talk to her now.

"Madame, it is late. Dr. Robinson means to say that we do not yet have all the information. You should return to your quarters, and we will contact you in the morning. I know this has come as a shock to you," JP says.

Marina's escorted to her car, and JP, Parker, Logan, and I pile into ours. Before Parker starts the engine, JP turns to Logan and me.

"Doctors, I would have preferred you speaking with us first." JP is angry with me. He's right, of course.

"I'm sorry. I just knew she would ask, and I didn't want to lie."

"Robinson, this is now a complex case—and no one knows you are here. We hoped that despite our suspicions, nothing would come of this."

"JP, wait. Before you continue. I have something to say." My voice is a little shaky because what I'm about to tell them will have inter-national ramifications. "The findings from this autopsy were so similar to those we found with Senator Steinman. They both had the same pro-cedure, a TAVR, and from what we could see, the President of Jokovikstan looks like he died of disseminated intravascular coagulation. That's the exact cause of death we found with the senator. And his artificial valve was impregnated with poison. So, if we find that to be true here, then there's a connection between the two deaths. I don't know what that could be, but we can't ignore it."

JP and Parker exchange looks of concern and surprise. JP only heard the details about Senator Steinman's death a short time ago when I revealed my conclusion to him back at the hotel. Chad was right when he said there had been no communication with JP and Parker while in Jokovikstan until recently.

"Shit, what are you saying? Steinman has this TAVR too?" Parker asks.

"Exactly. And it looks like the same brand of artificial valve was used in both cases," Logan adds.

"Jesus, JP. This makes this a hell of a lot more

complicated. I can't believe it," Parker says, shaking his head.

While Parker states the obvious, JP is thinking. I can see the crease in his cheek deepen, and his eyes look dark.

"Are you going to send these specimens to Hong Kong?" JP asks me.

Logan looks at me quizzically.

"Of course. The toxicology report will be crucial. If the findings are the same, both Senator Steinman and President Khan were murdered by the same person." The car is silent for a minute before anyone speaks.

"What poison did you find?" JP asks.

"An unusual scorpion toxin. One I wouldn't expect too many people to use. We can discuss it later."

Logan, who's said very little up until this point, leans forward in his seat, meeting Parker at the back of his. I see a quizzical look on his face.

"Why do I get the feeling that you three want to discuss this without me. I don't know what's going on. So let's get back to the hotel and sort this out after a good night's sleep. Okay?" Logan says, sounding as if he's pissed off. I don't know what he and I were expecting when we came to this country, but it wasn't this.

It's the middle of the night, and we're all tired. Once back at the hotel, each of us goes to our room, having agreed to meet for a fresh start in the morning. My eyes feel heavy, and the bed looks so inviting, but first, I take another shower to erase any lingering smells of death. JP and I want to pool our information and forge a plan. We'll cut Parker in on this when we can. Right now, we don't know what to do with Logan. He's a good man, and I'm sorry he got dragged into this mess.

The shower's like an hour's worth of sleep, and now feeling more comfortable, I want to climb into bed and pull the covers around me. Instead, there's a knock at the connecting door, interrupting my desire for sleep.

"JP, come in," I say, grabbing him by the shirt and pulling him on my side of the barrier. Now that I see him again, I'm hoping he can stay with me tonight.

"My Lily," he says as he kisses me, "This evening has presented us with some difficulties."

"No shit, my friend. I'm not sure what's going on, but it's too much of a coincidence for these two deaths to be unrelated. What could possibly link these two men?"

"Parker and I made some observations before you, and your colleague got here, but we dismissed it."

"What observations?" I ask, now giving JP a well-deserved back rub. His shoulders are so tense. He turns his head in a circle, and I hear his neck vertebrae crack.

"When Parker and I went to see Thomas Thornton—"

"Who's that?"

"Thomas Thornton is the U.S. Ambassador to Jokovikstan, *et*, during our visit, he dismissed the president's wife as hysterical and tried to steer us off. There is a certain irony here because we understand that it was Marina who asked Thornton to contact the U.S. for help."

"Well, JP, you have to admit it's more than a little odd for the wife of a dead president of another country to ask for our help."

"*Oui, c'est vrai*, this is true, but this is a woman who feels she cannot trust her own government. What is more, Parker believes she and Thornton are having an affair. Under ordinary circumstances, that could be a possible motive for the ambassador to have his rival killed. But these are not normal circumstances."

"I agree. My woman's intuition tells me that Marina loved her husband. I don't think she's putting on an act. Sometimes people stray from the relationship because they want sex, or maybe feel lonely or even angry. Her husband was very senior to her, and well, possibly he couldn't provide the physical closeness she required." I can feel the warmth spreading on my face. I'm sure my cheeks look red.

"*Et* would not explain the connection between Khan and Steinman, if there is one," JP adds.

"Of course. What would Thornton have to gain by this death? He may love Marina, but he'd have to obtain something far more valuable, like money or power. And JP, for once, I have more information than you do. I failed to tell you earlier that the death of Steinman may be connected to the Russians. You know that they're the ones that favor poison."

"The Russians? Again? Persistent bastards. What do you know?" JP asks me, his neck muscles feeling less tight.

I fill JP in on the details of my visit to Omair and his untimely death. My partner turns around and smiles at me when I tell him how I cleaned up the mess, no doubt proud that he trained me well.

"*Bon*. Other than poison as a calling card, is there anything else that points to the Russians?"

"Yes, the box I found on Omair's dresser, I believe contained the suicide pill, and that box had Russian writing on it. And before you ask me what it said, the answer is—I don't know. I handed it over to Chad."

"If the Russians are behind this, then we must discover what they had to gain if both these men were dead."

"JP, if you don't mind," I say, now nibbling his ear. "Could we continue this tomorrow morning? I'm exhausted."

"*Mais oui, ma chérie*," he answers, and we tumble into bed.

• • •

The next morning, Parker, JP, and I arrange to reunite before we see Logan. JP called Chad last night with the updates of our findings and is waiting for further instruction. I've straightened up the room so that we can gather here. I hear a knock at the door.

"Come on in. Hey, you two, I know we're starting early because you wanted to first meet without Dr. Pelletier," I say to them. JP and Parker head directly to the small table in the corner of the room, smelling the coffee and eyeing the familiar pastries waiting for us.

"*Bonjour*, Dr. Robinson. Chad got back to me early this morning concerning your colleague. He said that they had reviewed Dr. Pelletier's application and have cleared him to work with us as needed."

"What application?" I ask. I place my coffee cup back in the saucer with a clink.

"Apparently, after you two did the initial autopsy at Chad's request, Dr. Pelletier asked Chad what it would take to become, how should I say, a more regular member of the team."

"Chad never mentioned this to me. When did all this happen?" Why do I feel blindsided?

"Hey, Dr. Robinson, you'd still be our favorite pathologist. Right boss?" Parker says, turning to JP smiling while trying to relieve the growing tension.

"*Oui*. My guess is that Chad needed to do a little

more investigation into the doctor's background. *Et*, from what he told me, this Pelletier comes from a very wealthy family—hedge funds."

"Why the hell didn't he stick with the family business? Shit, that or cut up dead bodies. That's a no-brainer," Parker says, biting into a croissant. "Sorry, doc."

"All right, whatever. So why are we meeting without Logan now if he's got Chad's blessing?" I ask.

"In due time. Let us ease into the arrangement. The three of us have worked together for years and have a certain comfort level. I want us to review the case first, then bring him in," JP says, pouring himself a cup of coffee.

Is it something more, I wonder?

JP continues. "We have assumed that President Khan was murdered with the same scorpion venom used to kill Steinman."

"Ah," I say.

"*Je sais*, not confirmed. *Alors*, the link between the two men? Chad is looking into a possible connection. *Mais*, he tells me to tread as lightly as he, putting us all at a disadvantage. If, as Chad believes, it was someone close to the senator that betrayed him, then we do not know who we can trust."

We hear a knock at the door and assume it's room service with more coffee. So I get up to answer it.

"Good morning, Lily. I thought you and I could get an early start and talk," Logan says, stepping into my room. "Oh, I see that I'm not early at all. Apparently," he adds, seeing the other two men, "I'm late. Nice view from here. You're up a couple of floors from where I am. Hello, Parker. JP," he says, nodding his head in the direction of the others. "Mind if I join you for breakfast?"

Logan takes a seat next to JP and opposite Parker and me. Pangs hammer at my stomach, and I search my pocketbook for some antacids. Parker and JP give each other a look.

"So, what've I missed?" Logan asks, pouring himself a cup of coffee and picking up a pastry. He maintains a cool and relaxed demeanor despite the unexpected company. This man doesn't rattle easily.

"I am glad that you could join us, Dr. Pelletier," JP says, sounding stiff.

"Please, call me Logan."

"*Oui*, Logan. I spoke with Chad, and he has approved your continued collaboration with us. Your role is to provide a forensic perspective in concert with Dr. Robinson. Do you have any questions before we start?" JP sounds surprisingly blunt.

"None, thanks. But I welcome the opportunity to work with Dr. Robinson. She has extensive knowledge of poisons that I find could be useful in my line of work," Logan says, picking out a fruit pastry and giving me a warm smile with a wink.

JP drops the corners of his mouth, and Parker clears his throat loudly. It's not just me. I know that both of them caught the hidden meaning in Logan's words—and his flirtatious look. I will hear about this, I'm sure.

"*Oui*, so now that we are all together, let us review what we know. Both of you believe the same poison killed both Steinman and Khan."

"It looks that way, but I need the tox evidence to be sure," I say to JP, treading very carefully. "Most of what we know about scorpionism is from studies of people who've been stung by these arachnids. Our two cases are very different because they involved the isolation and concentration of one or more of the specific toxins from the venom to make it more potent. Unlike stings from other scorpions native to the Middle East, a sting from gadim, that's the local Iranian name for *Hemiscorpius lepturis*, would initially produce minimal pain, possibly causing delay in getting treatment. But after twenty-four hours, we'd expect to see skin necrosis at the sting site, and the victim, now having more pain, would seek medical attention. But by the time the localized effect's apparent, systemic toxicity may also be full-blown. And some patients might present with kidney injury, respiratory failure, coagulation disorders, and more. But, if the scorpion envenomation's recognized, then we can give them a multivalent scorpion antivenom. For some, it may be too late, and they may die, anyway."

Parker's eyes glaze over, and he shakes his head. "Thanks for all those details, doc. So what exactly did you two find during Steinman's autopsy?"

"The major finding in that case, and probably in the one we saw here, is DIC," I answer. "And I believe that if both these men had obtained medical attention quickly, they might've been saved."

"Agreed. Lily told me back in Washington that the poison was contained in nanoparticles within the animal tissue portion of the valve, and we think the particles probably broke down after several hours, probably longer in Senator Steinman's case. This would have allowed for a successful interventional procedure like inserting the valve and then obtaining an x-ray that revealed the implant's correct anatomic placement. Enough of a delay so that both patients could be sent home to recuperate. Bruising would've been expected at the groin site, so no alarm bells there. And one or both patients may have been given antibiotics for a few days," Logan adds.

"That reminds me. I have the medications, including the antibiotics that were given to

President Khan. They should be analyzed," JP says.

"We can do that," I say. "The president was taking an antibiotic?"

"*Oui*."

"Antibiotic use may depend on the cardiologist. We ruled out antibiotics as the cause of death with the senator. Anyway, what we need to determine is where each of these valve implants was obtained. They looked similar to Logan and me, so they may be the same brand," I say, seeing Logan nod his head.

"We can probably check to see if there's an associated serial number. Clearly, no matter what, they were tampered with," Logan adds.

"So, forgetting the antibiotics for the moment, what you're saying is that someone could have obtained these two devices, altered them, and somehow got them into the respective hospitals. Any indications that the surgeons were involved?" Parker asks.

"I'm guessing they weren't, Parker. It just doesn't make sense. I think they were handed down via the supply chain and targeted for these two patients. Whoever did this knew what they were doing and was content to wait while the tainted implants did their job," I say.

"Dr. Robinson, *s'il vous plait*. Perhaps you could follow up with Dr. Leigh. I would think that you would have a shortlist of those capable of this level of science between the two of you. *Et*, and, I do not know if there is any reason for you and Dr. Pelletier to remain in Jokovikstan. You have completed your part of the mission. Parker and I will finish up with the president's widow, and then we should take the investigation back to the United States."

I find this rather abrupt of JP to end the meeting this way. A severe look masks his face, deepening his wrinkles. Parker's already gotten up from the table before JP gives us our marching orders as if he knew this was coming. It's true that Logan's and my function here is done, but I believe the assassin resides somewhere in Russia. I'm sure I will learn more from JP when I see him alone.

"Who is Dr. Leigh?" Logan asks.

"He's the toxicologist I sent the specimens to for identification of the poison," I respond.

"Right. I don't think you mentioned his name. Just that you used a lab in Hong Kong. So Lily, since our business here's finished early, would you like to take a tour of the city with me? I'm sure that JP and Parker have important things to discuss," Logan says, giving JP a challenging look. The man is unflappable.

"Maybe later, Logan. I need to check in with my fellow to see if he needs any help with the clinical cases at the hospital. He's very capable, but you know how it is." I feel the heat creep into my face.

"Sure. Then maybe we could meet for lunch," Logan says and then turning to JP and Parker, "Maybe we should all meet for lunch. I'll spend the rest of the morning looking into the manufacture of the valve implants, the different vendors, and see if I can find any interesting connections."

Logan stands up to leave the room, shakes Parker's hand, gives JP a nod, and lets himself out. Parker soon follows, leaving JP alone with me. I go bold.

"You want to tell me what the hell that was all about? It didn't seem like you at all," I say to JP. I've got an edge to my voice, and maybe I do sound a bit defensive.

"Why, Lily, you sound agitated? I simply said that I believe you and Dr. Pelletier have completed your work here. You will wait for the toxicology results from Dr. Leigh, and then you will let me know. I, too, believe we will find a connection."

JP seems too in control for me, and yet the muscles in his lower jaw are clenched. After he told me that my daughter Rose was alive, there was a strain in our relationship. Even so, when I arrived in Jokovikstan, we were consumed by passion at our first meeting—more fireworks this time—as if JP were marking his territory. And I could think of nothing else but being in his arms and wanting him inside me. I don't intend to lose him, yet I sense that he detects Logan's interest in me, and that could prove dangerous.

"No, JP, let's get this out. What's wrong? I can feel it," I say, moving into him, my hands reaching to his chest. He takes my wrists in his hands.

"There is nothing wrong. I can see you have a certain, a certain friendship with Dr. Pelletier. I think he made that apparent this morning and . . ." JP stops mid-sentence.

"JP, let's talk about this. You know that you're the love of my life, my soulmate. I don't want to lose you."

He laughs. JP laughs at this. I feel hurt.

"*Ma chérie*, I love you, I will always love you, *mais*, I am not certain that I can ever possess you. We do not live together. There is sometimes an ocean between us, and although we have passion for one another, perhaps I cannot give you what you truly desire."

"And what's that, JP? What do I truly desire?"

"Since you learned of your daughter Rose's existence, I believe that you blame the Agency for those lost years, *et* perhaps, for the exploitation of your talents, as well. I am not sure if you also blame me. Lily, you told me you wanted Rose in your life. But I am the one who put limits on that. You wish to have a normal mother-daughter relationship, perhaps even a husband, maybe settle down. A different life from this one."

"A normal mother-daughter relationship—yes. A husband—no. Is there something in between for us?"

"That I cannot say."

"So, what do you want, JP?"

"I am wed to this existence until I cannot carry on. I do not see myself as a family man living a risk-free life."

"I would never ask you to. But do you have a past I don't know about? You've always been the mysterious man, the dark-haired man with the blue-green eyes. I still don't know the depths of you. Do you have any children? Did you or do you have a secret wife or a hidden mistress?"

Again he laughs, and I see some of the tension leaving his face.

"I have no children, as far as I know, Lily. Years ago, I had a vasectomy to ensure that would be impossible. I have no wife, although I have enjoyed many women but none such as you. My relationship with you is intense and consuming. But for you, Lily, I fear it is not enough," he says, stroking my cheek and moving an errant strand of hair behind my ear.

"No, JP, it's enough. Yes, there're times when I feel lonely, and more so now after living our fantasy holiday in France, and since I found out that Rose is alive. When I thought she was dead, I could drown myself in work and use these missions as a way to make up for the loss. But now? I don't know, JP. I just don't know," I say, flopping down on the edge of the bed, feeling slightly defeated.

"I think time will unravel all. You have your daughter now. We cannot feel guilty about who we love or who fills our loneliness, or even who we kill as a duty to our countries. I have told you before, *chérie*, be in the moment. Do not dwell on the past or try to guess the future," he says, kissing the top of my head. "Now, would you like to take a quick tour of the oldest part of the city before we get back to our assignment?"

"I'd love to." I let out a big sigh and take JP's hand.

JP goes back to his room to make some calls while I decide to linger outside the hotel and people watch before going in. The walk was good for us. Even though we didn't speak very much, I felt connected to him and somewhat comfortable thinking that my tryst with Logan won't cause any problems. But it's hard to tell. We talked about it without really talking about it. Like many other things in this organization, sometimes it's better to deny, deny, deny. While I'm sure he suspects that I've been with Logan, I don't imagine he wants the details. It's my business.

We're all planning to meet for lunch and review some additional aspects of the case. Before I'm about to return, JP sends a text asking me to meet at the small Chinese restaurant within walking distance from the hotel. He says Parker and Logan will be there. Since this country shares a border with China, it's not unusual to find authentic Chinese cuisine here. I walk alone wearing a long white linen dress with a silk embroidered jacket. My hair's pinned up and covered with a green print silk scarf. There's the restaurant just ahead, and I notice the streets are mostly empty.

The eight-foot-high metal door opens as I pull on formidable brass handles and enter a dimly lit, almost café-like eatery. I can see Parker and Logan at a corner table located several feet away from a family with two young children. No one else is in the restaurant.

"Hi, Lily. I thought JP would be with you?" Logan says, seeing that I'm alone. "I just got here too."

"No, I'm sure he's on his way," I tell him and then look over at Parker, who's nibbling on something.

"Yeah," Parker says with a mouthful of food. "Have a seat. I'm sure the ol' man will be here soon. So look, I ordered some dishes for all of us to share. Have a seat and dig in," he says, pointing to some bowls of soups, noodles and vegetables, and some kind of meat dish.

I'm glad JP's not here to hear that. He doesn't like it when Parker refers to him as the ol' man.

I settle into one of the wooden chairs, then pour myself some tea and wonder why the change of venue since we were going to meet back at the hotel.

"Parker, why are we having lunch here?"

Parker leans into me and speaks in a low voice. "Robinson, we thought maybe the optics were better if we looked a little more like tourists and less like operatives from another country," Parker says, giving me a wink.

Are we being watched? If this country's president was murdered, I expect that the murderer's still out there. Parker makes a little small talk while we're waiting for JP.

"So what do you do exactly, Dr. Pelletier?" Parker asks Logan.

"As a forensic pathologist? The usual. Investigate sudden and unexpected deaths. The autopsy usually determines the manner and cause of death. We give court testimony in homicide cases and give closure to families wanting to know what happened to their loved one, particularly if the death's not witnessed," Logan says, pouring himself some water.

"Usually determine the manner and cause of death? Not always?" Parker asks.

"Right. Sometimes we just don't know, and that we call undetermined."

"Right," Parker says. "So, you're in a different line of work than Robinson?"

"Yeah, Parker. We're both pathologists; we just specialize in different areas," Logan says.

Finally, JP arrives.

"*Bonjour*, hello, sorry I am late. Tied up on the phone with Chad. He stayed up late to make the call," JP says, charging over to our table and taking his seat.

"Great. We're all here. What can you tell us, JP?" I ask.

"Chad found something very interesting *et* something that the president's wife Marina alluded to. She told Parker and me that her husband was working on a deal regarding rare earth minerals, or elements. Jokovikstan's mountains contain considerable amounts of REEs, that is what they call them, and rather than sell them to either Russia or China, both bordering countries, who in turn would sell them to the U.S., Jokovikstan's president wanted to deal directly with the United States."

"What's so important about these REEs?" I ask.

"*Bon*, Dr. Robinson. Since China currently controls more than 80% of the rare earth deposits and does much of the processing, it can charge high tariffs during the export of its natural elements. Jokovikstan could be a direct competitor, so it's in China's interests to want control of the world's deposits. Other countries depend on these technology minerals, or REEs, and see China's control as a potential threat.

While there are treaties that address climate control and world markets that govern gas and oil, there is nothing in place for the disposition of REEs. These minerals are essential components in electronics, clean-energy functions, and high-tech military mechanisms." JP says.

"And," Parker continues, "Military applications for REEs are the most critical and have allowed some countries to excel at weapon production. China, for example, has created both kinetic and hypersonic weapons. A higher launch velocity of a projectile can be achieved with the use of magnetized plasma artillery."

"Magnetized plasma?" Logan asks. He scoops up some rice and vegetables with his chopsticks.

JP picks up the pace. Clearly, he and Parker have been looking into this.

"*Oui*, a magnetized sheath of plasma inside the body pipe reduces both the heat and the wear of the gun barrel, and with reduced friction, may also make the weapon more accurate. Railguns use parallel conductors—those are the rails—to create electromagnetic force rather than chemical energy to fire a projectile. Kinetic weapons, those that deliver death with incredible velocity, are a variation on a theme. Shells wrapped in another body and fired at high speed are hard, dense, and fast projectiles that devastate their target."

"Right, JP. You can imagine that a shell moving at 3,500 feet-per-second is traveling three times faster than the speed of sound. No longer are chemical explosives utilized to propel the shell fragments; in this case, it's the projectile's sheer velocity that does the damage."

Both Logan and I are quiet. For once, it's JP and Parker speaking a language we're not familiar with.

"REEs are also vital in communication devices, *et* essentially technology we use now and in the foreseeable future. *Tres, tres important*," JP emphasizes.

Parker lowers his voice. "So, if the President of Jokovikstan was about to make a deal with the United States, getting him out of the way would be crucial. We need to find out who is next in line to control this country now that Khan's dead, and what's their relationship with China."

"No, not the Chinese. The Russians," I say.

"The Russians?" Parker asks, putting down his bowl of soup.

"Assuming that we find scorpion venom in the president's tissue samples, then we must assume the Russians are involved, JP," I say, looking straight at him. "I told you that I found evidence that the Russians played a part in another death." I'm trying to give him the information without saying too much.

"*Oui, je comprend*."

"Holy shit," Logan says. "Listen, we use some of these REEs in medicine. Lily, you know we use gadolinium as a contrast dye during an MRI to improve visibility of the internal organs and other structures."

"Yes, of course," I answer.

"And we use titanium in several medical devices, like orthopedic implants, eye implants, pacemakers and—"

"Valve implants," I add. We're all now staring at Logan.

"So after breakfast this morning, I looked into the companies that make valve bioprostheses. There aren't all that many. One's a relatively new company called Trileaflet, Inc. And get this, they're manufacturing a new bioprosthesis with a metal other than titanium. Now it's not specified, but I'll bet it's some kind of rare earth metal."

"Jesus Christ, Dr. Pelletier, I am very impressed with your research. Chad was right about you," JP says.

"So, how does this all tie in together?" I ask.

"Lily, when we get back to Washington, you and I should track down the valve implants in our two cases. Of course, if the boss approves," he says, exchanging looks with JP. "I wouldn't be surprised if they're made by Trileaflet," Logan says.

"But that makes no sense. If this is a new company with a new product, why kill important people who have used these implants? That can't be good for business," I say.

"Look, I think whoever killed these two people banked on cremation or, in the very least, no autopsy. And they must've had someone in on both sides of the Atlantic that could see that that was the case. These implants were just a mechanism for causing deaths. It's what they had available. So, yes, I agree that they were not out to broadcast failures, and remember, the medical details of these two men were private. The important connection's that whoever did this had access to these products and could alter them without detection." Logan adjusts his man bun and pushes back from the table.

"*C'est vrai*, I agree with Logan. If we assume that the death of each of these men is somehow tied to these heart valves and REEs, we now know where to focus our attention."

"For fuck's sake, Logan, anything else on Trileaflet?" Parker asks, shaking his head.

"Turns out it's a subsidiary of a larger company that has holdings out of Russia, something called Global Tectonics. Gentleman, I would listen to your Dr. Robinson. You need to follow the trail to Russia."

Chapter 19

France

Alexis found her way into the rehabilitation hospital. The information she was given about her mother's recuperation proved correct. The facility was not very strict about visitors, so Alexis told the nurses that she was a family member, and they didn't question her further. She was brought to Adrienne's room, which appeared bright and cheery. A large window next to the bed allowed the light to shine through, and Alexis could see the warm sun hitting Adrienne's face. The vision unsettled her stomach, and she could feel the emotion creep up to her brain. The nurse introduced her.

"Good morning, Adrienne. You have a visitor. A family member has come to see you."

Adrienne turned her head and looked directly at Alexis. There was no recognition in her eyes. Undeterred, Alexis sat in the chair next to the bed and took her mother's hand. She turned to the nurse.

"Does she recognize anyone? Does she have her memory?" Alexis smoothed out her white cotton dress, cinched at the waist with a black belt, her lightweight coat, now in her lap.

"Adrienne has some recognition. She is very lucid on some days, and on other days she struggles. She is familiar with the staff who are working on her recovery. She also has a daughter who comes to see her regularly."

"A daughter? Do you know her name? Perhaps she's my cousin," Alexis asked, fully knowing that Rose was her adopted sister.

"Her name is Rose. She lives in the United States but has spent much time with her mother during her recovery. Adrienne suffered serious head trauma and has faced an uphill battle trying to restore her memory and some of her physical skills." The nurse looked at her watch. "Will you excuse me? I have to see another patient now."

The healthcare worker left the room, and Alexis had a sense of sadness as she looked at Adrienne, who had quietly been listening to the conversation. The lost daughter squeezed her hand and leaned in closer.

"Mother, mother, it's Bella. I'm here, mother," Alexis said.

Adrienne turned toward Alexis and spoke. "Bella? Bella is dead. I remember, Bella is dead." Adrienne's eyes filled with tears, and she felt the fingers of this stranger intertwined with hers and tried to pull away.

"Mother, I did not die. Do you remember the kidnapping? After I was kidnapped, I was taken to Russia and put to work in an organization."

Alexis wasn't sure that her mother understood her, so she continued talking softly to Adrienne about their life together on the plantation. She told her stories of how she and Rose played together within the walls of the Compound and reminded her of how Bella's gift of language had been encouraged and nurtured. By the time Bella was thirteen, she was already speaking three languages fluently. After some time, Adrienne's eyes seemed to move closer together and her mouth opened as if she wanted to say something. Startled by revelation, she examined Alexis's face with her hands.

"Bella? Are you Bella?" Adrienne asked, tears streaming down her face.

Alexis moved in closer and took Adrienne in her arms, and hugged her. The comfort of the physical closeness overwhelmed her, and she too, became emotional. Since Scottie had died, her existence had been lonely—without love and physical connections. Thoughts crammed into Alexis's mind jamming all her feelings like solar interference of radio waves.

"Yes, mother, it's me. I heard about your accident and came to France to see you. I'm on my way to America. I wanted to say goodbye."

"What do you mean, goodbye?" Adrienne asked, her clarity of mind now strong. She remembered.

"I mean that I have to go, but I wanted to see

you one last time. One last time to thank you for raising me under such difficult circumstances. I know it wasn't easy for you. Your Uncle Alberto was oppressive, and he kept all of us in isolation. Those were the circumstances that fed my desire to escape the plantation, but when I was kidnapped, it was terrifying. Yet on some level, it was also freeing. It's hard to explain," she said, giving her mother's hand another squeeze. "I just wanted to say that I love you." Alexis wiped the tears from her eyes.

The blond-haired daughter looked out the window and wished things were different but realized there was no escape now, just as there wasn't back then. Sergei was waiting for her right outside in the parking area, not about to let Alexis change any of the plans. They were on their way to the United States to finish the mission per their superiors. Their instructions had been made clear. As Alexis stood up, readying herself to leave, Adrienne gripped her daughter's hand tighter, refusing to let it go.

"Bella, please do not leave me. I found you. I have prayed to God, and he granted me my wish. Please forgive me. Your life is not your fault. When I was trapped on my uncle's Compound, I could see that he had dealings with criminals, but I could say nothing. I wasn't dumb or blind. I was scared. One night, one of these men, a Russian, entered my room and raped me. The moon was full, and in the light, I saw his face. His stormy gray eyes have haunted me ever since. But you, Bella, were my gift from that night. You brought joy and unconditional love into my life. Markovic was a brutal man, and when he took you from me that day after we visited the small village, I thought he would kill you. I thought he did kill you as revenge for Uncle Alberto's refusal to cut him in on his drug trade and because he wanted no evidence of the rape."

Alexis reeled at her mother's words. Adrienne said it was Markovic who had assaulted her and that she, little Bella, had been the offspring of that violence. My God, Markovic was her father! Alexis pulled her hand from Adrienne's abruptly with this revelation. A wave of nausea overcame her, and she grabbed for the chair to steady herself. Her hand could not stop the vomit that spilled out of her mouth. She staggered across the room to get to the sink and rinse out the bitter taste. Alexis swallowed hard and took a deep breath as she held on to the paper towel dispenser above the basin for support. Once settled, she pulled a couple of sheets of paper from the metal dispenser, wiped her dress, and cleaned up the mess on the floor. Disgust and fear blocked Alexis's mind, and she was at a loss for words. Her body shook, and her thoughts consumed her.

Alexis could not let go of the vision of this man who had abused her in every way. He was her father. Her gray eyes were his gray eyes, and her hair, light like his. Eyes closed, Alexis threw her head back and revealed her long neck and wished this wasn't true, but deep in her heart, she knew it was. She was predestined to be evil and unlovable. Why else would she have turned into the person she'd become—alone, addicted to cocaine, and involved with terrorists?

Alexis felt she finally understood those feelings she had as a child. Her mother had appeared sad when looking into her little Bella eyes. Bella, now Alexis, thought this secret explained the demons who lived in her mind, and the reason why she could never love herself. At that moment, she felt that her life was no longer worth living. Yet, a glimpse of Scottie percolated through her brain. Was that relationship real? She thought so at the time. She thought that perhaps he was the only person who saw the frightened girl beneath the horror. But Scottie was gone. And at last, Alexis wondered if her suspicion that her mother loved Rose more was because Rose's face didn't remind her of Markovic.

Alexis hugged her mother one last time. Adrienne had trouble letting go. She clung to her daughter and said, "I remember, Bella. The day we were in the village. Rose got a rose tattoo, and you got the—"

"The spider tattoo. I know, mother. I still have it."

"Yes, the spider tattoo. I should have gotten a dragonfly. I wanted to, but I . . ." and Adrienne stopped. She closed her eyes as tears fell down her cheeks and onto her flowered shirt.

Alexis bit her lower lip and hugged her mother goodbye, convinced that this would be their last meeting. It had been bittersweet. And sad. How would her life have been different if she hadn't been kidnapped? The discovery that Markovic was her biological father, as well as her abuser, left Alexis with a hollow in her center and self-loathing. She left the room feeling empty and broken.

After Rose dropped her bags at the estate, she drove to the rehabilitation hospital to see her mother. This was one of the weeks she would be in France. For now, she was dividing her time between Boston and Reims. Rose, although exhausted from the trip, felt buoyed by her budding relationship with Dr. Kelley. After their lunch at the sushi restaurant, they had spent more time together visiting some of the Boston museums and even took a trolley ride to see the historic parts of the city. They walked the Freedom Trail, visited the Old North Church, and enjoyed cannolis in the North End. This union was a bright spot in Rose's life and helped her fight her depression caused by a burden of tragic circumstances that had already stained her young life. When Rose reached the rehabilitation facility where her mother was recuperating, she was immediately greeted by one of the nurses.

"Hello, Rose," the nurse said, "I was going to call you, but I remembered that you told us you were going to be back today. Your mother is very agitated. She has been in quite a state since she had a visitor an hour ago. I was about to give her something to calm her down but seeing you should make all the difference. Please let me know if you think I should call the doctor."

"What visitor? The only visitor that I know she has is the priest, Père Berger."

"No, this was a young woman, about your age. She said she was your cousin."

Uneasiness swept over Rose. She had no cousin. Why would someone visit her mother and say otherwise? Rose's mind ran unfettered. Maybe this was someone trying to steal her mother's estate, knowing that she is incapacitated while recovering from her car accident. Rose felt the heat sweep her face. Her steps got longer as she hurried to her mother's room. "Mother, it's Rose. How are you feeling?" Rose sat on the edge of the bed and touched Adrienne's arm, rubbing it, hoping to soothe her.

"Bella, Bella," Adrienne said, her voice agitated.

"No, mother, it's Rose. Bella's gone, remember?"

Rose held onto Adrienne's arm with a tighter grip as if to squeeze her mother into reality. Exasperated, she let out a sigh, worried that her mother was having a relapse. Adrienne's progress had been rocky. Some days her mind seemed clear, while other days, she had difficulty remembering people and events. Adrienne grabbed Rose's hand and looked directly at her. Her face, still showing evidence of the healing laceration on her forehead, appeared sullen, and she stared at Rose.

"Rose, I know I have had a difficult time with my memory of events and recognition of people. But as of this moment, my mind feels clear. I had a visitor today. A young woman. It was my Bella. Your sister," Adrienne said, now up out of bed. Rose saw her shaky balance and helped her into an oversized recliner chair by the window. Still slightly wobbly with transitions from supine to upright, Adrienne steadied herself using Rose as a brace.

"I don't understand. Bella was kidnapped, and we never heard from her again. Everyone assumed she was dead. Even your Uncle Alberto said so. How do you know this was Bella?"

Rose felt uneasy and still guilty over having read the letter Adrienne had written and given her years ago. It was only meant to be read after her mother's death, but on an impulse, Rose had removed it from its safekeeping and cried at its admissions. Somewhere deep inside, Rose felt Adrienne's accident was retribution for the letter's reading. A punishment for going beyond the bounds.

"Listen to me, Rose, it was Bella. She knew about the spider tattoo. Bella came to say goodbye. Rose, I told her the truth about her father. I've never shared that with anyone except my uncle, who knew at the time. I told her that I was the victim of rape and that her father was a Russian named Grigory Markovic. I wanted her to know the truth. I want you to know the truth."

Adrienne slumped down in the chair, now feeling exhausted by the day and its revelations. Rose debated whether to tell her about the letter but then forged ahead.

"Mother, I need to tell you something. Before your accident, when I was back in Boston, I read the letter you gave me when I was in high school. I didn't wait like you said. I thought that if I knew the contents, there'd be something in there that I could help you with. I had no idea it would reveal the rape and how I was found alone in the jungle."

Adrienne stared out the window as if she were collecting her thoughts. She knew this day would come. The intersection of truth and deception. It was time. She needed to tell Rose everything she knew about Bella, the drug trade, and how Rose ended up on the coffee farm. Now that she knew

Bella was alive, there were decisions to be made. Her mind, tired, once again became cloudy. The truth would have to wait. She pushed herself up out of the chair and into Rose's arms. They gave each other the kind of hug reserved for moments of uncertainty—about the future and the unknown before them.

Chapter 20

Boston

Jokovikstan seemed like a blur. JP sent us packing—Logan took a flight to D.C., and I came home to Boston. It felt comforting to me to be in my own space. My gray chenille couch had a cozy, fuzzy nap that invited me in when I reached the condo. There was time to reflect on my trip abroad while I wait to hear from Dr. Leigh and pull on one more loose thread.

This morning I'm connecting with Senator Steinman's staffer by video conference. She's the one who alerted Chad with her suspicions regarding her boss's death. Chad agreed that I could reach out to her. I'm pulling up the link on my computer now.

"Hi, Maryanne. Thank you for talking with me. I know you spoke with Chad Jones."

I can see a young woman wearing a white blouse and brown cardigan, her dark hair tied up in a ponytail.

"Hi. Nice to meet you, doctor. So, how can I help?"

"Maryanne, Chad mentioned that when you spoke with him, you said that Senator Steinman was very upset the week before he died. Was he working on anything in particular?"

"Well, as Chair of the Subcommittee on International Development and International Economic Policies, he was involved in so many things. It's hard to pick out just one thing."

"I'm sure he was. But was there some specific project, or maybe someone who had come to see him during that week?"

"Let me see. I have his calendar right here." She looks away from the screen and thumbs through a desk calendar.

"Yeah, it looks like he had several meetings that week. That's not so unusual, but I see that he met with James Andrews more than a few times. Just looking at the senator's calendar makes me upset. He was such a good man," she says with a sniff.

"It's okay. I'm sure it's been quite an adjustment for you. So please remind me, who's James Andrews?"

"Deputy Secretary James Andrews of the Interior Department."

"Oh, of course. What kind of business would they be discussing?"

"It could have been anything from economic policies, possibly a trade agreement, mining rights; it kind of runs the gamut. If you like, I can try and see if there's anything in the files. Right now, I'm trying to organize some of Senator

Steinman's projects that he and I were working on so I can transfer them to another senator."

"Maryanne, you've been a big help. If you do find out anything more, please contact me. And thanks again." We shut down our video cameras after a nod and a smile, and I'm wondering just who James Andrews is and why he was meeting with Senator Steinman.

I've got one more call to make. A nurse I used to work with in Boston, who's now down in D.C., staffs the OR at the same hospital where Steinman had his procedure.

"Hi Linda, so good to hear your voice."

"Gosh, it's been a while, Lily. How are you?" Linda says with enthusiasm.

"Good, thanks. Listen, Linda. I wonder if you can look into something for me. Could you check with your cath lab and see what kind of aortic valve implants they use? I'm interested in any sales staff who may have shown up at the lab with some new products in the last few weeks. I'm doing a little research project, so if you find out anything, just pop me a text message."

"Sure, no problem. Didn't know you were doing cardiac pathology now. Hey, you still happy in Boston? We can't bribe you to come down here?" she says with a laugh.

"No, I'm good. Listen, I've got to run. Thanks again and take care," I say and hang up the phone.

Checking my watch, I see that Lisa should pop in any minute. Here she is.

"Good morning, Dr. Lily. How was your trip?" she asks, looking smart in a blue blazer, her hair swept back in an up-do. Those dark eyes sweep over the mail collected on my desk.

"Great, Lisa, thanks. You know how these trips are. Science, science, science. It gets boring after a while." I nearly choke on the words.

"I know you've quite a bit of catching up, and Dr. Kelley says he wants to review cases with you, but that medical student, Rose, is very anxious to see you today if you have the time. I've checked your calendar, and I could fit her in now before your other meetings if that works for you. Should I call her? She left me her cell phone number."

I feel my heart skip a beat. A chance to be with my Rose!

"Lisa, please give her a call. I'll see her now. It must be something important."

While I wait for Rose to show up, I buzz through some of the emails. There's one here from Leigh who acknowledges that he's received the specimens and will get in touch with me later in the week. He already has a good idea of what to look for, so I'm thinking he's going to dive right in analyzing for toxins from *H. lepturus*. I see there's another email from Logan. I wonder what he wants now.

"Excuse me, Dr. Lily, but Rose is here to see you," Lisa says.

I look up from my computer. "Wow, that was fast. Come on in, Rose. Take a seat."

"I was just over in the medical library trying to study. I got back from France last night."

There's no lovely smile lighting up her face. Her eyes are puffy, as if she's been crying. I'm concerned. "Rose, is everything all right? Is your, your mother okay?"

Tears start falling down her face, and I hand her a tissue from a box containing wipes to clean a microscope lens, not dry tears.

"Thank you. I'm sorry, Dr. Robinson. I'm sorry. I keep showing up in your office crying. I didn't know who else to turn to. I really have no family other than my mother, and well, she's still recovering. I just feel so alone," Rose sniffs.

"It's all right, Rose. I'm glad to be of some help to you. Tell me what is going on?"

I hope I don't sound too clinical. It's hard to balance the joy of seeing my daughter with the sadness that she can't know that I'm her biological mother.

"Well, I've been going back and forth to France while my mother's been in the rehab hospital. We're hoping she could come home soon, you know, get home care with a full-time attendant. But this last time I was at the hospital, something very strange happened."

"Strange? What was strange?"

"I don't remember if I told you about my sister."

"I don't think so, Rose. What about your sister?" This hadn't come up before.

"When I was a young teenager, my mother took us for a celebration to a town on the very outskirts of our coffee plantation for our birthdays. It was an exciting day for us because my sister Bella and I had never been off the farm in our lives. When we were there, I'm a little embarrassed to say, our mother let us each get a tattoo to celebrate the occasion. I got a Rose, and my sister Bella got a spider."

Rose does seem a little uncomfortable by this admission. I can see her wringing her hands, her eyes tilted to her lap. And frankly, I'm a little surprised that Adrienne let the girls get tattoos. I would have been worried about blood-borne diseases. But that's me. While Rose takes a pause, I realize that she has no idea that she lived with me in the States before Colombia. Her trauma must have blocked her memory too. Her prior life is a blank to her.

"It's okay, Rose, go on. What else happened in that little town?"

"Well, that same day when we were on our way home, our driver was shot and killed, and Bella was taken from the car by a man I'll never forget. He had hard cold gray eyes, and wispy blond hair, and big feet." Rose's hands shake, and she twists in her chair.

"How awful." I let out a little gasp. God, I'm thinking that sounds like a description of Grigory Markovic.

"I'm sorry, I'm rambling a bit," she says with a sniff.

"No, it's okay, Rose, go on."

"We never heard from Bella again. My great uncle tried to find her, but we never did, and so we all assumed she, she died. But, when I just saw my mother, she said that Bella came to visit her," Rose says, now starting to cry again.

I'm listening intently now.

"Rose, you told me that your mother had a traumatic brain injury. And I also believe you said she had memory problems. Isn't it possible that she just imagined that your sister was there?"

"That's what I thought too. But the nurse told me that my mother had a visitor about my age with blond hair and gray-blue eyes who claimed she was a cousin."

"Still, that could have been anyone."

"I know. However, they talked about the trip to the little town we took, and Bella finished the story saying she had gotten the spider tattoo. Adrienne, my mother, was fully aware at that point and recognized Bella. It was the eyes. Bella has her father's eyes."

"Who's your sister's father?" I ask, now fully engulfed in the story.

"It's the man who raped my mother. His name's Grigory Markovic. Dr. Robinson, my sister Bella's alive, and she said she's coming to the United States."

I'm spinning now. Blindsided. Markovic! That bastard. Will I ever be free of that man? The screw turns ever tighter. I need to talk with JP. I'm trying to remember what he told me when we were in Seoul and in Reims—about the little girls in the photograph that Scottie found in Alexis's room. If JP knew about this, what else is he not telling me? Is it possible that Bella and Alexis could be the same person?

"Rose, I'm so sorry. It must be shocking to find out that your sister's alive after all these years. Did Adrienne tell you why Bella said she was coming to the United States?"

"I don't think so. Bella told my mother she wanted to visit her to say goodbye. I don't understand why she wouldn't want to stay in contact with her family if she just found us. And where has she been all these years? Doing what?" Rose says with some intensity. Her face is flushed, and her green eyes are filled with tears that catch the light. She plays with her beautiful red diamond ring, making me conscious of my own gold band—a serpent with a ruby head.

"Those are all good questions, Rose. You must

feel very confused. What did your mother think about the visit?" I ask, hoping JP can make some discreet inquiries.

"I'm not exactly sure. She appeared to be thinking clearly, and after she told me about the rape, I admitted to her that I already knew. Poor Bella, I can't imagine how she must feel knowing her real father's a criminal," Rose says, the tears falling again. She grabs a few more wipes from the box on my desk to blot her eyes. "When we were young, we used to make up stories about who our fathers were. At least Bella knows who her biological mother is. I have no idea where I came from," Rose says, still drying tears.

Now my heart is breaking. As much as I want to tell Rose the truth about her life—her father, an extraordinary scientist and her mother, a doctor whose despair and loneliness propelled her into a life of deceit, I can't break my vow to JP. Not right now. Doing so could put Rose in jeopardy. What I need to do is call Chad.

"Rose, I can see you have a lot to process. Why don't we plan to meet again and soon? I'm glad you felt you could confide in me. Listen, I know Dr. Kelley's in his office today. Maybe you could stop by there and see if he's free for lunch."

"Thanks, Dr. Robinson. I'm sorry for breaking down."

"Rose, you're hardly the first medical student, resident, staff member, faculty, or even patient that has cried in this office. Please, don't give it another thought."

I lead my daughter to the door, my arm around her shoulder, give her a little hug, and Lisa gives me a knowing look as I watch them walk toward Kelley's office. I can't wait to get out my phone and dial my Agency contact.

"Chad. This is Dr. Robinson. When you get this message, please give me a call right away; it's important. And have JP call me too."

I hang up and find my computer screen staring back at me, begging me to work on my email. I try not to look at the number of messages accumulating in my inbox. So hard to focus after my conversation with Rose. Logan's message is flagged as high importance and confidential, so I start there.

Of course, it's cryptic, and it has to be. He would like to meet and talk over the details. He's looked at the microscopics from our most recent case and confirms that it's disseminated intravascular coagulation, DIC. He sees microthrombi in all the organs we were able to take samples from. So the two cases have the cause of death in common. If the etiology's the same, then both cases will be considered a homicide. Death at the hands of another. But whose hand?

My secure phone rings. It's Chad. I tell him that I want to meet with him tonight and ask if JP can join us. He agrees to come to my office later and lets me know that JP is still in Jokovikstan looking into Thornton. I hang up, knowing that I have so many questions for both Chad and JP.

Bringing my brain back into focus, I begin to tackle the folders filled with clinical cases when there's a knock at my door.

"Excuse me, Dr. Robinson. The micro lab needs you to take a look at an insect they pulled off a patient. They have it waiting for you under the stereo microscope," Lisa says.

This is welcome. I need to get out of my office, move, and shake off the building anxiety from all the morning's revelations. To the lab, it is.

"Let's see what you've got," I say to the lab tech who's working on the case.

"It's a tick, Dr. Robinson, but which one? We usually let the clinician know if it's a deer tick, *Ixodes scapularis*," the newly minted graduate says.

I sit down at the scope and look through the binocular lens. I can see the tick, its back to me, isolated on the stage.

"You're right, Jane. It's a tick. But it's not *Ixodes*, and we both know everyone worries about Lyme disease with that tick. *Borrelia burgdorferi* is the spirochete that carries Lyme disease. It also transmits other organisms that cause diseases like babesiosis. We see that in Massachusetts, particularly on the Cape and Islands."

"I know what Lyme disease is, but what's babesiosis, Dr. Robinson?"

"Babesia are organisms that invade our red blood cells and lyse them. As a result, patients have intermittent fevers, headaches, fatigue, and some additional generalized symptoms. The good news is that we can see these organisms under the microscope. They look a little like malaria parasites inhabiting the red blood cells."

"So if this tick's not *Ixodes*, what is it?"

"This is the Lone Star Tick, *Amblyomma americanum*. You see that little white spot in the center of the back? That's how it got its name. This tick's also important clinically because it carries organisms that transmit disease. But unlike *Ixodes*, it's more common in the southeast United States than in Massachusetts. Where's this patient from?"

"Oh, I think the doctor said they were up from Georgia. So I guess that makes sense. Thanks for double-checking me. There's just so much to learn."

I leave the lab thinking how we couldn't do our jobs without the hard-working technologists that operate the instruments that do the bulk of the analyses, prepare all the specimens, and do the manual work too—anything that needs to be observed under the microscope or analyzed by a non-automated assay. A lot of knowledge goes into generating a result for a patient.

• • •

I'm now waiting for Chad to show up. I spent most of the day catching up with emails, colleagues, paperwork, and cases. I'm also putting together a new lecture on the opioid crisis. It's still raging; so many people have died of drug overdoses, and we must address ways to deal with it. I hear Chad outside my door.

"Chad, thanks for coming. I'm glad I caught you before you go back to D.C."

"No problem, what's up?"

"Two things, really. One is that I spoke with the staffer who worked with Steinman, and the other is that Rose Moreau came to see me this morning. I assume you know who Rose is, right?"

I can see Chad fidget a little in the seat in front of my desk. He leans forward and starts drumming his fingers on my table.

"Let's start with Rose. What do you want to know, Robinson?"

"JP told me that my daughter was taken in by a woman from a coffee plantation after the massacre of, of my colleagues in Colombia all those years ago. This woman, Adrienne, raised my daughter as her own. Did you know that she had another daughter?" I say, my voice sharp. Chad doesn't answer. "Don't lie to me, Chad. I need to know the truth."

There's quiet in my office. The air's still since there're no words to move it.

"Yes," Chad says after a long pause. "I knew she had a sister."

"And, that photograph that Scottie took from Alexis while he was with her in Moscow tracking down Markovic, it was a picture of two young girls with an older woman. JP told me that you identified one of the girls in the picture as Alexis when she was younger."

I feel the anger building. I only heard part of Alexis's story while we were in Seoul. At the time, Intelligence asked Scottie to track down Markovic through a woman named Alexis Popov.

Chad's really squirming now. He leaves his seat, turns his back to me, and walks to the bookcases snug on the far wall. His fingers run along the volumes while he ponders what to say.

"Yes, we did identify the young woman as Alexis. But at the time, we didn't know who the other little girl was. I swear it, Lily. Look, we've never shared all the details with you for your own safety. You know that."

When Chad calls me Lily, it's a rare occasion. I think we've forged enough of a relationship to share some honesty.

"Well, Alexis is headed for the United States. Or she may already be here. Don't know where, but I have a good guess." I throw it out there and see if it sticks.

"What the hell are you talking about?" His voice is agitated, and he comes back over to my desk.

"I'm telling you that my Rose said her mother got a visit from her dead daughter named Bella. Now I assume Bella and Alexis are one and the same. Yes?"

Chad pauses.

"Yes, yes, that's correct. What in bloody hell's going on?" His fist hits my desk.

"You tell me. I want to see JP. Where is he, Chad? I will not allow my Rose to be in any danger. I was told that I could not have an open relationship with her because it would put her in jeopardy. You goddamn people have been screwing around with my life for years. And for what?" I'm yelling at Chad and shaking all over.

Chad backs away from the desk. Both his hands are raised, and he is moving them back and forth to indicate calm. Is he aware of the sign on my door? *Keep calm and ask a toxicologist.* I'm furious, and I didn't realize how angry I was until now. Buried emotions spew forth like ash from a volcanic eruption.

"Robinson, please. We can protect your daughter if it comes to that." His voice is even.

"If it comes to that? No, we need to find out what the hell's going on now. My intuition says what's happening in Jokovikstan and in D.C. has something to do with the Russians. I know it, Chad. I just know it."

"We're looking into that, Lily. You know we are."

"Let me ask you this. Did you know that Alexis was Markovic's daughter? That piece of shit was sleeping with his own daughter."

I can tell by the look on his face that this is news. He lets out a large sigh and bites his lower lip while I reach for the bottle of antacids, taking two. The chalky mint feels soothing, and I wash it down with my disgust and some bottled water.

"And the staffer, Robinson; what did you find out there?" Chad asks, changing the subject, hoping my anger will subside.

"Steinman had several meetings with a man named James Andrews. Turns out he's Deputy Secretary of the Interior, and one of their priorities is to create energy security and develop critical minerals for the U.S. You think maybe those REEs we talked about fall into that category, Chad?" I know I have a slight sarcastic edge to my voice, but I'm still fired up.

"Okay, Robinson. I'll send you back to Jokovikstan to work with JP. See if you can find out if Thornton knew about Andrews. I'll work it from my end. Now get your goddamn bags packed and get going. And by the way, how the hell do they let you keep working at this hospital with all the time you take off?"

"You have no idea, Chad."

Chapter 21

The Republic of Jokovikstan

Right before I left for my second trip to Jokovikstan, Maryanne called me with some additional information. Going through the senator's work, the staffer discovered that Steinman was reviewing some Executive Orders— specifically 13817 and 13953. Attached to the file, there was a sticky note that read, "see Andrews." When I looked up the EOs, they addressed our country's dependence on imports of critical minerals from foreign adversaries, particularly China. However, Jokovikstan's not an adversary of the U.S., and conveniently, their mountains are a hotbed of REEs. So, maybe a partnership with the U.S. would give a small nation greater financial independence and get the U.S. out from under China's thumb. But what if the Russians wanted in on the deal?

Now that we are at cruising altitude, I release my seat back into a comfortable position and realize this is one of the fastest turnarounds I've ever done—I've been ping-ponging across the Atlantic for the last few weeks. Jet lag's practically nonexistent since I've had almost no time to acclimate. But I am tired. I emailed Lisa (again), saying it was an emergency and that I had to leave immediately. I also left a message for Kelley telling him I wouldn't be available and asked him to look after Rose; after all, she was upset when she came to see me last and needed a little TLC. But he probably knows that.

I look forward to seeing JP, and once I touchdown in Jokovikstan, I plan on pressing him about Rose. He's meeting me at the airport. I'll close my eyes for just a minute.

The airport's busier than I expected. "JP, thanks for picking me up. Is Parker here?"

"*Bonjour*, my Lily. No Parker. He is back at the hotel. Chad contacted me and said he was going to put you on the next plane to us. He did not give me many details but said that you would," JP says as he picks up my suitcase.

"Let's go straight to the hotel. I'm exhausted from the flight."

Fatigue has followed me from one country to the next, and I'm in desperate need of a shower and a change of clothes. JP sees my struggle and takes my arm as I drag my feet. We walk to the car, and once the doors are shut, he turns to me.

"*Ma chérie*, what is it? I can see anger behind those tired eyes." He leans over and gives me a kiss to soften the moment.

"Let's wait until we reach the hotel. There's just so much to say; I don't know where to begin."

"*Mais oui*."

• • •

We drive to the hotel, and I'm lucky to get the same room that I had before—room 646. Clouded with brain fog, I must remember to put my scorpion antivenom in the fridge so it doesn't spoil. I never travel to the Middle East without it. A trick I learned from Omair. I ask JP to let me take my shower first, and then we can talk. The man's agreeable and leaves me for now. After I wash and dry my hair, I notice the bed beckons me for a short rest. Lush pillows on a cream spread appear inviting. So I give in to my exhaustion and close my eyes. Sometime later, I'm awakened by the knock at the adjoining door. It's JP. I unlatch the lock, and he spills into my room, smelling and looking fresh. Maybe he had a shower too.

"Hi, JP. Come on in."

"Lily," he says, his arms surround me, and I feel his strength and hear his heart.

"So, you are back to Jokovikstan. This is not an easy destination to get to. What have you found out?"

"First, I want to talk about Rose," I say, and relate to him all I had told Chad. He listens patiently. "So it's true? Alexis is Rose's sister, and Adrienne's her mother?"

"*C'est vrai*, Lily."

"I thought we said that there'd be no more secrets." I'm not counting the secret I have about my short affair with Logan in this equation.

"*Oui, mais*, sometimes, keeping you safe is more important than the truth."

"You know, you're full of shit," I explode in anger. These last few weeks, emotions, usually under control, have surfaced again and again. "I don't know what to say. For years I cried over having lost Rose, and now that I've found her, I don't want to lose her again. Did you know that Alexis is Markovic's daughter?" JP sits next to me on the bed, an arm around my shoulder, seeing that I'm upset.

"Chad mentioned that on the call, but he gave no details. I did not know it before," he says, now hugging me close. Physical comfort helps soothe the volatility simmering inside.

"Yeah, well, here we are. If the Russians are involved in this, I'll bet Alexis is too. Rose told me that her mother said Bella—Rose doesn't know her by Alexis—wanted to say goodbye. That's what the visit was about. Shit, JP, you don't find your mother after all these years just to say goodbye unless you know you're never coming back. And I have the feeling that she wasn't planning a trip to the U.S. for anything other than trouble. You guys should be all over that."

"I understand that our agents in Moscow were following her for a time. Alexis apparently continued to work at her old job. *Et*, if you remember, when we were chasing Markovic, we thought she was picked up by Russian Intelligence, but it is hard to know for sure."

"Do you believe she's aware that Markovic was killed? Do you suppose she thinks that Markovic's still alive? I have so many unanswered questions."

"I do not have all the answers, my Lily. Have you heard from Dr. Leigh yet?"

"I might hear from him as early as tonight. And since you're changing the subject, what more have you found here?"

"Parker was right to suspect that Thornton and Marina are having an affair. We spent some time following her, and I think it is clear they are together."

"Do you think she told Thornton that I suspected her husband was murdered? If they were intimate, I would expect so."

"*Oui. C'est possible.* Since he was the one who initially dismissed her concerns, I think we should pay him another visit and see what he has to say."

"Tomorrow, please; Right now, I'd like some dinner followed by a good night's sleep. Umm, in between perhaps a little love," I tell JP. I caress him with soft kisses and run my fingers through his dark hair, sprinkled with streaks of gray. Yes, my anger is subdued for now, but I still feel it bubbling under the surface and mixed with uncertainty.

"In that order, or can I change the order?" he asks, running his forefinger along my jawline.

"Please do." And I close my eyes and inhale the pheromones like vaping an intoxicating drug.

Room service provided dinner, and now Parker has joined us for dessert so the three of us can pool our information. We sit at the small table that had been rolled in with our dinner, the ends fully extended so we can all dine together.

"Hey Parker, do you want an espresso or decaf?"

"I'll take the decaf. Thanks, doc."

"Robinson is here to fill in some blanks," JP says, sipping his espresso.

"Right. We're all looking for the connection between the two deaths. I found out that Steinman had been talking to James Andrews."

JP raises an eyebrow. "Andrews works in the Department of Interior. *Oui*?" JP says.

"You got it; second in command. Turns out it was Andrews negotiating the deal between Jokovikstan and the U.S. on the REEs. But with President Khan dead, obviously, the deal is off."

"*Oui*. Kill the deal," says JP.

"So what was Steinman's role in all this?" Parker asks.

"The senator was Chair of the Subcommittee on International Development and International Economic Policies. That's with the Foreign

Relations Committee. And Steinman's assistant said he had several meetings with Andrews the week before he died, which upset him. Her boss indicated that he was about to take action, but exactly what, I don't know."

"I think we need to figure out what Thornton knew about this. I don't like that guy, and I don't trust him. I'll follow up on Andrews too," Parker says, dipping a biscuit in his coffee.

My phone buzzes, and I swipe to the right seeing that it's from Leigh. Fingers crossed.

"John Chi. Hello. What've you got for me? Did you find any poison?" I ask, my voice hurried with impatience.

"Dr. Robinson, the most interesting case. The answer is yes, but what I found was more isolated toxins rather than venom."

"What? You mean compared to the first set of specimens I sent you?"

"That is correct. In the first case, I found a much more crude venom from our *Hemiscorpius*. In this case, it looks like whoever did this took the venom and extracted the various toxins. I found evidence of hemitoxin in higher concentrations compared to the other components."

"And the heart valve, John?"

"Microencapsulation of the poison. It is the same signature we saw in your other case."

"Who is capable of pulling this off?"

"Ah, that is where it gets fascinating, Lily

Robinson. I have heard much chatter in our circles about an obscure assassin from the past. He may have resurfaced. This could be his work."

"God, who the hell's that?"

"He is only known as the Tsar."

"The Tsar?" I say, looking at both JP and Parker, who have been following the conversation intently. Parker shakes his head, and JP stares into space.

"John Chi, do we know anything about this guy?"

"Only his reputation. No one knows what he looks like. He is a master at disguise. It is said that he worked for the KGB developing various poisons and toxins for political gain and for chemical warfare. I have not heard anything about him for a long time. But I remember his techniques. We once had dueling histories for the title of Poisoner-in-Chief. He is formidable, Lily Robinson."

"Where will we find him?"

Leigh laughs at this, and even Parker and JP, listening on speakerphone, give each other a look.

"I do not think you will find him, but he may find you. And when he does, I will be there. Give my regards to Jean Paul and Parker." And Leigh disappears off the radar once again.

I feel that physiological ping in my stomach—too many moving parts with no schematic available.

"Okay. You heard Leigh. Who the hell's the Tsar?" Parker asks.

"That was a surprise," JP says, letting out a big breath. "I can remember something of him. No one has heard about the Tsar in some time."

"Shit, JP. You know of this guy?"

"*Oui*. He must be an old-timer by now. Like Leigh said, he was thought to have worked on some of those initial political kills backed by the KGB. I believe many assassinations were attributed to him. *Mais*, no one ever confirmed his identity, although there was plenty of speculation." JP's face is drawn. His fingers comb through his hair, and I hear him clear his throat. Something in his past?

"So if this Tsar *is* involved in the deaths of these two men, who's he working for? And if these are Russian hits, that could explain why Alexis is coming to the U.S.," I say.

"*C'est possible*." JP pushes his chair away from him. His eyes cast downward, with his fingers bent over his mouth, elbow on the table; he's thinking.

"Next steps, boss?" Parker looks eager to move.

"Tomorrow, Parker, you and I will see Thornton. Dr. Robinson, how would you like to pay a visit to Marina. See what you can find out. She may feel more comfortable talking with a woman and perhaps even a doctor, *oui*?"

"Yes, JP. I'll go under the pretext that I've more information about her husband's death."

"Do not share anything we have learned from Leigh tonight. You can tell her that you are still looking into the case. Perhaps broach the subject about her asking Thornton for help."

I can see Parker squirm in his chair—he's itching to leave. It is getting late. "Okay, guys, on that note, I'd like to call it a day and say good night."

Parker leaves us, and JP and I finish the last remains of the coffee and the crumbs from the luscious chocolate cake. He knows I have a sweet tooth.

"So, what do you think, JP?"

"Steinman was killed because he was about to reveal something or expose Andrews. What more did Andrews know about the rare earth minerals negotiations? Remember, Khan died first. Perhaps the original intent was to kill the president and stop the deal. But the plan leaked."

"And Steinman found out about it. And maybe this Tsar had to strike twice," I add, a chill moving up my spine.

The moon has settled in for the night, a crescent of its former self. This slice in the dark is like a crack through a partially opened door beckoning us to enter a forbidden world. I have one step over the threshold, close my eyes, and wait for the fall.

Chapter 22

Hong Kong

John Chi Leigh had held back some of the details from his colleague, Lily Robinson, on the late-night call. The renowned chemist was more familiar with the Tsar than he let on. The Russian was known to be a dangerous man, and Leigh had tangled with his archrival in the past, each one determined to kill the other. Both had survived, and after years of the Tsar's untold political assassinations, he suddenly went quiet. Leigh assumed his nemesis had gone to ground like a fox. Yet, for all the sonar soundings released over the subsequent years, the Tsar was untraceable. Hidden by the equivalent of the espionage thermocline, Russian Intelligence effectively shielded the master assassin from view like a savvy submarine captain.

Intrigue swept Leigh's mind. Not soon after the disappearance of the Tsar from center stage, another man exited the wings and caught the interest of Russian Intelligence—Grigory Markovic. He was not a man of science, but he knew the power of poison and operated independently from the Russian military intelligence, the GRU—and they were all too happy to sit back and watch Markovic cultivate his terrorist faction. Years later, those charged with oversight of growing extremist activities began buzzing about mass poisonings and chemical warfare as Markovic carried out several plots to disrupt world order. But with his death, Leigh wondered if someone else would fill the void. Was it time for an old assassin to rear his ugly head?

If there were a plan in the works for Russia to take control of Jokovikstan, that might be reason enough to resurrect the master assassin. Someone who had the know-how to create the nanoparticles that could hold onto the scorpion toxin just long enough until it released its deadly catch. It was said that the Tsar had been the one to design and engineer the pellet that was fired into the Bulgarian journalist from the tip of an umbrella at that bus station in London. But no one knew for sure.

Leigh resolved to find this assassin after all these years of quiescence. He had reviewed his old notes on the Tsar and would utilize all his known contacts in his consortium to track down the Poisoner-in-Chief before he could kill again. If Leigh could succeed, the United States and Jokovikstan would certainly cheer at the death of a man who had murdered the president of a struggling nation.

John Chi Leigh wanted to refine a new toxin he was working on. While he often oversaw the analysis of the more complicated drug cases in the central laboratory, he was only truly happy when in his own private space, used to analyze and synthesize various drugs or toxins. After the success he and Lily had had with the derivative cone snail toxin used to eliminate the missile scientist from China, Leigh decided that he would make another derivative toxin, in this case, an analog of bufotoxin. Toads from the genus *Bufo*, produced toxin in their parotid glands, the modified mucous glands located on either side of the head behind the ear and the eye. Bufotoxins are cardiac glycosides and act in the same way as digoxin which is given to patients to help regulate their heart, but as with either a drug or a toxin, it's the dose that makes the poison—overdose leads to fatal cardiac dysrhythmias and death.

Leigh had spent several weeks working on the analog, a related structure to bufotoxin, but with a slight change in the molecular arrangement to increase its potency and reduce its detectability. His objective was to aerosolize the toxin since there was an advantage in spraying poison in the victim's face if the circumstances were right. This approach would take his target down quickly. However, it was tricky to get a toxin weaponized so that it could be small enough to be inhaled into the deepest depths of the lungs. Undeterred, Leigh played with different options knowing that one or more would be successful. He embraced the challenge of working with various natural toxins and the unique methods for their administration—it was the joy of science that he shared with his colleague Lily Robinson. Leaving the workbench, the chemist went back to the fume hood where his flasks and beakers were waiting, donned his gloves, and secured his mask. He considered the possibilities. Either way, he wanted to have something for his meeting with the Tsar.

Chapter 23

The Republic of Jokovikstan

Marina Khan is waiting for me. JP's dropped me off at the private presidential rooms while he and Parker go and visit Thornton. I'm an expected guest, and my visit is announced when I arrive. An escort takes me to Marina's sitting room. A glimpse of the space highlights the grandeur with its tall ceilings and crystal chandeliers.

"Dr. Robinson, thank you so much for coming to speak with me. It's much appreciated."

"Madame, you're most welcome," I say with a polite nod of my head.

"Please come in and sit down."

She leads the way into a lovely room with dark blue velveteen settees. Marina sits on one, and I sit on another. She's wearing a plain navy sheath dress adorned with pearls and kitten-heels. If it weren't for her golden blond hair piled in an up-do, her form would melt into the sofa like fudge sauce on chocolate ice cream.

"Dr. Robinson, would you like some tea?" Marina asks.

"No, thank you, I'm fine."

Marina turns to her attendant and asks them to leave the room so she and I can be alone.

"Madame, I'm sorry to bother you again, but I had a few questions for you." I decide to start gently. "I'm terribly sorry about the loss of your husband."

"Thank you, doctor. He was, he was a good man and trying to do good things for this country," Marina says, her eyes staring out the window rather than capturing mine.

"I'm sure he was. But what made you think that his death was not a natural one? Please forgive me, your husband was eighty and had undergone a medical procedure. While it's a little unusual for patients to die after a TAVR, given his advanced age, it's not unheard of."

She hesitates and turns from the window to look back at me.

"After you saw him, Dr. Robinson, you said you also thought he didn't die a natural death. Have you confirmed that? Was my husband poisoned?" She ignores my question.

"I'm still working on that. May I call you Marina?"

"Please do. I believe someone put something in his soup. Although he is, was, fond of that dish, I don't think that was an appropriate meal. It was too heavy for someone coming home from the hospital. A clear broth would've been better."

"At the time, who did you share your concerns with?"

Marina looks out the window again as if she's weighing her options.

"Dr. Robinson, I loved my husband. Yes, our age difference was significant, but I was looking for stability, and what he wanted was companionship. I provided that. Before the marriage, he revealed that he was unable to have children because he was impotent. He recognized that we would not go through with the wedding if that had been critically important to me. So, we both entered our partnership with our eyes wide open. While I had all the emotional comfort, care, and financial support that a wife could expect, some desires still needed to be satisfied. And my husband understood this. The physical love that he could not deliver would be gotten elsewhere. I'm embarrassed to say, but as a woman, I'm sure you can appreciate this."

"I'm not here to judge you, Marina. I want to understand the circumstances around your husband's death. Am I to assume that maybe you and Ambassador Thornton are close? After all, you asked him to call his contacts in the United States to help with an investigation."

Marina is quiet now, her lower lip trembling and a tear emerging from one eye, then the other.

"Yes, Dr. Robinson, the ambassador's my lover. His wife wants nothing to do with him and spends most of her time stateside, hoping their children will marry and produce grandchildren. I guess you could say they're somewhat estranged. But Thomas fulfilled a physical need. I don't believe he loves me." She takes her handkerchief and blots her eyes.

"Thank you, Marina, for being so honest with me." I pause for a moment while she composes herself. "When you asked the ambassador to contact the U.S. for help, what did he say?"

"He said I was hysterical. He was dismissive of me. He said my husband died a natural death as confirmed by his physician and that we should cremate him and provide a laudable funeral."

"But you resisted his advice. Why?"

"Doctor, I don't need a man to tell me how to live my life or what to do. That was the gift of my husband, who saw me as his strategic partner, not a silly hysterical woman. He gave me that confidence."

"Do you know of anyone who benefits from the death of your husband?"

"I don't. I know many in his Cabinet worked well with him, but there were some advisors who were clearly against him. I can get you a list of names if you need to know."

"Thank you. That would be helpful. Marina, did you share with the ambassador my suspicions regarding your husband's death?" My voice is soft and caring. I understand how hard this is for her.

"Yes, of course. I wanted him to know that he

was wrong and that you were going to look into it further."

"I see. One last question. Have you ever heard Ambassador Thornton speak of a man named James Andrews?"

"Off the top of my head, I really can't say. I have to think about it."

"Okay. Thank you again for speaking with me. Listen, at this point, it's hard to know who to trust, so I would not say anything about our meeting to anyone, including Ambassador Thornton. Let's keep this conversation between the two of us. If you can think of anything else, you can reach me at the World Hotel in the old part of the city. I'll be staying there for the next few days."

"Thank you, Dr. Robinson." She sniffs, blotting her nose. I feel sorry for her.

Marina rises and shows me the way out.

Within no time, I'm back at the hotel. I haven't heard from either JP or Parker, so I look at my watch to see if there's time to call Boston. It's late there, but I expect Kelley will be up.

"Kelley, I hope I didn't wake you. Is everything okay?"

"Dr. Robinson? No, you didn't wake me. I'm young, remember?" He laughs. "I don't go to bed this early. What's up?"

"I just wanted to check in with you about our medical student Rose. How is she?"

"I think she's doing better. She was quite upset about her mother. I guess she told you all about it. Listen, are you going to the chemistry conference? It's next week. It should be interesting."

There's a knock at my door—the one between the connecting rooms, so JP must be back.

"What, Kelley? Sorry, I have to go now. I'm glad you and Rose are all right. Talk later."

"Just a minute, JP," I say as I go and unlock the door; he's standing at the ready.

"My Lily, Parker has gone to get some food. We had an interesting meeting with the ambassador. *Et*, how was Marina?"

"I confirmed what both you and Parker suspected. She's having an affair with Thornton. I don't think there's any love there. Just sex. Women can have sex without love, too." He must wonder why I'm making a justification for this. Is it for Marina or for me?

"I have said nothing, Lily. You do not have to make a case with me."

"Right. Anyway, I asked her if she ever heard Thornton talk about James Andrews. She couldn't recall but was going to give it a little more thought. How was your meeting with the Ambassador?"

"The most interesting finding of our visit was Thornton's lack of information. It was almost passive-aggressive. He admitted that the president's wife confided in him about your suspicions but again dismissed this as a fantasy of a grieving widow and the overreaching, *eh*, overreaching hand of a woman pathologist. Those are his words, *ma chérie*, not mine. I do not think there is much respect for women there. However, he was shocked to learn you and Dr. Pelletier were here and conducted an autopsy. He seemed most unhappy about that. *Et*, frankly, it is unfortunate that he was told. This may jeopardize our investigation."

"I think Marina was more interested in a 'told you so' than anything else. She did mention that the ambassador was close with some of her husband's advisors and was going to see if she could get a list of a few names for me. Maybe someone other than Thornton was working with Andrews."

"Thornton admitted nothing. Parker is looking into any communications that the ambassador may have had with the Department of the Interior."

"You would expect something, JP, if the two countries were looking at a deal involving rare earth minerals."

"*Oui*."

Jean Paul and I hear a knock at the door to my room. Parker? I check the peephole and find that it's someone from the hotel.

"Excuse me, madame, but I have a note that is for you," he says, handing me a cream-colored envelope. There are no other markings on the outside other than my name.

"Thank you," I say as I close the door and turn to JP. "Who would send me a note here?"

I eagerly open the letter and find that it's a message from Marina.

"JP, it's from Marina. I did tell her that if she found out any additional information, she could contact me at the hotel."

"What does it say?"

"I'll read it to you."

> Dr. Robinson,
> I have come across some new and alarming evidence regarding the death of my husband. Please meet me after dark at my husband's mausoleum, where we can discuss these new findings in private. Tell no one.
> Marina

"So, what do you think? Could she have come across some information regarding her husband's advisors? Or something about his burial, which is why she wants to meet at the mausoleum. I'm going to meet with her and see what she has to say."

"I do not care what she says; you are not going there alone. If she has new information, then she can share it with both of us. So there is no specified time to meet, *oui*?"

I glance back down at the message again for the details.

"No, she says just after dark, nothing more specific. It is rather strange, but she may be feeling paranoid after my meeting with her today. You really don't have to come with me, you know."

"*Oui*, I do." He says this with a thought-provoking smile.

"You think this is a trap, right?" The look on JP's face changes—eyebrows knitted together in suspicion.

"I do. *Mais*, we should still follow through and see what we can uncover," JP says.

"Would you like to wear one of my disguises?" I let out a loud laugh, and he shakes his head. "*Mais oui, monsieur*, as you would say. You know, I do travel with both conventional and unconventional items in my bag. You never know what you might be up against. Would you like me to do your make-up too?"

Finally, he breaks. JP laughs, and we make a plan to see Marina. What's she up to?

JP and I spend the rest of the afternoon assembling the puzzle pieces we have so far. I'm feeling more fatigued lately, and by now, the jet lag has finally overtaken my body. Chad's still chasing down the details of the negotiations between the U.S. and Jokovikstan—and at turtle speed. He's worried about tipping off the murderer.

I'm hoping that Steinman's staffer will find a solid connection that ties him to the REEs deal and contact me directly. Meanwhile, Parker has been looking into the relationship between James Andrews and Thomas Thornton, assuming there is one. Is this why Marina wants to meet tonight?

Night is beginning to fall, and it will be time for JP and me to meet Marina. We have a plan that also includes Parker. We all assume that Marina will have someone with her, as I doubt she would meet me alone. Parker's going to drop JP off somewhere in the cemetery not too close to Khan's mausoleum. Then he'll let me off near the mausoleum and drive away to wait out of sight. I'll stay outside the crypt for a while until JP shows up, so we can go inside the tomb together.

It's time. I make my way down to the rental car and let myself into the back seat, where I wait for Parker and JP. They arrive, ignore me, and I remain hidden from view as they pull out of the garage. It's dark now, and we're counting on the cover of the night to keep our secret. Parker gets to the cemetery and drops JP off at a different mausoleum nearer to the graveyard entrance before he stops closer to where President Khan is buried. I slip out of the car, then Parker drives away. We plan on sending a signal to him once the meeting's finished so he can pick us up.

I can see the burial chamber up ahead, and I wait in the shadows until JP catches up.

"Ready?" I ask, and we slip inside the unlatched door.

Marina's there waiting for us in the vestibule, holding a lantern for light. It's as dark as it was the night we did the autopsy. So, I've brought a flashlight, and JP has one too.

"Marina, it's Dr. Robinson. Are you all right?"

"Dr. Robinson, you said you would be meeting me alone," she says, pointing to JP.

"Oh, sorry. You've met Agent Marchand before."

"Madame, no need for any alarm. I did not want Dr. Robinson to be alone. I assumed you would have someone with you as well."

"But your note said I was to come alone. That you had additional information for me regarding my husband's death, and you wanted to show me something in the burial chamber. I don't understand." The pitch of her voice is raised, and Marina's pacing the chamber.

"Wait a minute. I got a message at the hotel from you, Marina, saying to meet you here. Now you're telling me you got a note from me saying I asked for the meeting? JP, quick, check the door. We were right; this is a setup."

But JP is already on it before I finish my sentence. Of course, the door's locked. Of course. Well, at least Parker knows where we are.

"JP, did you contact Parker to come and get us?"

"*Mais oui*. It seems as if the signal is jammed."

"Well, even if it is, if he doesn't hear from us soon, he's bound to come knocking at the door."

"Marina, who could have possibly sent both you and me a note forcing us to meet here?"

"I don't know. There were only a few people from my staff that knew you came here to do the autopsy. Otherwise, I told no one."

"*Mais*, you did share the information from the autopsy with Ambassador Thornton?"

"Yes, yes I did. But only later. I only told him after."

"Someone wants us out of the way," I say, looking at JP in the yellow light.

"I'm afraid that if you go missing in Jokovikstan, it's not a big news story. There are factions in the country that are known for political murder. It's why I was sure my husband was poisoned. Ow!" Marina says quite unexpectedly.

"What is it, Marina?"

"I don't know. I thought I felt a little pinch at my ankle. But I don't see anything, so it's probably nothing. I'm just feeling a little claustrophobic, that's all." Marina's breathing quickens, creating shallow breaths. "Monsieur, Marchand, have you been able to contact your colleague?"

"No, not yet. Something is jamming the signal."

JP shines the little light we have into the rocky corners to see if he can detect anything. He's got all of us looking around the interior to see if there's another way we can get a signal out. Marina and I soon grow tired and cold.

"JP, we've been here for an hour. Why isn't Parker showing up? He must realize that something's gone wrong."

"There may be another way. Let me have your phone," he says, taking mine, and then adds, "*Et*, Dr. Robinson, please, the president's wife is looking pale. Can you attend to her?"

I look at Marina's face, and she does look white and sweaty.

"Marina, how are you feeling? Are you all right?" I ask, putting my hand on her forehead. She feels warm.

"Not so well, Dr. Robinson. I feel nauseous, and being shut in this chamber is making me anxious."

"You know, I'm also feeling a bit nauseous. Try and take some slow deep breaths and focus on your breathing."

I sit next to Marina and take my own advice.

"JP, both Marina and I don't feel well. How about you? We all need some fresh air."

He looks at me, shaking his head as if to say, no shit, then says, "*D'accord, mais*, I cannot get a goddamn signal. I tried to boost it, but nothing. Are you worried about carbon monoxide poisoning?"

"I'm worried about dying in this damn tomb. We've got to get out." Now my voice sounds anxious, and I feel like we're spinning our wheels. "Where the hell is Parker?"

Marina looks worse; her eyelids appear heavy as if she's fighting sleep. I touch her shoulder to stimulate her.

"Marina! Marina!" I shout.

"Ahh, why does my ankle hurt so much, and why am I drooling? Ugh, I'm going to vomit," Marina says, doubling over in pain. She leans over and vomits in the chamber.

I pull her away from the mess. It makes me gag. I'm so nauseous too, but I fight it. "Marina, let me take a closer look at you."

I take the flashlight and hold it close to her face while my fingers feel her wrist for a pulse. Her forehead's warm and wet, she's struggling to breathe, and her heart's racing—hyperthermia, tachycardia, hypersalivation, nausea, and vomiting. Oh, God, I know what this is.

"Marina, let me see your ankle."

I push up her pant leg and can see swelling and redness in the area.

"JP," I yell. "Get over here."

"What is it?"

"Marina's losing it. I think her symptoms are from a scorpion sting at the ankle. All her walking around the chamber after the sting has only caused the envenomation to get worse. My guess, given this is Jokovikstan, we're probably dealing with a sting from Leiurus quinquestriatus."

"Not the scorpion we found in—"

"No, not that one." I give JP a look to indicate

say no more, and he stops. "She's reacted badly, and we may lose her airway if we don't get her to a hospital soon. JP, while you're looking for a way out, please check the crevices for a fat yellow scorpion, and if you find it, kill it. These arachnids aren't like bees who can sting only once. This guy has enough juice for another round. And, he may have friends. Let's get as much light in the area as we can."

"I have been systematically searching this damn place looking for what is jamming my signal, and I have not seen any scorpions." JP hesitates, then says, "What can you do for Marina? She looks bad."

"Wait a minute. With everything going on, I forgot that I have something here we can try. JP, hand me my bag."

JP throws me my bag, and I dig in until I find a metal vacuum Thermos. I guess it's lucky that I forgot to take it out of my pack earlier. I quickly unscrew the cap and remove a syringe, a 50 cc sterile vial of saline, and polyvalent anti-scorpion serum. It's only cool in the Thermos, not cold, but I have no choice but to act quickly.

"Marina, Marina, can you hear me? I'm going to give you an injection through one of your veins to help you. Try and stay with me."

I've reconstituted the antivenom with the vial of saline. What I'm about to do should take place within a hospital and through an IV, but I have to improvise given the situation. I hope she doesn't have an anaphylactic reaction, but an epinephrine autoinjector waits its turn if needed. I've always traveled with a medical kit. You just never know.

"I can't find my phlebotomy tourniquet in my bag. JP, tear off a strip of material from your shirt. Now!"

He tears from the shirttail of his white cotton dress shirt. "Take it."

"Got it," I say, catching it mid-flight.

The cloth's wrapped and knotted around Marina's arm. Her circulatory system's collapsing, making it hard to find a vein. I pick the best one that I can visualize in this darkness and cross my fingers. Christ, my own fingers are shaking.

"JP, more light, please." I can feel my heart racing as I talk to JP.

I inject one cc at a time, going slow, so Marina doesn't die from shock. I, too, have an overwhelming feeling of nausea trapped inside this chamber, but I hold it together for Marina's sake. Is there futility in trying to save the wife of a dead president when we might all die in this tomb anyway?

An hour later, we're still trapped. Marina's flat on the cold ground, her head resting on a jacket, but she's still breathing. JP's finally located a small device in the mausoleum that may be the cause of the jammed signal. It was camouflaged so well he kept missing it. Now, he's trying again to reach Parker.

"Lily, I have finally gotten through to Parker. He, too, was sent a message earlier pulling him away from the cemetery. A diversion, no doubt. He is on his way to Marina's residence to contact her assistant, who helped us originally. It is assumed that they will be able to get us out."

"JP, we both know this was a trap. Marina's note was a message in poison. Someone wanted me out of the way. You were a bonus."

"*Oui*, you think the scorpion was planted?

"It's hard to know. The deathstalker is native to this region, which is why I happen to have the necessary medical supplies in my pack. I carry the antivenom when I travel to the Middle East. I hope Marina makes it."

It's quiet now. JP and I have not seen any scorpions, and the damp chamber feels as if it's shrinking around us. I start to doze, fatigue kicking in. Marina's head rests in my lap, and mine is leaning on JP's shoulder while he's propped up against the wall. I open my eyes for a second and see a fat yellow body, pincers flared, creep toward JP's head. Is it a dream? I let out a scream.

"Shit, shit, shit—watch out!" and JP moves aside quickly, allowing the creature to drop to the ground. He stands up and raises his foot, aims, and stomps. A flattened scorpion shudders as it's kicked to the side. Marina hasn't moved, and I'm shaking.

After a long wait, we hear the door to the chamber open, and Parker enters with some of Marina's attendants and medical personnel, who take the president's wife out on a stretcher to a waiting ambulance. I refuse any medical treatment, my nausea subsiding once I hit the cool night air. After the ambulance departs, Parker collects JP and me, and we head back to the car.

"Jesus Christ, Parker. What the hell happened out here? Even though I could not get through to you, I assumed you would show up if you did not hear from me."

"Sorry, boss. I thought it was strange that you didn't contact me, but then I got word from the president's residence that they had already picked you, the doc, and Marina up and were headed back. I thought it was a pile of shit but decided to check it out. When I tried to get back to the cemetery, the road was blocked with construction trucks," Parker says, trying to explain what happened.

"Parker, someone tried to kill us or, at the very least, intimidate us into letting this case go. Let's get back; I'm exhausted. I need a warm bath and a good night's sleep," I tell them.

"Sure thing, doc. Hop in the car, and I'll take you to the hotel," says Parker, giving me a hand.

My hotel room awaits me, and after dumping my bag, I enter the bathroom to fill the tub with bubbles. I would've asked JP to join me, but I need a little alone time following our harrowing ordeal. My reflection in the mirror is of an exhausted woman with newly formed dark circles under her eyes. I step into the warm water, sink to the depths, and wish myself back in Boston. Life seemed simpler when most of my time was spent at the hospital and the medical school. Now so much more of my life consists of fighting in a world that has become ever-threatening.

After a nice soak, JP shares my room and my bed. The security of being in his arms, in a safe space, is all I need now.

"Hey," I say, leaning over on an elbow facing him, "did you think we were going to die in that place tonight? The thought crossed my mind."

He strokes my hair and kisses me softly.

"*Ma chérie*, I think every day brings a chance for death in my business. *Mais*, I try not to dwell on it. We could have died tonight, *et* my last night on this earth would have been with you." He smiles. A closed smile with no teeth, but a warm smile.

This is our life together. Danger followed by romance. We are by no means a normal couple. Far from it. But I take what I can get, and so does he.

It's a bright start to the day, and JP's gone off to see Thornton, again. Marina's still clinging to life, and I worry that the antivenom may not have worked. Her systemic symptoms were too severe by the time I gave her the injection, and there was too long a delay in getting her supportive hospital care. In most cases, if a scorpion sting's recognized, the sooner the patient's taken to the hospital, the better chance they have. And at the very least, the patient shouldn't be walking around circulating the venom in their body. But we didn't realize Marina had been stung. Then too, the antivenom had been in my bag for some time without the proper storage—probably resulting in destabilization. I meant to put it in my mini-fridge when I arrived in Jokovikstan but forgot. Still, I had to try. Doctors always feel bad when they lose a patient. Yet, if Marina dies, it was because she was murdered, not because of something I did or didn't do. Someone locked us in that chamber, blocked our signal, and diverted Parker away from the site. This was an attempt to trap us in there long enough for the scorpions to do their job. I believe that those creatures were placed in there deliberately.

I'm on pins and needles waiting for JP to return from his meeting with the Ambassador. Finally, a knock at the door.

"Hey, JP. What've you found out?"

"Not very much. Thornton already knew about Marina's impending death." He charges in the room, fired up and frustrated.

"How did he seem?"

"Not particularly sad. *Rappelles-toi*, he does not know that we know about his affair."

"Maybe Thornton let your earlier visit with him slip, and someone either with or without his knowledge set up the meeting at the crypt."

"I do not know. The man says little. *Mais*, we are looking into the whereabouts of Thornton over the last twenty-four hours. However, I doubt that he alone would have found and used scorpions, so if it is him, he must be working with someone else."

"I agree. And I hope Marina makes it. I'm not sure if she was one of the intended targets or just the bait. When I saw her earlier, she told me that Jokovikstanian law states that the republic must hold an election for a new president within sixty days of the previous president's departure or death. She was going to try and find out who in the Cabinet, or maybe which one of her husband's advisors, might be in the running, but she never got a chance to tell me."

"*Oui*. This country is in a state of flux, and a power grab is currently in play."

"Yeah, not like the States where we all know which of our politicians want the job."

"Not politicians, Lily. Russia wants control. It has the resources and the motive to kill the president."

"And Senator Steinman."

Chapter 24

The Cottage

After Jokovikstan, I made a quick stop in Boston to review some cases at the hospital before heading up to the cottage. My turnaround was so fast I didn't even get a chance to see Kelley or Rose on the return. Lisa said my fellow's been busy preparing for the influx of new medical students, and Rose's been shadowing him in the lab whenever she gets a chance. Lisa also let me know that she thinks Kelley and Rose are an item now. I told her that I thought so too. She has no idea how happy that would make me.

A few days at my Cape Cod cottage with blue skies, pounding waves, and the daily long calls from the herring gulls are what I need before I go back to D.C. and try and wrap things up with Logan. I always look forward to the drive along the coast, knowing that I'll enjoy the solitude and beauty of my surroundings. Tucked away behind the dunes is a small house with weather-worn cedar shingles and wood trim outlined in robin's egg blue. The mahogany porch is enclosed by creamy drapes that float in the wind on a breezy day and keep out prying eyes.

My poison garden, hidden around the back,

and bordered by clumps of beach grass and sand, waits for me to harvest nature's defenses when its fruit is ripe. The wild's a mixture of life and death held in a delicate balance, tipping one way or the other in the eyes of the beholder. This is my escape, a place to think, to mourn, to change. It's where transformation took place, from a simple doctor to a stealthy assassin. An unimaginable transformation. In nature, caterpillars turn into lovely butterflies, not the reverse. At this coastal retreat, magnificent flowers bring either joy or death.

On this morning's misty dawn, a large brown bird feeds on the marsh, and one that big can only be an eagle—a juvenile feasting on a large fish. Unlike his adult counterparts, white feathers haven't completely replaced the brown feathers on his majestic head. Predator and prey. Expected in the kingdom of animals—but there are boundaries in that world—no gratuitous murder. Unfortunately, man's intellect permits him to desire more than he needs, and he does, despite the consequences. Like Logan said, murder's committed for selfish desires: greed, jealousy, power, and revenge. I continue to be troubled by the deaths of two men who were only out to help their countries. Will we ever have peace on this planet and work together as one united earth?

Contemplation pushes into my afternoon as I watch the creatures that stand in the eagle's footprints. Three turkey vultures, their pink naked heads glowing in the light, form a single shadow on the marsh. This characteristic crown, with no feathers to soil, allows them to plunge deep within the carcass. And aided by an ebbing tide that secretes them in the seagrass while they devour the remains, I take stock of the wonder before me.

Striking red sunrises greet me in the morning while burning sunsets fill the open expanse of sky, unimpeded by dense trees or city dwellings. And at night, out on the deck in the quiet of the dark, I scan the stars for the Pleiades, seven sisters veiled in the constellation Taurus. With no city lights to hide them, each star appears brighter and a reminder that there may have been a plan grander than we know.

JP, too, should be back from Jokovikstan by now, having followed my exit by a day. I'm expecting him at the cottage. Unusual for him, it's only happened once before that I can remember. We have so much to talk about. For me, a casual weekend day, dressed in jeans, a navy blue tank top, and flip-flops for a change. I feel so much shorter, missing my high heels now secluded in a closet until I return to Boston.

JP's here. His gray company car sits in front of my house while he walks the stone steps to the porch. Then parting the drapes, he takes that leap of faith and enters my domain. I look forward to our quiet weekend together.

"*Bonjour*," I say, pulling him in.

"*Bonjour*," he says, kissing me on one cheek then the other. A warm hug follows with a more intense kiss on the lips. JP's not creative with his wardrobe—black pants, black shoes, and a light blue dress shirt, with his Luminox Nighthawk watch peeking out from his French cuff. I'm not sure he even owns a pair of flip-flops.

"How was your trip back from Jokovikstan?"

"Long."

"I know how you feel. Please sit down. Would you like a cup of coffee?"

"*Oui, merci.*"

I go to the kitchen while JP makes himself comfortable on the ivory-colored cotton couch. Light furniture anchored by a wavy blue striped rug, reminiscent of seaside colors, provides the serenity I seek. He picks up a magazine from the coffee table and thumbs through it.

"Here you go. I have a few warm croissants, chocolate, and almond if you're interested." I smile, knowing he will jump on this.

"Wonderful, *mais oui*."

A warm pastry and cups of joe rest on the table—his cup imprinted with the word "LOVER" and mine with "SWEETIE."

"So, what can you tell me about Jokovikstan? How's Marina?"

"Marina is still in hospital. She was quite ill, as you know. We arranged some protection for her, but she will have to vacate the presidential residence now that her husband is dead. Her staff is taking care of that."

"That'll be hard for her, I'm sure. And Thornton, where was he when you, Marina, and I were trapped in the mausoleum?"

"He was in his apartment which his staff verified. *Mais*, you know that does not mean he did not have a hand in it."

"True. But Marina told us that he was particularly close to one or more of the men working with President Khan. Maybe it's one of them."

"*Oui, mais* who? So it is hard to say. Getting people to talk has been *très difficile*. That bastard Thornton is passive-aggressive. It was easier when Marina was available. Chad is still looking into his background."

"You believe now that she wasn't involved?"

"It looks that way, but there is always the possibility that she worked with someone who double-crossed her," he says, edging his "LOVER" cup closer to my "SWEETIE."

I nod my head. "Listen, JP. A nurse friend of mine looked into the OR supply chain at the hospital where Steinman had his procedure. Turns out that a Trileaflet rep came in the day before and pushed the new, improved aortic valve implant. She said it wasn't part of their usual stock, but since the vendor spoke so highly of the product and, and was willing to give the hospital a huge price break, they went ahead for it. Coincidence?" I add, knowing it's not.

"Not surprised. Nice work, Lily," he says.

"So, are you going back down to the Capital to meet with Chad? Because I was going to go as well. I'm planning on following up with Logan."

"Not certain where I will be and when."

"Oh, here we go. The mysterious Frenchman," I say sarcastically.

"*Encore du café, s'il te plaît.*" He changes the subject.

"*Oui, monsieur.* Are we going to speak only French now?" I give him an elbow in his side; the corners of my mouth spell out my disapproval. My platinum bracelet, his gift to me, catches his eye.

"Sometimes, my Lily, when I am tired, I revert back to my native language. There are some things I cannot change." He is who he is.

"All right, I'll get you some more coffee, but I want to bring up something else." I feel that knot in my stomach.

I leave him hanging on my words and retreat to the kitchen. I pour another cup for him, black, while I add skim milk to mine.

"Another croissant while I'm up?"

"*Merci.*"

I hand him his cup and sit down on the ottoman so I can pull it up close to him and look into his blue-green eyes.

"JP, I don't think I can keep my relationship

with Rose a secret. She has a right to know, and I have a right to claim her as my child. You, of all people, know how painful this has been. And when do you plan to share with your cousin Adrienne that she has family she thinks are long dead? It's not right." I hear the anger creep into my voice.

"Lily, this will be between us if you let it. I told you at the time it is for Rose's safety. I have no doubt that you love her, and want to tell her she is your daughter. Perhaps you will, one day. But not now. I am sorry."

"You do know that you can't stop me, right? I can call her up tomorrow and tell her all about my time in Colombia on that scientific expedition. I can tell her that her Maggie, the woman who looked after her, was massacred. I can tell her everything, and you can't stop me." I'm standing up now, towering over him as he sits on the couch, stoic and quiet. I feel tears sting my eyes, and heat burn my cheeks.

"Lily, *c'est vrais*. *Mais*, I do not believe you will do that. Not now."

"By that time, she'll hate me for not telling her. Goddamn you. Rose has suffered too. All these years not knowing who her parents are. It's a shitty mess, and I blame the Agency." My teeth clench, and so does my heart.

"You are not listening, my Lily," his voice now raised, matching mine. "We should assume

Markovic was not the only one who knew your name. Right now, only a few of us at the Agency know Rose's true relationship to you. *Et*, one way to get to you would be through your daughter. It is a classic move, *n'est-ce pas?*"

JP's words make me stop, and I use the back of my fingers to wipe the tears. Seeing my distress, he stands up with open arms, and we fall in together, his frame towering over me, his bear-like grip encompassing my shaking body. He strokes my hair and kisses the top of my head. He's a man who shows little emotion, and I've learned to live with it. Who knows what made him emotionally shut down and enter a life where danger suffuses all his waking hours. The minutes go by, and the emotion drains out the bottom of my feet, no longer stoppered by a blunt cork. I would never put Rose in danger. My shoulders drop, and I squelch the sobs within my chest, swallowing bitter liquid running from my eyes and nose. I feel his chin rest on the top of my head.

"A walk on the beach?" he asks, breaking our hug into two.

"Sure, but you can't wear those shoes."

"*Oui, mais,* I have sandals in the trunk of my car," he says with a smile.

I let out a big sigh and take his hands in mine.

CHAPTER 25

Washington, D.C.

As a man who followed orders impeccably, Sergei Petrikov had always been a reliable soldier in the service of his country and was impatient to return home. But loose ends, like unraveling aging telomeres, had to be extinguished. Posing as a married couple, an older man with a younger woman, Sergei and Alexis, had flown to the American capital after leaving Reims. Once settled, Sergei contacted his connection in the U.S. government and arranged for an "information" exchange at the National Zoo. The park would be busy enough during the summer months with children out of school and parents looking for easy entertainment.

Only a short distance from the hotel, Sergei, with Alexis in tow as his interpreter, followed the path from the visitor's center off Connecticut Avenue, along Olmstead Walk, until they reached the center loop that took them to the lower zoo. They waited for a time outside the area designated as Amazonia before they entered the concrete building. The two Russians stood at the back, away from the huge tanks filled with large fish, amphibians, and other aquatic life from the Amazon River.

The exhibit felt like a relatively secluded place in the zoo, with dim lighting emanating from overhead. Smaller tanks contained fish vulnerable to larger predators, and terrariums held colorful frogs that once inhabited the trees and dense foliage found in the Amazon rainforest. A Roseate Spoonbill waded into the water pool after flexing its wings. Sergei surveilled the area and saw nothing suspicious. A few families eyed the tanks, and some scholarly types observed the exhibits in great detail, notebooks in hands, scribbling facts. He scanned the room for his target, quietly placing his hand on those of his accomplice, and waited.

At the other end of the park, Rose and Dr. Kelley were on an afternoon break. Rose was giddy to be on holiday with her new boyfriend, and he was excited to have her there. While not exactly a holiday, it was close enough. Kelley was attending an annual summer conference for chemists in D.C. It was a good place to share ideas, learn about the new assays and techniques, and most importantly, network with colleagues. Kelley had been dating Rose for some months now, and he used the scientific meeting to ask her to accompany him on the trip. An attempt to let Dr. Robinson know about his plans had been made, but not unexpectedly, she was brief in her phone calls and missed the details. Kelley sent her a message but had not heard back from his mentor. He was concerned that she was becoming less attentive to her emails. That her absences had become more frequent and more prolonged in duration had not escaped Kelley's notice either.

A lively panel discussion, one in which Kelley presented his work on a new method for the detection of fentanyl analogs, had occupied the morning. Later, both Rose and Kelley boarded the Red Line from their hotel and emerged at the Cleveland Park Station to walk the remaining distance to the National Zoo. Rose aimed to see the panda bears, and a stroll among the lush plants and exotic animals provided a means of relaxation. Thoughts of her mother occupied the silent fissures in her mind, and the Boston student knew she would soon have to return to France.

After gaining entrance to the zoo, they'd purchased tickets for a ride on the Conservation Carousel, which Rose had read about. She wanted to experience the animals from the four different habitats represented by aquatic, forest, grassland, and desert species. Intricately carved animals moved up and down while the landscape of the various environments spun by. Rose and Kelley waited in line behind families eager to pick out the species of their choice. Rose hoped to ride on the cuttlefish while Kelley was aiming for the naked mole-rat. As Rose waited in line, she saw a man on the other side of the carousel who looked familiar. He reminded her of someone she'd crossed paths with in her life, but she couldn't quite place him. Quickly distracted by their final entry to the carousel, the romantic pair scrambled to find animals next to each other that they'd enjoy. They settled on a zebra and a tiger, with Rose at least feeling as if she were once again on an equine of some kind. As the carousel spun around, she could see the familiar form standing alone as if he was waiting for someone. Dressed in a long raincoat with a wide brim hat, Rose noted that he had peculiarly large feet and wondered if he needed to have custom-made shoes.

After the ride, the two walked hand in hand along the elephant walk and stopped by several other exhibits along the way. By the time it was getting to late afternoon, they had only gotten as far as the bald eagle enclosure after strolling some distance along the American Trail. However, Rose was soon distracted by the majestic fowl trapped in their coop. Perched on sizable branches, these large birds with heads of bright white feathers waited patiently for their next meal. Rose and Kelley had their noses as close as they could to the fencing watching the birds of prey watch them. The sun dipped behind the clouds darkening the end of the day.

Sergei Petrikov was eager to complete his mission before linking up with another associate.

Once the job was finished, he and Alexis would leave by way of the park's American Trail as planned. Looking at his watch, his impatience grew, and the hot and humid air in the exhibit became stifling. Now was the time. The exhibit house had trickled down to only a few visitors, and Sergei's mind raced for a solution. But before he had the answer, the Russian caught a glimpse of a man in his sixties with white hair swept over his head and sunglasses covering his eyes. The red carnation in his lapel was a signal, and Sergei walked over to engage the man believing him to be his contact. With Alexis at his side, he listened as she said something in English to the American. While Sergei could speak English, he wasn't as fluent as his companion. The American nodded his head in response, indicating that they'd made contact.

"Good morning, a nice day for a boat trip down the Amazon," the man said.

"Yes, but beware of the piranhas; they feed when they are hungry, and they are very hungry today," Alexis replied, confirming that he was the associate that Sergei was to meet.

The group of three moved further into a corner away from the few people eyeing the fish, and any cameras so they could converse quietly, the American speaking with Sergei and "the interpreter" working to communicate the conversation to both of them.

"Why was it necessary to murder your senator? This only brought more attention to our arrangement," Sergei said.

"Yes, it's unfortunate, but Senator Steinman discovered that I'd killed the agreement in favor of Russia. I had to get rid of him. If I didn't, I would've been exposed as a traitor, and the plan would have come to light. Once we found out that the senator was going to have the same medical procedure as Khan, it made it all the easier. Thanks to your people, I arranged to have a similar implantable device, one made by your Trileaflet, available to the cardiologist. The doctor was none the wiser. And, the senator was not aware. Very unfortunate."

Sergei moved closer to the American so he could whisper in his ear. This time he spoke in English.

"Most unfortunate. We all agree, no loose ends," he said, and Sergei removed a small bottle from his pocket and sprayed a mist into the American's face using his gloved hand, his scarf pulled up around his nose and mouth.

Sergei immediately backed off his target when he caught a glimpse of a man in khaki pants coming at him. He kept the bottle out to use again, but Alexis grabbed his arm, pulled him toward the opposite exit, and they headed for the American Trail. Their victim, unable to cry out, his throat filled with mucous, coughed and sputtered before collapsing to the floor. A spoonbill grunted at the commotion, wings aflutter, catching the attention of the few remaining visitors who then gathered around the dying man, unaware that they could also be in danger. There was little they could do for the man caught in a death roll, fluids seeping out from his eyes, mouth, and nose—urine creating a puddle under the watchful eyes of the piranhas.

After Lily Robinson had found the connection between Senator Steinman and the Deputy Secretary of the Interior, Agent Parker had been tasked with dogging James Andrews. Parker had spent several days tailing him, hoping that he could turn something up. This day, the agent found it curious that Andrews was headed to the zoo and figured he might be meeting someone. It paid off. Parker could see that Andrews conversed with two people, but their hats, scarves, and dark glasses in the already dim light made it difficult to identify them. One of the two moved away at one point, but the other continued talking, moving closer, and Parker thought he saw something sprayed into Andrews' face. It happened quickly, the spray unexpected, and Parker moved in as the Deputy Secretary clutched his throat and dropped to the floor. He pushed back the spectators for their safety and watched the assailants leave from the other exit. Parker realized what had occurred and knew he couldn't help Andrews, so he left the body in place and called JP for backup. With his phone still in his hand, Agent Parker ran out of the exhibit to track down the two people he saw assassinate Andrews.

Parker followed the American Trail assuming that would be the route the two suspects had taken. Near the other end of the path, Parker emerged with his pistol neatly tucked inside his jacket, having picked up his pace since contacting JP. He cursed that innocent bystanders were in the area and didn't want them to become collateral damage as he focused on the two people up ahead.

Rose and Kelley turned their backs to the bird enclosure, and Rose saw a woman across the other side of the path in the company of a man. Rose stared at her, a quizzical look on her face, as she reached back into her mind. Although the woman wore dark glasses, her gold hair was striking, and Rose thought she looked familiar. On a hunch, she took a chance. Embarrassment would be the only risk. But recalling her mother's words about Bella made her bold.

"Bella, Bella," she shouted as she ran toward the woman in the cream coat. "Bella, it's me, Rose," Rose said, her arms opened wide as she moved in for an embrace, thinking there was nothing to lose other than some dignity.

Sergei turned, saw the approaching Parker, and, seizing the opportunity, grabbed Rose before she could hug Alexis. Now in the daylight, Parker recognized Alexis from the photographs and stopped.

"Stop," Sergei shouted, waving a gun.

By this time, Kelley was headed toward Rose when Parker grabbed him by the shirt.

"Don't move; stay behind me," Parker said, his feet planted firmly on the path.

"What the hell's going on? Rose, Rose are you all right?" Kelley said, knowing full well she was not.

"Do not move," Sergei said, the barrel of the gun at Rose's temple. With his protective gloves and scarf gone, he could no longer use his poison.

Alexis spoke up. "He means it. Stay back, and no one will get hurt."

Agent Parker and Kelley watched as Sergei concealed the gun back in his pocket yet held it to Rose's back as he pushed her forward. Alexis grabbed her sister's arm while she and Sergei disappeared.

"What the hell? Who are you? Why the hell didn't you go after her?" Kelley asked Parker, his voice agitated and shaky.

"I'll need you to come with me," Parker said, holding onto Kelley.

"Get your hands off me. I'm not going anywhere until you tell me what the hell's going on and why that man took my girlfriend. I've already called 911, so the police are on their way."

Parker decided to wait until JP, who was with Chad at the time of the call, arrived. Agent Parker skimped on the details over the phone but emphasized that additional agents were required immediately. By the time JP arrived, the local police were also on the scene and interviewing Kelley. JP flashed his credentials and pulled the officer in charge to the side. Understanding JP was taking over the case, the Metropolitan police left.

"Wait a minute," Kelley said, "Why did you send the police away?" Kelley was beside himself at this point, pacing back and forth, his face red.

"I am sorry about this. Agent Parker said you are Mr. Kelley, *oui*? I cannot give you many details, but please understand that we will do everything we can to get your girlfriend back safely. Can you give me the name and a description of your friend?" JP asked.

"It's Dr. Kelley, and the person they took is Rose Moreau, and we're both from Boston," Kelley said. His hands made fists and battered against his sides.

JP stopped for a moment, looked at Parker, who shook his head, and then looked at Kelley. "Why are you two in Washington, D.C., if I may ask?"

"I'm here for a scientific meeting. I had a presentation to do, and Rose came with me. Listen, I was filming when the eagles were eating, and as Rose ran to that woman she called Bella, my camera was still on."

Kelley ran the video of the incident, and in the picture, although shaky, both Sergei and Alexis could be seen.

"Again, I am sorry, but I am going to have to take your phone. Agent Parker will accompany you to your hotel."

JP met with Chad at the safe house, a small nondescript white stone building outside downtown Washington. The misleading sign out front read *Society for Climate Intervention*, and JP was buzzed in after a retina scan. Chad walked past a few agents busy checking their computers' updated data and ushered JP into a small conference room with a rectangular table covered in cheap veneer and flanked by metal chairs.

"So, I guess you're going to be the one to talk with Robinson? Unless we don't tell her." Chad said.

"I do think that we need to tell her." JP thought back to the conversation he had with Lily regarding secrets and Rose. If he didn't let her know about Rose's capture, she would never forgive him. "What do you make of the video?" he asked after showing him the clip from Kelley's phone.

"That's a fucking lucky break. And you're correct; the woman's Alexis, aka Bella. Her accomplice may take a little more time to track down. I'll let the staff out front play with it. This guy's probably someone working in the deep, and we just blew his cover."

"With the pressure on, his next move will be his undoing," JP said, placing his hand on his colleague's shoulder. "And the body found at the Amazonia exhibit?"

"Didn't Parker tell you? It's James Andrews. Parker was all over that guy after Robinson made the connection with Steinman."

"So he was killed because he was getting too close to the truth or because he had something to do with Steinman's death?"

"Or he fucked up the deal," Chad added.

"Where is the body now?"

"I had him taken to Dr. Pelletier's shop. I'll ask Robinson to work on the toxicology. But if we assume this is a Russian affair, then whatever got into Andrews's face was poison—probably another goddamn nerve agent. Let's meet later tonight over at Logan's. I need the quiet of the morgue," Chad said, trying to make light of the situation.

JP left Chad and returned to his hotel, and prepared himself for the call.

"Ah, Lily, I am glad I caught you. Where are you?"

JP was surprised to hear that she was already in Washington, thinking she was still in Boston.

"*Écoutes*. Lily, write down the name and address of my hotel," JP said, giving her the details. Then he patiently listened to her express disappointment that they only just discovered they were in the same city. She reminded him that he told her he wasn't sure where he'd be, or when. Once again, he heard the anger in her voice.

"Lily, *je comprends*. We can discuss it later," he said, trying to soften the blow. "You must come right away. It is about Rose."

JP waited, and as expected, there was silence on the other end of the phone. No questions asked. That would take time. Just a quiet halt to the call. He checked his watch and assumed that Lily would be at his hotel as soon as she could find a taxi—still time for a ten-minute shower. The day had been long, and JP knew how Lily would react to Rose's abduction.

CHAPTER 26

Washington, D.C.

The fear that took hold of Rose's mind and settled in her belly had been there before. Dark rear windows dimmed the view, stoking Rose's imagination, and the car's speed forced her to slide around in her seat. There had been no time to put on the safety belt after she was shoved into the backseat and held in place by her sister until the car took off. Rose could feel her heart thumping in her chest and her mouth dry. It made a smacking or sucking sound when she tried to open it.

Dread had occupied Rose's being after Adrienne's car accident in France when she thought she would lose the only mother she'd ever known. Terror ended an afternoon in Colombia when Adrienne had been rendered unconscious, and her sister Bella abducted. And then there was a time even farther back in her mind that produced a feeling of panic when she was a child lost in a hot and steamy jungle. All she could remember was her calling for her mother, *mommy, mommy*. A new cloud of desperation and abandonment positioned itself before Rose's eyes. Looking over at her sister, Rose could see Bella's gray-blue eyes surrounded by red rims as if she'd been crying. Bella's blank look was more of a vacant stare. Rose tried to get her sister's attention.

"Bella, I don't understand. What's going on?" Rose's voice sounded weak, her heart climbing into her throat.

"Don't call me Bella. My name's Alexis," her sister said, sweeping Rose's hand away.

Rose recoiled at her sister's hard and stern response and could no longer hold the emotion inside her. She started crying; tears dripped down her cheeks faster than she could wipe them away. "I don't understand; what's happening?"

Alexis never expected to see Rose again. She turned her head away from her sister and looked out the window. Beyond the darkness, the scenery blurred as Sergei drove, weaving through traffic, leaving anyone chasing him behind. Alexis bit her lower lip and saw her world crashing in around her. She imagined this would end badly. There was no escape. She and Sergei had been sent as a couple to tie up one loose end—the American that had killed the senator. A wildcard who'd overstepped the line and had to pay the price. Alexis didn't care. She found herself only going through the motions of life now. It didn't matter anymore. Since she'd learned that her father was Grigory Markovic, she could barely look at herself in the mirror without loathing.

Rose couldn't get Bella to talk. Silence followed over the next few hours of mindless driving, penetrated only by an occasional horn blast or tire screech on the pavement.

They were a long way from the National Zoo, near a green space, when Sergei finally stopped the car and pulled over to the side of the road. He told them to get out. The street, dark despite the lighting that ran the edge of the park, was quiet, except for the trees rustling in the breeze.

"Alexis, hold onto to her," Sergei said, speaking in Russian while pointing to Rose, "and keep walking. I will be behind with a gun pointing at our little hostage."

Alexis nodded her head and grabbed Rose's arm, squeezing it as tight as she could, jerking Rose off her feet. Rose cried out, and Alexis took the flat of her hand and covered Rose's mouth, trying to squelch her. Rose persisted.

"Bella, I mean Alexis. But you are Bella? I don't understand."

"Shut up. You don't know me." Alexis looked only forward, not at her sister. She would not acknowledge the relationship for fear of harm coming to Rose. Alexis fought the memories of their childhood together so tears would not come to her. She pushed out the images of their silly girl musings all those years ago when she and Rose wondered about the fathers they never knew. As Bella, she recalled her mother telling her that her father was a coffee plantation worker who died in an accident. Disappointed at the time, Bella imagined him as a foreign diplomat—dashing, in Colombia on a secret mission, and then unexpectedly called home. The truth was, her father was a monster. No, the safest thing she could do for Rose was to push her away. She had to convince Sergei to let her go.

"Sergei, this woman's no use to us now. Let her go. Killing her will only call more attention to us."

"No. I do not think so. Do you know her? She seems to think she knows you," he said, now catching up to them on the walk.

"I've never seen her before."

Alexis hoped the feeble lie would work. Sergei had turned out to be more clever than she initially thought, and yet, he was different from his brother Maxim. When Maxim Petrikov and Grigory Markovic were together, they created strategies. Plans to terrorize their adversaries. In her eyes, Sergei Petrikov couldn't live up to his brother.

"Don't move. He will shoot you," Alexis whispered to Rose, halting her in her spot. She then pulled Sergei off to the side.

Too terrified to run, Rose's feet felt planted in the ground.

"Sergei, true she has seen us, but she doesn't know who we are or what we've done. Another killing will only draw more attention. Let's leave her here, get our things and go home."

Alexis hoped the appeal would work. She bit her lower lip while she checked Sergei's face for any signs of agreement. It was blank. Sergei said nothing for a few moments.

"Possibly a bargaining chip, but I think it is best to get rid of her." Sergei's eyes turned dark as he weighed the possibilities.

Undeterred, Alexis tried again. "Sergei, we can head to the airport now—"

"No," he interrupted, "I have some unfinished business." Having made up his mind, he screwed the silencer on his pistol while Alexis watched.

"Give the pistol to me. I will do it. Please, let me show you I can do this," Alexis said. "She'll be more cooperative with me and not try to escape."

Sergei grabbed Alexis's arm and twisted it until she flinched. His eyes bore deep into her, and she sensed his anger. When Sergei felt the buzz in his pocket, he dropped her wrist and pulled out his phone.

"Do not fuck this up, or I will kill both of you. *Da*, make it fast." He handed Alexis the gun and walked away with the phone to his ear.

Alexis ran to Rose and jerked her toward her.

"Follow me. Don't scream, and don't try to run."

Rose shook and started crying again, dragging

her feet as Alexis took her into the woods. Once they were behind a large tree, they stopped. Alexis spoke.

"Rose, say nothing, or he'll kill us both."

Rose's face was pale, and the tears streamed down her cheeks and dripped off her chin. She swiped them away.

"Bella, I don't understand. What's happened to you?"

"I'm not Bella anymore. I'm the daughter of a saint and a monster. This conflict lives within me and must stop."

"I don't know what you've done, and I don't care. I know what your father was, but you are not a monster. You're not your father," Rose pleaded.

Alexis stopped at this. Adrienne must have told Rose about the rape. Rose might know his name and his deed, but she couldn't know all the evil Markovic's life created in this world. She doubted Rose knew much at all. Alexis leaned in close to Rose and spoke.

"The sun-browned man told us all those years ago, remember, Rose? The rose tattoo was a symbol of promise and hope, while the spider represented treachery. It was preordained."

"Bella, that's not true. Please." Her sobs became louder.

"What is taking so long?" Sergei said, ready to step in. Alexis made her move and whispered in Rose's ear.

"Quick. Get your phone and turn it back on. Put in the password." Rose's hand shook as her fingers moved around the keypad.

"Now give it to me. What's the name of your boyfriend?"

"What? It's Kelley. You're not going to hurt him, are you?" Rose's sobs became loud and irritated Sergei.

"Let us go, *now,*" Sergei yelled.

Alexis took the butt of the gun and struck Rose on the side of the head, knocking her unconscious. She quickly typed a text into the message icon then placed the phone underneath Rose's body. Holding the pistol in both hands, she aimed and pulled the trigger before running back to where Sergei was pacing, smoking a cigarette. He took it out of his mouth, tossed it in the air, and stomped his heel on the ground where it landed. He looked at Alexis. His face seemed taut, and she felt uneasy, and vomit crept to the back of her throat. She swallowed hard.

Alexis knew he would kill her eventually, here, or maybe in the hotel, leaving her body for housekeeping. Once again, she wished she could roll back the stream of time and dip her toes into the youthful spring of freshwater before it all flowed downhill. A do-over. But she was too far down the river, and lost. She flailed against the rocks in the rapids while the sound of the impending waterfall screamed in her ears. Cocaine would chase the feeling, and she craved the white powder that had dusted her for most of her life.

Chapter 27

Washington, D.C.

By the time I reached the lobby, a taxi was already waiting for me. I only wished it could've been faster. It's that impatience gene. But I'm here now, and pounding at the door to JP's room.

"Jesus, JP," I say as I blast past him without even a hello, "What the hell's going on? You said it was about Rose."

"Lily, sit down. We need to talk."

"Oh no. Not another one of those we need to talk talks. God, JP, please tell me she's all right." I can feel my body shaking, and my voice has an uncharacteristic tremor.

"There was an incident that occurred at the National Zoo today."

"What about Rose?" My heart is going around the bases at a sprinter's pace. "*S'il te plaît*, Lily, sit down and listen," JP says, his voice raised.

I sit on the edge of the bed, and JP fills me in on the assassination of Andrews and the abduction of Rose. I'm sick to my stomach. I had no idea that Rose and Kelley were in D.C. How could I have missed that?

I get up and stand, shaking my head. "JP, do

we know where Rose is?" I feel the dread swirl around in my chest.

"No, not yet."

Another big breath escapes my lungs, and I fall back to the edge of the bed, my hands cradling my head. All the years I thought she was dead, my only companion was guilt. Now I still own the guilt, but it's been overtaken with fear and worry.

"The plan?" I must focus.

"*Oui*. This complicates many things. I do not believe that they will link Rose to you. But it is possible they will consider that Alexis/Bella, has a sister. My guess is that they will let her go. For now, she may be a bargaining chip."

JP's sitting next to me now. My head's resting on his shoulder, his arm around me. I can feel the closeness and warmth of someone who loves me, who cares about me.

"A bargaining chip? For what?"

"They murdered our Deputy Secretary of the Interior, Lily. Rose could be their ticket out of this country."

"Oh," I say, clenching my teeth. I let out another sigh and close my eyes. JP squeezes my hand.

"*Eh*, we have Kelley's phone if Rose tries to contact him. You cannot call your fellow since he does not know of your involvement in our operation."

I can see JP raise an eyebrow, and the corners of his mouth turn down. He looks tired too. I bring my knees to my chest and curl up into a ball. My poor Rose. She must be so frightened. How did she feel after she was taken from me all those years ago? A tiny stranger in a foreign land. And once again, I can't be there to help her. Well, heaven help the bastard that took her.

JP redirects the conversation. "Lily, I had Andrews's body taken over to Logan's place. You should go over there and take your mind off this. Parker and I will let you know if we hear anything. I know Chad has men working on the identification of the man with Alexis."

"I'll do it. But only because I don't want to put Rose in any jeopardy. Promise me that the second you know something, I'll know it too."

"*Mais oui, ma chérie.*"

I kiss JP goodbye and squeeze him so tight he probably finds he can't breathe. But I'm the one with shortness of breath. I'm the one who fears the impending loss of my child all over again.

"Good to see you again, Lily," Logan says. "Another unfortunate circumstance."

He's so professional. No hint in his tone that we had an affair. It's good to move forward.

"What've we got?"

"I have the body in an isolated section of the morgue. Parker said he saw something sprayed into Andrews's face and thought it might be toxic. Since this is not my area of expertise, I had everyone who handled the body wear PPE. Lily, please wear your Powered Air Purifying Respirator."

"Oh, you have PAPRs here? Great, because if this was a Russian hit job, then I think we should expect poison. I'll collect some specimens for the tox lab. Let's take a look at the body."

Logan and I dress in space suits. That's what I like to call the kind of personal protective equipment we're wearing. If Andrews was poisoned, his secretions could be contaminated and put us at risk. I hope the transport people took precautions getting the body here. We go to a remote room in the morgue with negative pressure, so air is apt to flow into the room rather than out. This will help keep those in the rest of the building safe. The body's laid out on the stainless, and we'll conduct a focused autopsy given the circumstances.

"Lily, I don't see too much on the external exam other than blunt force trauma on the back of the head. That could be attributed to the fall he took during the assault. There are also secretions around the nose and mouth as well. We found evidence of urine and feces on the clothes."

"Sounds like a cholinergic response. My guess is that whoever did this used a nerve agent. These are organophosphate compounds that have been used for chemical warfare. I've seen this recently. Let's proceed with caution."

"I won't ask you how you know that. You scare me, doctor. So, okay, if you're ready, let's open him up and check out the heart, lungs, and anything else you want." I can see Logan's eyes inside the PAPR mask, and his eyebrows are pushed toward the bridge of his nose. He's intense.

"No, that's fine. We can check out the heart for infarction and take some samples to embed and then put under the scope. Although I doubt he had a heart attack. Same with the lungs. I might want a piece of liver. Did you already collect blood?"

"Absolutely. Both heart and femoral."

We open the chest and cut away the breastplate so we can look into the thoracic cavity. Everything looks anatomically correct. Logan cuts into the pericardium, the small bag of tissue surrounding the heart. No abnormal pericardial fluid's observed. Then he cuts away the heart from the chest and places it on a table. The dissection begins after Logan examines the coronary arteries. They appear normal. He picks up the scalpel and makes transverse slices starting at the apex and works up to the base of the heart where the large vessels like the aorta originate. I can see a large postmortem clot in the left ventricle. Nothing to worry about. Logan takes some small slices to fix in formalin to look at the tissue under the microscope. He then moves on to the lungs.

"Logan, these are heavy and look congested," I say, looking at the lungs.

"I agree. But other than that, I don't expect we're going to find much more." He pokes down through the diaphragm so he can collect a piece of liver for me. "All right, I say we wrap this up. I'll wait for the toxicology report from you before we call this. If it was poison, then we can rule it a homicide."

"Agreed, I'll get these specimens sent off to Hong Kong."

"Still using the Hong Kong lab? Don't trust the ones in the States?"

It's complicated. It's not that I don't trust the labs here, it's just that when it comes to this kind of work, I prefer the one run by John Chi.

"Yes, I am. It's someone I work with regularly, so it makes it easy. I'm going to get out of the spacesuit and shower. I'll meet you back in your office."

What I really want to do is check my phone, no make a call, to see if there's any word on Rose. I'm out of the jumpsuit and the shower in record time. There are no messages on my phone, so I call JP.

"Hey. I'm worried sick. Do you have anything for me?" I feel tears reaching the brim.

"No, nothing yet. Sorry. But we have everyone

working on it. Lily, I am betting they will not harm Rose."

"Don't you dare bet with my daughter's life! These are crazy people," I say, biting my lower lip and feeling the stress eat at my gut. Where are those antacids? "Sorry, JP. Look, Logan and I just finished the autopsy on Andrews. No tox yet, but if you and Chad want to meet us here, we can talk about it."

"*Oui*. Anything interesting?"

"Well, there might be when we get the tox back."

"Let me check in with Chad and then come over. Parker has been working the abduction and is going to head over to Kelley's hotel in a little while."

God, I have to worry about Kelley too.

"K, see you soon." I hang up the phone and wait in Logan's office. It's not long before I see the handsome doctor appear.

"Wow, you were fast. Showered already, I see," he says. Logan smiles and spreads his arms wide open as if modeling his scrubs. "Me too."

The poor man probably spends most of his day in blue hospital garb. Most of my day is filled with sleek shoes and fashionable outfits. Tonight I have more important things on my mind.

"You okay?" he asks, putting his arm around me noticing my subdued response.

"Yes, I had to make a few phone calls. Chad

and JP should be here shortly. Not sure if Parker will make it over."

"You seemed a little preoccupied back there. Anything else on your mind? Anything you want to talk about?"

"Nothing, thanks. That's kind of you."

We both sit down at the round table in the corner. My foot is bobbing up and down as the right leg rests on the left knee. The waiting's torture. They must have heard something by now. Logan asks me if I'd like to review some microscopics with him. Something to do.

"Come on, Lily. I have a case just for you. Drug overdose. Here let me pull the slide with the lung tissue. Tell me what you see."

He's trying. I'll try too.

"First thing I notice is congestion. There's fluid in the air spaces," I tell him and then see something that catches my eye. I focus the scope up and down until the image is clear. "Logan, you see this area?" I say as I switch to polarized light.

"Yes, the Maltese cross pattern caused by starch. Good pick-up so quickly into the case."

"A lot of heroin's cut with starch or talc, so when it's injected, these excipients get trapped in the lungs causing pulmonary hypertension or infections."

Logan's about to drive another slide when my phone buzzes. It's a text message—from Kelley, or is it Rose? It's a group text.

"Logan, I have to take this call. Would you mind?" I try and sound calm but inside, I'm screaming.

"No worries," he nods and walks out of the room.

In my haste, I dial Rose's number. Come on, Rose, pick up, pick up. Then I actually look at the text message. It's on the text string from Rose to Kelley and me about setting a future lab visit. Kelley had added me in on the text at the time. But I think this message is meant for Kelley, not the both of us. A chill moves up my back as I focus on the text: *Sergei Petrikov the Willow Hotel 6457*. I say the words out loud, grab my bag, and bolt for the door.

"Logan, oh, you're right here. Listen, I have to go. I'll check back with you later."

My body creates a stir rushing from his office before Logan can say a word. Petrikov. I know that name.

"Logan, good to see you. What've you got for us?"

Chad enters the office with JP expecting to see Lily at the microscope. He's kept the team small, choosing to do some of the previously delegated work himself for fear of those who might betray him.

"Where's Dr. Robinson? She was to meet us here."

"She was here. You just missed her. Only left a little while ago. Like a banshee on the wind," Logan says, whisking one hand up into the air.

JP, who was on the phone, perked up and turned toward Logan. "Did she say where she was going?" JP put his phone down with a look of concern at Logan's revelation.

"I've no idea. That woman has a mind of her own."

"Did Robinson say anything before she left?" Chad asked, shooting a look across the room at JP.

"No. We were at the scope when it sounded like she got a text. Then she said she had to make a call. I gave her some privacy, and when I got back to my office, I heard her say something but didn't have time to question her. Man, she just bolted."

"What did she say, for God's sake?" Chad said.

"She said something like Sergei Petrikov, the Willow Hotel 6457. I don't know. An address to meet someone?"

JP felt the hackles rise at the back of his neck. Petrikov. How Lily would know that before him was remarkable. She could be in danger, or be dangerous. Either way, JP would charge to be at her side.

"*Merde*, I am leaving now," he said, shaking his head. "Chad, call Parker and let him know." JP moved like a blur, and Logan could feel the air swirl as JP flew out of his office.

Turning to Chad, Logan said, "Shit, I don't know what the hell's going on, but I'm sure you do."

"Look, sorry. Let's connect later." Chad left the office and hurried back to his base of operations. Maybe it was time to bring in some other players.

Chapter 28

Washington, D.C.

This is a risk. I've been there before, and I'll be there again. I hope Sergei Petrikov, or whoever he is, is on the other side of the door. I have no clever plan to work my way in. No matter. Go bold. I knock.

"Who is there?" I can hear a Russian accent, so this must be the right place—sixth floor, room 457.

"Mr. Petrikov, I have a message for you," I say evenly, fighting the growing fear.

My chest is pounding. Each beat hard and responding to the adrenaline, pushing blood out faster to my brain and my limbs ready to explode. I will brace myself for whatever lies ahead. The door's opening.

"*Da*, your message?" Not that he will be fooled. He knows what he's done and that he's wanted.

"May I come in, Mr. Petrikov? I'd like to talk about Maxim." I'm not sure how well he speaks English but assume he understands some of it. As the door swings a little wider, I can see a man who resembles Maxim holding a gun. I don't wait for a response; I just push past him knowing that the gun is now pointed at my back. I feel my chest tighten, my breathing quicken as I turn around and look at his face. Can he see my fury? Anger trumps fear.

"Mr. Petrikov? You're related to Maxim Petrikov, *da*?" Establish the connection. My eyes scan the room. I don't see Rose. No one else is here unless she's in the bathroom, or maybe the closet. I expected Alexis would be here too.

"You knew Maxim? How?" he says, keeping his distance and waving the gun to drive me off to the side of the room. I twist my platinum bracelet, hoping JP's paying attention. I let out one of those laughs that aims for provocation.

"Know Maxim? I didn't know him. I killed him."

"Ah." He laughs back at me. A good laugh, too, and then his eyes narrow. "Why are you here?"

There's disdain in his voice. The corners of his mouth tilt down. His hazel eyes are like his brother's—clear and determined. I wait for an opportunity.

"Where's the girl, Petrikov?"

"Not here."

I grit my teeth, forcing my emotions back in the bottle. "Where's the girl?" Petrikov's face wrinkles. He sniffs. He knows he has the upper hand—doesn't have to answer me. He's annoyed. Not worried by my presence. I'm not a threat.

"Who the fuck are you to care?" His gray polo shirt's wrinkled at the hem, where he tucked it into the front of his pants. He was probably getting ready to take it off when I knocked on the door. Sergei pushes what he can back into the waistband with the hand not holding the gun. "You killed my brother? I will enjoy killing you." He nods his head.

"By all means, you bastard, but first, I'd like to know where the girl is if she's not here?"

"Someone will find her body," he says, waving the gun at me.

Her body? I block my fear and tears and ask one more question before I kill him.

"It was you who visited Omair?"

"Omair? I do not know anyone named Omair."

"The scorpion dealer."

"*Da*, the schoolteacher."

Oh God, that must be it. Omair taught school, and this bastard must have threatened the children. I should've known. That explains the photograph.

"Who would be interested in obtaining such an unusual venom? Is it the Tsar?" And Leigh told me that I wouldn't be able to track down the Tsar.

The barrel of the gun drops to the level of my chest as Sergei's arm bends at the elbow. He's surprised. Another sniff.

"I am not sure who you are. You admit to

killing my brother, and you ask about the Tsar. Who do you work for?"

"Let's just say I'm an independent contractor. I took care of Grigory Markovic, too." Actually, Leigh did.

I can tell that I'm getting under his skin. There's a flash of anger in his eyes. He shifts his weight from one foot to the other.

"Markovic? *Da*, we can all be replaced." Sergei's voice reflects irritation and impatience.

My time's almost up.

"Senator Steinman found out about Global Tectonics, didn't he? And James Andrews had to murder him. That's why you killed him—no loose ends."

He walks to the desk, shaking his head in disgust, and opens the top drawer to retrieve something. He screws on a firearms suppressor at the end of his pistol. Both the gun and the silencer look like they may have been made in a 3-D printer. A ghost gun. Easy to get once he was here in the U.S.

"Andrews talked too much, just like you."

"What's your plan, or the Tsar's plan?"

"The plan?" He laughs. "More than a plan. It is control of the world. You think in such small terms."

"So, the deaths of Khan and Steinman were necessary for your plan to go forward?"

"What did you say your name was?"

"I didn't, Sergei."

"No matter." He raises his arm, the gun now aimed at my forehead.

I drop the quarter I've been holding in my hand, its shiny surface enticing his eyes momentarily to look toward the ground. I lunge toward him with a warrior scream and grab him at the shoulders, throwing him off balance. A good hit with a knee to his groin sends him forward in pain, allowing the heel of my stiletto to strike. Sergei winces as the jab penetrates his leg, yet he manages to knock me hard with his elbow, sending me sideways, and I hear the gun go off. A soft pop sounds within the room, and the bullet burrows into the carpet, missing my body by inches. With another stab from my heels, the gun drops, and I kick it as far away from him as I can.

"You want to know my name?" I yell through my teeth. "You can call me the queen of all poisons."

In a final flash of anger, I claw at Sergei's face and drag my nails along his cheeks, drawing blood. He clutches his face in agony, feeling the burn, and in the end, he will kill me if I don't escape. I race to the door, my ragged breath slowing me down from the pain in my ribcage. My heart's in overdrive, hurling me down the hall. I pound the elevator button with my fist, hoping to buy time, and instead take the stairs at the pace of a sprinter, my shoes in my hands. When I reach the front of the hotel, I gasp for breath in the fresh air, splinting my ribs with my hand, and hail a cab.

I had no choice. The demon took Rose. Never get between a mamma bear and her cub.

Chapter 29

Washington, D.C.

By the time JP reached the Willow Hotel and Sergei's room, it was too late. He deftly entered the room, gun drawn, only to find it empty. White bloodied towels were heaped on the bathroom floor, and traces of blood skirted the rim of the sink. There was no evidence of Lily Robinson or Sergei Petrikov. JP sat down on the wooden chair near the desk and ran his fingers through his hair. Did Sergei take her as a hostage, kill her, or did she escape? Looking at the scene, it was hard to know. His phone rang. It was Parker.

"*Oui?*"

"Shit, boss. You okay?"

"*Oui*. No sign of Robinson here. Do you have Rose?"

"Yeah. After that text came through on Kelley's phone, we used cell phone triangulation to locate her. Kelley's phone was off after we pushed out the video, so we initially missed the text."

"Jesus fucking Christ. That is sloppy work."

"You're right."

"Where is Rose now?"

"They took her to the hospital to have a head wound checked out, but she should be okay. If the hospital releases her tonight, Chad's putting her and Kelley on a train. No ifs, ands or buts. He's preparing for fucking Armageddon. Says they just happened to be a couple of innocent bystanders. Feels sure this was just one of those coincidences. Wrong place at the wrong time."

"*C'est vrai.*"

"You think the bastard took Doc Robinson?"

"I do not know. There is blood here, Parker. Someone is hurt." JP's voice sounded strained, and his mind wandered for a second. He needed to get back to his hotel, get his briefcase and use his tracking device to find her. She couldn't have gotten that far. When he found Sergei, he would kill him. No questions asked.

"I am going to check the room and then head back to the hotel. Robinson has shown us to be capable in the past. She may be hiding." JP said this, believing in his lover's strengths, yet worrying about her life nonetheless.

He hung up with Parker and tried calling Lily. The call went directly to voicemail. JP took in a big breath, released it, and started a search of the room. Two queen-sized beds filled the space, and the closet contained only a few clothes, primarily women's clothes—a dress, a pair of shoes. There was one pair of men's slacks draped over a wooden hanger. JP turned out the pockets. In the right front pocket was a crumpled piece of paper. He opened it, scanned the contents, and put the note in his own pocket.

• • •

JP reached his hotel and settled into his room. He poured himself a glass of bottled fizzy water and sat down on the chair by the desk. He realized that Lily had become more reckless over time, and particularly since she found out Rose was alive. It seemed contrary to what he or anyone would have guessed. He would have expected her to be more careful, preserve her time at the medical school teaching, and mentor her daughter. Maybe he was too hard on her. Maybe the Agency had gone too far this time, and Lily was beginning to bend under the strain.

He walked to the closet and removed his briefcase. The seasoned asset flipped the top and pulled out a device he used for tracking a signal. As he sat waiting for the pulsing light, a memory going back more than twenty years popped into his mind. He could see himself, a handsome young man, looking in a mirror, admiring his fit body, biceps bulging, abdominal muscles toned, and a full head of dark hair. While in France, on holiday in Paris, he met a woman who captivated his imagination with her bright eyes, delightful laugh, and most importantly, her free spirit. He didn't mind that she was a little older than he, not that anyone could tell. Her youthful face carried a smile that he loved, and he told her that it was her prettiest feature. *Très jolie*. They would walk the streets of Paris, talking about literature, art, and science, and her stories filled him with desire and admiration for her intellect. They once stopped by the river Seine so a street artist could capture her image in colorful charcoals. He was sure he still had that sketch in a drawer somewhere at his flat. Jean Paul closed his eyes, felt the warmth, and remembered what it was like to fall in love. To be consumed by love. It was God's gift to humanity. To be young with your whole life ahead of you. Jean Paul fell in love with the woman with the bright pink streak in her hair.

In time, he learned that she worked for a secret agency that few people even knew existed. There would be clandestine missions gathering intelligence, assassinating terrorists, and working to subtly shift the balance of good versus evil. She seduced him first as a lover and then as an operative. She was the best in the business—at both. She could recognize talent and would exploit anyone to get what she wanted. She had recruited Lily Robinson soon after her scientific party was massacred in the Colombian jungle. JP had only recently learned the details of Lily's background since Lily's memory had been blocked, and no records from that time existed at the Agency. Pixie Dust was a maverick. Brilliant. Recruiting Robinson and setting her up to be JP's working partner had been a stroke of genius. By that time, Jean Paul's love affair had been long over. Pixie Dust had brushed him aside and focused only on the business. And, in time, Lily Robinson turned out to be another independent woman who stole his heart and tortured his mind. The doctor had been molded in the image of her mentor, Pixie Dust.

Pixie recognized that poison was still a valuable weapon, not to be underestimated. Used correctly, it could be difficult to prove in assassinations and challenging to trace. She was always on the lookout to find and recruit a poison expert and did so when she happened to find a small paragraph of highly classified information from the drug enforcement branch of the government on finding the remnants of a bloodied scientific expedition in cocaine country. Lily Robinson had been so traumatized it had been a relatively easy sell. Pixie found a recruit—albeit reluctant and naïve—whom she could shape and incur allegiance. It was serendipity at its best.

JP remembered Pixie Dust telling him about her new find, assuring him that the doctor would make him a great collaborator, but she would need hand-holding and encouragement. "Beneath that austere academic facade lurks a woman looking to escape her world," Pixie used to say. JP was tasked with providing the framework that would support a series of assassinations—by poison—for over a decade.

Hidden in the recesses of JP's mind was a conversation with Pixie, who had hinted at a plan for hunting down one of the most formidable Russian poisoners, referred to either as the Poisoner-in-Chief, or more commonly, the Tsar. She set her sights on him—no one had ever confirmed the Tsar's identity—to follow his exploits, researching what she could find from files of the old KGB days. He never knew if she found him. But he did know that Pixie Dust's body was discovered in Paris, near the river Seine, where a sketch artist plied his trade for tourists. JP was sure he had that sketch, too, the one of the woman with the pink hair sleeping on the bench by the river. No cause of death was ever determined.

Pixie Dust thought she had identified the master himself, primarily through dogged research and by a little chance. Rumors circulated that there was a chemist out of Hong Kong who was also after the Tsar. But Pixie Dust wanted to find their archrival first and traveled to Russia to confirm her findings. She followed the man back to Paris, got close to revealing the true identity of the Tsar, and readied herself for the inevitable confrontation. But the Poisoner-in-Chief got the upper hand. Pixie had finally met her match.

The white light on the screen was pulsing, bringing JP back to the present and letting him know the whereabouts of Lily Robinson. He closed his eyes, let out a sigh, and shut his briefcase.

Chapter 30

Washington, D.C.

I'm back at my hotel now. I've got at least one fractured rib, and I'm expecting a big bruise on the side of my chest. With my blouse off, the mirror confirms a large blue mark level with my elbow. I'm sore. Sergei got me good, but he didn't kill me, and I expect that JP will soon be at my door. I'll call him after I wash off. He's going to be pissed.

    The water feels good. Although the warm spray soothes my aches, I will still need some surgical tape for my ribs. Stepping out of the shower, I wrap myself in a towel, plop down on the bed and consider my surroundings. The standard hotel fare, lush dark brown walls contrast with a brown leather headboard framed in white. It looks inviting, so I want to close my eyes and sleep—just for a few minutes, the exhaustion catching up with me. But I need to keep moving. Towel drying my hair proves a little challenging with the pain, yet I'm able to apply some eyeliner and lipstick with no problem. A washcloth removes the blood from the heels of my shoes, and I step into a black pencil skirt with a red silk chemise—and call JP.

• • •

Someone's at my hotel door. I look through the peephole and recognize Jean Paul, who was on his way over when he got my call.

"JP, come in," I tell him, peeking out of the room and down the hallway. It's empty.

"*Ma chérie*, are you all right?" he asks with a combination of concern and anger.

He moves in for a hug, and I push him off.

"What is wrong?"

"Just a few fractured ribs or just one. Not a big deal. More importantly, did you get Rose?"

"Parker put Rose and Kelley on a train back to Boston. You should know that Rose was checked out at a local hospital for a concussion. She received a nasty blow to the head, *mais*, otherwise is okay. Chad is certain that they were in the wrong place at the wrong time. No one believes there is a connection to you."

"My God, JP. I didn't realize that Rose was injured. I tried to find her but found Petrikov alone. And, I'm not so sure that there isn't a direct connection to me. I should call Rose, or at least Kelley, and see how they're doing."

"This time, my Lily, you went too far. You should not have attempted to take on Sergei Petrikov by yourself. Why not contact me? Parker and I could have gone to the Willow Hotel." I can see a flare of anger behind his eyes.

"Did you get him?" I ask, ignoring his question.

"No, I did not. Chad has some men out looking for him, but your folly caused us a setback."

"Sorry about that. I thought he would still be there by the time you—"

"*Merde*. You could have been killed." JP takes my hand and kisses the palm. This is a conversation we've had many times before, and the anger in his voice is not a stranger to me.

We both hear a knock at the door, and JP pulls out his gun before he looks through the peephole. Then he turns to me.

"It is Parker." He opens the door, and in spills Parker smiling to see that both JP and I are intact.

"JP, you want to holster that thing. I'm not a danger to either of you. Good to see you, doc. You do know you pissed off the boss here. You okay?" He has a large grin on his face. He means well.

"Yes, thank you, Parker. I was just telling JP that I'd hoped you would have found Petrikov at the hotel, but I'm told he got away. He won't get very far."

"How do you know that?" Parker asks.

"Poison."

"What do you mean?" JP perks up.

"It's your shoes, right? You wore your poison shoes?" Parker asks.

"No, I did not. But I did get in a few good stomps with my stilettos. I'm sure his leg is hurting."

"So, how'd you do it?" Parker's ears perk up.

"Think about this, Parker. One of the ways people try to beat their drug test is to adulterate their urine." I can see the quizzical looks on their faces wondering where this is going. "They smuggle salt, hidden under their fingernails, into the bathroom where they're going to take the test. Then, after they pee in the cup, they dip their fingers into the urine and stir. This salt adulterant interferes with the instrument readings."

"Stirred, not shaken?" Parker smirks.

"I do not understand," JP says.

"I used the same trick but with a poison exploited by the San Bushmen who hunt in the savannah region of eastern Namibia and western Botswana. They use diamphotoxin found in the larvae of the beetle from the genus Diamphidia. The hunters traditionally used a bow and arrow and, like other cultures, dip the arrow tip in poison. In South Africa, this poison was used to hunt large mammalian prey. It's not a fast-acting poison, so the Bushmen would track the slowly dying animal and wait for their death."

"So the poison wasn't in your stilettos, right, doc?"

"Exactly, Parker. I had the crystals of poison under my fingernails and scratched Petrikov's face, drawing blood. The poison's now in his bloodstream, and like the wild animals in nature, he'll die a slow death. Diamphotoxin will increase the permeability of his red cells, causing hemolysis. Think of it this way. All those ruptured red cells will mean there's less oxygen getting to his organs. Over time, his muscles will slowly become paralyzed. And, dying red cells release a lot of potassium, and hyperkalemia or increased potassium will produce cardiac dysrhythmias. So in short, he'll become paralyzed and bleed to death."

"Jesus Christ, Robinson. You are a menace. Shit, though, I'm glad you're okay," Parker says, shaking his head.

"Most interesting. *Alors*, we need to look for a man with scratches on his face who may be bleeding and paralyzed. Chad will be most happy." JP shakes his head too, and I see a look of concern on his face. His lips are pursed together, his jaw clenched.

"There's one more thing. I went after Sergei Petrikov because I think he's our Tsar, and I believe he's orchestrating the REE Jokovikstan grab for the Russians. It makes sense to me."

"I am not so sure, Robinson. Have you spoken with Leigh?" JP asks.

"I haven't, but I will. Why don't you think Petrikov's the Tsar?"

"At this point in his career, I think the Tsar would be pulling the strings, not center stage."

"Either way, I tried to take this bastard out. He threatened my Rose." I let out a humph and let it go.

My phone rings. It's Logan.

"Hey, Logan. Yeah, I'm all right. What? I'm going to put you on speakerphone. I'm here with JP and Parker." I make the switch.

"Great," Logan says. "I just got some info back from the lab that I wanted to share. I couldn't get through to Chad, so that's why I'm calling you."

"Logan, this is JP, what have you got?"

"Both aortic valve implants, the one for Steinman and the one for Khan, were made by Trileaflet, Inc., and both implants had been packaged similarly to valves that each surgeon normally used, so nothing seemed out of the ordinary."

"Yes, we know this, and I confirmed with a nurse at Steinman's hospital that a Trileaflet implant was used for the senator's case," I say with some impatience.

"But what you don't know is that titanium was not detected in either implant. In this case, ziyantium comprised the mesh used for the support of the attached xenograft or animal tissue that formed the biological component of the manufactured valve. And ziyantium is that rare earth mineral recently found in the mountains of Jokovikstan. It took a very sophisticated metals laboratory to pull that out of a hat."

"Wow. I just came across a journal article on ziyantium. Even though it's lighter, it's stronger than titanium, and also less reactive with acids than scandium. So it has significant potential for use in medical devices. Implantable valves could be a moneymaker for Trileaflet since a recent assessment of the global market for cardiac devices indicated that sales would soar over the next decade in both the U.S. and in Europe in concert with the surge of heart disease. TAVRs would become more commonplace, and Trileaflet would hold the majority share with its superior product," I tell them.

"*Mais*, you are overlooking the most important use for ziyantium— computers, and weaponry— military applications. It would revolutionize the manufacture of critical technologies. Whoever controls the source and the distribution would, in essence, control the future," JP says, scratching his chin.

"Logan, you were correct about Trileaflet. It's a hot new company, and its stock's definitely on the rise. But more importantly, Chad was able to confirm it's a subsidiary of the Russian-held company called Global Tectonics," Parker says. "Just like you thought. And their core business is ziyantium."

"So Global Tectonics had Khan killed because he was going to give the U.S. a free shot at this deal. And someone paid off Andrews to foil it," Logan adds.

"And Senator Steinman, being the Chair of the Subcommittee on International Development and

International Economic Policies, found out about Andrews and Andrews had him killed, or killed him," I say.

"I'll check to see if Andrews was getting stock in Trileaflet, and if so, whether Steinman uncovered it," Parker says.

"Guys, I've got to get going. Just wanted to fill you in and check to see if Lily was okay."

"Thanks, Logan." I hang up the phone and think for a minute before I speak. "Sergei Petrikov was the hired assassin for Andrews, but was he the creator of the scorpion toxin embedded valve implants? That took some real poison know-how."

"*Oui*. The Tsar."

"Yes, and I haven't yet ruled out Petrikov despite what you think, JP. Parker saw Petrikov assassinate Andrews, but who was Andrews' connection in Jokovikstan? Was it Petrikov, or someone else? There had to be an intermediary."

"That dumbass Ambassador Thornton? I didn't like him when we met him. Don't you think so?" Parker asks.

"No, not Thornton. I think he's just guilty of sleeping with the president's wife. We have nothing concrete linking him to this. Who's his counterpart from Jokovikstan?" I say.

"*Oui*, I agree. Taz Chernsky is the ambassador from Jokovikstan to the United States. Anything on him, Parker?" JP asks.

"Don't know much about him. But you can be sure as shit, I'm going to check into his profile when I leave here," Parker says.

"Let us see what we can find out. Get an ID of this guy and see where he goes, who he meets. I'll follow up with Chad on this," JP adds.

We're all silent for a while, taking in the moment, and then I venture forth. "You know, Global Tectonics is like the tectonic plates found in the Earth's outer shell. This company can shift world power not by creating mountains or volcanoes or earthquakes but by controlling who can make better weapons, faster and more stable computers, and communication devices. That's a pretty powerful idea."

"Communication satellites, more likely. And the Russians will be in control if they run Jokovikstan," JP says.

"Speaking of which," Parker says, "Chad said the elections are underway for the new president in Jokovikstan."

"We can only hope that the election is free and fair," I tell them.

"And, if it's not, we will have a hand in it." Parker nods his head in agreement. "Nothing like shaping world politics."

"Russia, and I guess China, has been putting so much pressure on Jokovikstan to follow them. When will we know who was elected?" I ask.

"They are waiting to make an announcement

after all the votes have been recounted—security problems," JP says.

"Oh shit," I say, and we end it there.

They leave my room, seeing that I'm tired and want to rest. Now alone, I take the opportunity to call Kelley. He must be back by now if he's taken the high-speed train to Boston. His phone's ringing.

"Hi, Kelley, I'm so glad I caught you. I got a call from a government agent who said that you gave him my name after you and Rose were involved in an incident in D.C. Are you both all right?" I try and not let on that I know what's happened.

"We're fine. Look, we're just pulling into the station. I can give you details later, but that was the scariest thing that's ever happened to me in my life. I'm sure it was worse for Rose. She's been very quiet."

"I'm sure. The agent did give me a brief outline of what happened. Absolute hell. Kelley, please put Rose on the phone."

"Sure, doc. Rose, Dr. Robinson wants to speak with you."

"Hello." Her voice is distant and quiet.

"Rose, I know you've had a terrible trauma and must be very scared. Let's plan on meeting after you've had a few days of rest. How's your head feeling?"

"It's okay, I guess. It hurts. But I've cracked my head before, you know."

"Rose, I got this strange text message from you earlier. Maybe it was meant for Dr. Kelley."

"Yeah, but I didn't send that text. And it was meant for Dr. Kelley but got sent to both of you instead. I don't know what it means."

"No worries. Did you recognize the people who took you?"

"Only my sister. I'm sure it was Bella. I think she pretended not to know me to protect me. I don't understand why she was with that horrible man."

"Anything else, did she say anything else? Or was there anything unusual about the day?"

"No, but there is one thing that's bothering me. When Kelley and I were on the carousel at the zoo, I saw a man who reminded me of someone, but I just can't place him. I have a memory for shapes and faces, details you know."

I laugh to myself. She takes after her mother and will make a fine pathologist. "What did you find familiar about him?" My curiosity's piqued.

"I know this sounds weird, but the size of his feet—they're freakishly big."

I find this so strange that I don't have a comeback to Rose, so I tell her, "okay, that's interesting," and decide I really do need to lay down and rest. Rose wants to talk a few minutes more. I can hear the conductor in the background telling everyone that this is the Back Bay Station and to exit right. I know that route all too well.

"Dr. Robinson, I don't know how I'm going to get over this. You've been so kind to me. One day I will share with you how I was lost in the jungle. That same terror clawed at me hours ago."

My heart drops in my chest. "Listen, stay with Kelley. Keep him close." And then she's gone.

After JP and Parker left, they sent up some surgical tape to my room so I could bind my ribs. Deep breathing hurts, but I try not to take shallow breaths since I want my lungs to expand, thus avoiding future respiratory problems. It's time to put my head down for a few minutes.

I hear a knock at the door. I must have dozed off. I check my phone for the time, and I see that it's the next morning. Oh crap, what have I missed? I struggle to get out of bed, grab a bathrobe and get to the door. Peering through the peephole, I'm surprised to see an old friend. How did he track me down?

"John Chi! I'm so surprised to see you. What are you doing here?" I practically pull him through the door and into my room, his frame smaller than I recall.

"Lily Robinson, I told you I would come."

"You did not. I was not expecting you." I know my head's a little woozy, but I think I would have remembered if John Chi Leigh was coming to see me.

"The Tsar is here. But he's my nemesis, not yours."

"So, he *is* here in Washington?" My eyes light up.

"From the chatter in our circles, I would say yes." His black hair's gray at the temples and engulfs the ends of his dark-framed eyeglasses. He's wearing his khaki pants and a dark blue sports coat over a light blue shirt. His uniform.

"John, I think the Tsar is Sergei Petrikov. I tried to take him out."

"You are playing a dangerous game, Lily Robinson. You are a physician and sometimes operative."

I think about what he says. It's the same message from JP. "I know, you're right, but I took the opportunity handed to me. He took a young woman I know," I say, stopping there.

"Never put personal into this line of work. It clouds the mind and creates danger."

"So, what do you think about Petrikov?"

"It is not Petrikov. He is the wrong age and does not fit the clues. But, tell me what you know."

"Clues? Well, I don't know that much. He's, of course, the brother of Maxim Petrikov."

"And he confirmed the deaths of Steinman and Khan were related?"

"Yes, but that much we already figured out. It was Sergei who went to the Middle East to collect the scorpion toxin, and left the cyanide kill-pill. I believe he used the venom to kill Khan so Russia could take control of the country."

"Where is Sergei now?"

"I don't know. They're out looking for him. He'll be easy enough to find because I poisoned him with diamphotoxin."

"Diamphotoxin? Ah, from *Diamphidia nigroornata*. How amusing. It produces red cell lysis. Why would you pick a slow poison? In our business, the quicker the better."

"It was a little project I'd been working on. Happened to have it in my bag. Had to improvise."

"Your delivery technique?"

"Tucked the powdered form under my fingernails which I used to break the skin and get the poison into his blood."

"Clever, Lily Robinson. Lyophilization. I believe you are getting to like this aspect of your life a little too much." Leigh has a troubled look on his face, almost disapproving.

"I don't like being threatened or like having anyone I know threatened."

"I expect that Sergei felt the same about his brother." John Chi is right.

"So if you don't think Sergei Petrikov is the Tsar, then who is? How will we find him?"

"In the old days, information was harder to come by. There were no computers and no cell phones. Now many articles are digitized, and we have ways to search the internet for seemingly insignificant clues."

John Chi has me totally glued to his every word. I tighten the tie on my bathrobe and lean into his voice.

"I came across a newspaper story about a house explosion in the outskirts of Moscow in the 1970s. A family with two brothers and a mother and father narrowly escaped, but the body of the older brother's twin sister was never found. The cause of the explosion was assumed to be a gas leak, although authorities could not confirm that had been the case. Accompanying the article was a photograph of the family standing in front of the splintered remains of their dwelling. The brothers were sandwiched between their parents, the oldest boy nearest his father. The remarkable thing about the picture was that the father had uncommonly large feet—a genetic mutation—and from what I could see, his children had inherited this distinguishing trait."

I let out a little gasp. I just heard something about big feet. Where was that?

Leigh continues. "The caption under the photograph read, 'Annika and Leonid Markovic with their two sons, Grigory and Igor, survive a devastating explosion. Twin sister, Anastasia, was sadly lost.'"

"So, what are you saying, John Chi?" I ask while I scribble the names of the Markovic family.

"I am taking a leap of faith. Perhaps poisoning and terror started with the older brother, Igor, and continued until Grigory reached adulthood."

"You think he's still out, don't you?"

"No one knows exactly what he looks like. We must keep our eyes and ears open. He is mine if we find him."

"I think you may have to get in line for that one."

Chapter 31

Washington, D.C.

Sergei left the hotel soon after the encounter with Lily Robinson and after tending to his wounds. The scratches on his face still burned even after he had washed his skin with cold water. The mirror's reflection showed the claw marks deep into his cheeks, almost as if they had been caused by a wild animal. Using some of Alexis's make-up, Sergei tried to conceal the appearance of the red marks. Yet the wounds oozed, and the pain in his left leg where the heel of the stiletto had stabbed into his flesh throbbed. Sergei pulled up his pant leg and saw the quarter-sized bruise surrounding a dime-sized puncture, blood trickling down his ankle. Another cold compress soothed the discomfort, but his mind burned at the raven-haired woman who marred his face, and said she had killed his brother.

Sergei had one more job to do for the Tsar. Although the two had never been formally introduced, he was aware of the Tsar's reputation. Orders had always come down to Sergei from others in their organization, yet he hoped that the Tsar would reveal himself one day. Perhaps once Sergei completed his mission.

Although Sergei called several times, Alexis had not answered her phone. The thought crossed his mind that maybe it was Alexis who had betrayed him. How else would the woman in the stilettos know where to find him?

Alexis had spent the last day holed up, trying to figure out an escape from her current nightmare. There was none. She closed her eyes, knowing she would have to face Sergei, or he would hunt her down and kill her. Not that it mattered all that much. Alexis peered in the mirror and saw the spider just below her right hip. She could not erase the tattoo that had heralded her treachery, or the evil that ran through her blood, a gift of Markovic. As his daughter, she deserved to die.

For some time now, Alexis had been disturbed about the meeting she and Sergei had with the burly man from Moscow. His mission for them had been direct and clear. They were given orders to travel to the Middle East to pick up a scorpion toxin. Alexis had hated going to the dusty hovel, and she had felt sorry for the schoolteacher. Her relationship with Scottie had softened her just a little, and she now shunned some of Sergei's behaviors that she'd not seen before—cold, harsh, and unsympathetic. He had wanted to kill the schoolteacher on the spot, but Alexis begged him to spare the man's life for the sake of the children. She'd argued that they had gotten what they came for. Sergei conceded and left the terrified man a cyanide pill, telling him they would return and murder all the children at the schoolroom, and their families, if the teacher talked. It was one thing to kill adults, but Alexis wanted no part in killing children.

Their contact in Moscow had had little to say at the time, and she never saw him again. His dark hair, heavy beard, and thick glasses were a barrier to those around him. Out of fear, Alexis dared not look directly into his face. She had stared at the ground and at his feet, which were unusually large. She had seen large feet like that before, on one man, and one man only. And that was Markovic. But Sergei said Markovic was dead. Still terrified, in her dreams she imagined he had escaped his grave, would find her, and drag her back down to hell to keep him company.

It was time to answer Sergei's call. Alexis was well aware that he could kill her for her temporary desertion, but more significantly, she feared that he would harm her mother. She'd led him directly to Adrienne in Reims when she begged him to let her say goodbye. But one alternative she considered was that she could kill Sergei first.

"*Da*, Sergei?"

"Alexis, I have tried to call you several times," he said. Alexis thought his speech sounded strange, perhaps a little slowed.

"Sergei, are you all right? You sound different."

"I feel weak and need help."

Alexis worried that this could be a trick. Maybe he was enticing her to meet with him to kill her. She listened and spoke.

"What do you want?"

"Meet me at the National Air and Space Museum at 5:00 this afternoon. I have one more job to do before we go back to Russia."

His words made Alexis freeze. She would die here before she would go back to Russia. But if Sergei was weak, she might be able to push him over the edge—literally.

"*Da*. Where in the museum?" She could hear him coughing and struggling to breathe.

"The Skylab exhibit." He hung up the phone.

Sergei Petrikov felt his muscles tighten and noticed that the blood continued to drip from his nose. The inflamed scratches on his face oozed. He took a cool cloth and held it to his cheeks to quell the pain. One more assassination for his country, and then one more for his family's honor. Curse the woman who did this to him, who killed his brother. He would track her down and kill her too.

Jean Paul waited for Parker to meet him outside the hotel in the busy National Mall. He pulled the note he found in Sergei's pants pocket and reexamined it. It had been in Russian, but after scanning it with a translate app on his phone, he knew a meeting was going to take place later this afternoon. He picked up his mobile and called Chad.

"Chad. One more thing. Have someone who speaks Russian meet me at the National Air and Space Museum at 5:15 this afternoon."

"You got it. I'll have ops send someone over. Hey, guess who's back in action but in a new capacity?"

"Who?"

"Jackson Scott. Not sure if he's around, but you remember him, right?"

"*Merde*, I thought he was dead."

"We all did," Chad said.

"Parker is with me, but be on alert for backup," JP said and hung up the phone.

"Hey, boss, guess who else is coming to this party? Taz Chernsky. Been checking out his calendar, and X marks the spot," Parker said, pointing the way. "Glad we're leaving doc Robinson out of this one. It's going to be a fucking shoot-out like the OK Corral."

JP shook his head. He hoped it wouldn't come to that, but he wasn't surprised that Chernsky was headed in the same direction. Capturing, not assassinating, Sergei Petrikov was the plan. What they wanted was more information if they could squeeze it out of him. Robinson had jumped the gun.

The two operatives arrived at the formidable

cement and glass structure late in the afternoon. They waited outside the National Mall entrance looking for the interpreter en route from the Agency. JP wondered if Scottie would be meeting them, and although they'd never met in person, the dark-haired man with the blue-green eyes assumed he could identify the Agency's interpreter by the description of his clothes—a three-piece suit—and a pin on the lapel of his jacket. While JP knew that Sergei spoke English, he wanted a field operative present who could speak fluent Russian.

Seeing no one they recognized, JP and Parker walked up the front steps, flashed their credentials to the guards at the door, and passed through security. Most of the museum was by now empty, but there were still some visitors gathered in the first-floor atrium. JP and Parker assumed that Petrikov would want to make contact in a relatively secluded area in the building. A clandestine meeting followed by an innocuous exit with the remaining visitors. JP hoped they weren't too late.

Once inside, JP and Parker scanned the first floor and blended into the thinning crowd. Fully aware of their surroundings, they walked through the Milestones of Flight moving around the Mercury Friendship 7 spacecraft, passed the Viking Lander, and walked toward the west Gallery that held the multiple flight simulators, realizing their target could be anywhere in this over 161,000 square foot space.

Sergei was already up on the second level and waiting for his mark. Sequestered in the Skylab exhibit, he had not seen or heard from Alexis since the phone call earlier. His watch ticked past the designated hour, and sweat drenched the wristband. He mopped his forehead. Time was running out. Each breath had become more difficult, and the continuous drip of blood from his nose had not stopped. Taking the escalator up to the second floor had been a challenge. Now, Sergei wasn't sure that he would make it out of the museum and to the airport to catch his flight to Russia. Not able to wait any longer, he left the confines of the Skylab, and took the down escalator, clinging to the side rails, to the first level near the Independence Avenue entrance. Sergei hoped that Alexis would be there to see him through.

Alexis had already reached the museum sometime earlier and had been hiding in one of the flight simulators. She wanted to get in ahead of Sergei to make sure she wasn't being set up. A few children popped in and out of the exhibit, but soon their parents shooed them out, making preparations to leave the museum. Finally, she exited exhibit 103 and headed east down the corridor toward the Skylab.

Before reaching the end of the corridor, Parker

looked back east over the path they had just walked, and saw a man standing by the Skylab Orbital Workshop. He wore a gray tweed sports jacket over black slacks and carried a briefcase. Parker tugged at JP's arm, causing him to turn. His eyes landed on the man in Parker's sights. It was Taz Chernsky, the ambassador from Jokovikstan. JP knew that he must be Petrikov's contact, so they moved off behind the Spirit of St. Louis and waited for Sergei to appear. As the floundering Russian neared the first floor, a man with blond hair wearing a three-piece suit and an American flag lapel pin entered the atrium from Independence Avenue. Scottie was in the wrong place at the wrong time.

Disoriented, Sergei stepped off the escalator, bumped into Scottie, and held on to him, assuming the man meant to attack him. Sergei moved the man's neck into the crook of his arm and held him like a shield. The Russian was delirious and had difficulty discerning what was real and what was imagined. Alexis could now see Sergei across the corridor. He appeared unsteady yet had a familiar form draped in front of him. As she cautiously approached, her heart exploded in panic. There was a gun in Sergei's hand.

"Sergei, stop. What are you doing?" Alexis cried out.

"Stay back, stay back," he shouted in Russian and in English.

Parker kept his eyes on Taz Chernsky, who was now frozen in place, while he and JP moved closer to Sergei and his human shield. On the second floor, a man who had been hiding, watched the events unfold like a grade B spy movie. Although this was one loose end that needed to be tied up, he decided it was more important to escape the chaos. He quickly walked down to the far end of the museum and trotted down the stairs, his large feet providing a secure platform for his burly frame. Unnoticed, he slipped out the emergency exit door, setting off the alarm. Startled by the sound, Sergei jerked his head around and started shouting.

"Do not move, nobody move," Petrikov shouted in Russian. The man in his arms repeated the words out loud in English, then spoke to Sergei in Russian.

"Let's just put the gun down, nice and quiet like," Scottie said. Sergei only increased his grip and pressed the gun into the side of his hostage. Although he was weak, the gun gave him a distinct advantage.

JP whispered to Parker, "I think I can get a shot and take him out. Cover me."

Parker aimed his gun at Chernsky while JP crept closer to Sergei and Scottie. As he was about to squeeze off a round, Alexis raced up to Sergei, ignoring his threats, and blocked JP's view.

Sergei raised the gun and aimed the tip of the barrel into the struggling hostage. "Stop there. I will shoot him; I will shoot the fucking bastard."

Alexis screamed, "No, no, not my Scottie, my Sasha!" Heart pounding, desperate to save Scottie, she rammed into Sergei, causing him to fire the gun.

Jackson Scott squirmed free and fell to the ground, allowing Sergei to stagger back out the exit door, still brandishing the gun. JP looked to fire off one round, but scared onlookers now scattered near the exit door blocking a clear shot.

Seeing Alexis sprawled out in front of him, Scottie gathered her limp body, pulled her close, and cradled her in his arms, blood soaking onto the front of his suit. Alexis stared at his eyes and tried to speak.

"Scottie, it's you; it's really you." She choked. A thin stream of red liquid trickled from the side of her mouth. "Was it a lie, was it all a lie?" Her cough splattered red droplets in his face.

"No. Alexis. It was all real. I loved you. I still love you. Hang on. Don't give up," Scottie said and kissed her forehead. His voice cracked as he tried to keep it together.

"Better this way." And Alexis closed her eyes for the last time.

Scottie couldn't find a pulse and sat down fully on the cold floor. He bit back the tears and grabbed his belly, thinking of his own gunshot wound. Alexis had tried to keep him warm and stem the blood draining from his body before the Russian Intelligence stole her out of the car and left Scottie for dead, only to be rescued by friendly operatives.

Parker raced over to where Ambassador Chernsky had been crouching to avoid gunfire. The agent secured him and nodded to JP, who was on the phone with Chad telling him to send in the backup, and an ambulance. He signaled to the growing number of museum security guards to clear the area of any remaining visitors and indicated that he would take control of the scene. Then JP jogged over to where Scottie and Alexis were sprawled on the floor before following Sergei out the door.

"Jesus Christ, *mon ami*. You must be Jackson Scott. You know we all thought you were dead."

"I was, well, almost. Just got back to the States only last week to do some translation and interpretation work for the Agency." His face was pale and his eyes watery.

"Sorry about Alexis. She tried to save you," JP said, putting his hand on Scottie's shoulder and looking toward the exit where Sergei escaped.

At that moment, they both heard another gunshot outside the museum. They had expected that Sergei would have dropped by now, but it was clear that the amount of poison given by Lily Robinson had not been enough.

JP ran, pushed open the glass doors, and saw Sergei on the ground, his body piled on top of another body—collateral damage. The agent could only hope to keep this all contained. He pulled his gun out of his holster and approached the bodies cautiously. He swallowed hard. JP recognized the woman's shoes.

Chapter 32

Washington, D.C.

I know JP asked me to stay in my room, but I overheard him talking to Parker about going to the National Air and Space Museum, so I thought I'd check it out. I'm feeling much better now. Probably just a hairline fracture of a single rib. The extra-strength acetaminophen I took earlier for the pain has already kicked in.

Before I left my room, I called Kelley for an update on our toxicology consultation service and, more importantly, to check on Rose. Kelley told me that she was still very shaken. Her usually bubbly self was subdued, and Kelley's worried about her. Rose remains traumatized by her mother's car accident, her childhood abandonment, and this most recent abduction has compounded her depression and anxiety. Kelley's recommending that she see a mental health counselor. I agreed with him, and when I get back to Boston, I'll get more involved. The demon who took her during an otherwise blissful outing is still out there. I'm sure he's suffering, so I hope when JP finds him, he finishes him off.

I hear those words reverberate through my brain and feel disgusted with myself. How is it that I have become so vengeful? I can hardly recognize the doctor trapped in this body. Fatigue and intermittent nausea have plagued me over the last few weeks. The stress has exacerbated my stomach issues, and I need more antacids to quell the discomfort. Concentration has become difficult, too, and I find my thoughts meander aimlessly. Focus, Lily. Drill down with the fine focus and come back to your comfort zone.

The hotel where I'm staying has put me in the middle of all the beauty in D.C. Secluded in the Southwest waterfront, the distant Tidal Basin fills the view outside my window, and I imagine the spring when the cherry trees would have been in full pink bloom. It's a lovely afternoon for a walk in the National Mall, and I leave my room looking for an end to this chapter of my life.

What's this? I have to laugh to learn that my hotel's only a short distance from the International Spy Museum. This formidable steel and glass structure towers above L'Enfant Plaza. How would it be if I ask JP and Parker if they'd like to tour the Spy Museum with me? Is there information hidden in there we could learn from? I linger for a minute and sit on the metal platform supporting the bright red letters spelling out SPY. I make a quick call to Logan, who tells me that he'd like me to come to his place to review a case he suspects could be a poisoning that was initially missed. I tell him we'll do that later. I continue on my walk past the Spy Museum and down 12th street. From there, I can easily get to Independence Avenue, and I'll be right there at the Air and Space Museum. My phone rings. It's John Chi.

"Hello, my friend. What's happening?"

"Lily Robinson, I always find your choice of words perplexing. Where are you now?"

"I'm taking a walk in our nation's capital and enjoying the fresh air. Why do you ask?"

"The chatter has picked up on the Tsar. He is close, Lily Robinson. Situational awareness. Pay attention to every detail of your surroundings. I will be in touch." And just like that, he hangs up the phone. I think Dr. Leigh likes being a little mysterious.

One moment to look around me—Tsar, are you near? No, only ordinary appearing people enjoying a beautiful afternoon—nothing ominous. But I'll heed his advice. If John Chi Leigh suspects that there may be a danger, I'll keep a close eye on everything and everyone.

Up ahead, a tall spire, Ad Astra, the polished stainless steel sculpture by the artist Richard Lippold, touches the sky, its triple star-like cluster gleaming in the fading sun. A man hurries toward me. Why would he be in such a rush on a lovely afternoon? His full beard and thick dark glasses obscure his face, yet he looks at me and nods. I can't help notice his unusually large feet. Wait, both John Chi and Rose told me about seeing a man with uncommonly big feet. I turn to follow him, but he has disappeared into the throngs of tourists. Where in my memory have I seen other men with such a distinctive characteristic? That fact should be right where I can easily access it, but not these days. My mind feels blinded by some treacherous fog.

When I get to the bottom stair of the Air and Space Museum entrance, I see a man stagger out of the building. He looks sick or injured from the way he's moving. I tread closer to help him before he falls down the steps. My God, it's Sergei Petrikov! He's still alive. I thought he might be dead by now, but it seems that my new experimental poison was not very effective. I move in close and confront him.

"Sergei Petrikov, I thought I killed you." My voice is harsh, and I can see the startled look in his eyes. The scratches on his face are oozing, and he's clearly disoriented. I'm torn. A moment of self-reflection. There's too much time to think on this. Not good. The physician part of me is moved by his suffering, and I feel I should do something to help. Yes, reach out and help him. Let the authorities handle his crimes.

"Who is there? Who is talking to me?" he asks. He squints his eyes and focuses on my face. "You bitch, you did this to me." I can see recognition in his eyes.

He falls toward me, grabs my shoulders, throwing me off balance. I feel the tip of a gun in my belly. I didn't see that before. I never would have engaged if I thought he had a gun. He squeezes the trigger, and there's a soft pop, but I manage to get in one good stab at him with the heel of my bootie before I drop. We both fall to the ground, Sergei pinning me in place on the concrete. Sticky red liquid leaks from my body, and Sergei grunts as I try to move him. Nausea creeps up my throat, my heart now beating time and a half. I'm going into shock.

I'm not sorry for the end. It was worth the risk. I always said that the good of the many outweighs the good of the one. I pray that my Rose stays safe. I only wish I had more time to get to know her, to mentor her, to love her. Kelley will have that job now. He'll stand by her and take good care of her. And JP, my love, I hope you can forgive me for dying and for betraying our love. I'm so tired. But I must do one more thing before my final rest.

It'll take all the strength I have left. Sergei's body leaves me buried underneath, blood trickling from my abdomen, soaking us both. Blood drips from his nose and mouth, and I can feel his dying twitches. We are a pile of mangled killers vying on different sides of the equation, the net of which is now zero. I struggle to pull my body up and around so I can whisper in his ear. He smells of death, and terror, and I know that scent all too well.

"You goddamn bastard. Rest in hell with your brother and his comrade. You asked my name. It's Lily Robinson."

My mouth tastes like sawdust, and my throat is sore. Is this what death feels like? Darkness punctuated by beams of brightness. The last thing I remember is tangling with Sergei Petrikov. There was a gunshot, then pain in my belly. I remember stabbing him with my boot heel—the ones that deliver poison. Parker's a fan of these shoes too. Actually, these booties are the best weapon I own. Or owned? Pure stealth. No one sees it coming. And after I kicked that bastard hard in the leg, all I could see was blackness, and all I could feel was the warm ooze soaking my blouse.

I'm okay with death. In some ways, it brings peace and quiet. There's little conflict once you cross the River Styx and leave the Earth behind. Will I see Sergei on my journey down the river? I know he's gone too, and I keep my dead eyes open and look for him and his brother Maxim as I ferry along. This time I used a fast-acting poison. My poison, a gift from Omair, is inspired by the mythical sea monster Charybdis. She created an inescapable whirlpool driving the sailors closer to Scylla, the monster with the face and breast of a woman. I took the charybdotoxin from the freezer of the scorpion wrangler when I was in the Middle East and saved it for later use. I loaded it in the syringe within my shoe, just as a precaution. *Leiurus quinquestriatus hebraeus*—not a mythical sea monster, just a deadly scorpion whose toxin blocks cell channels. To live, those channels must allow ions to flow freely through the strait without getting trapped by the monsters that lurk on the rocks bound to either shore.

My mind is still fuzzy. Have I reached the end of my journey? I force my eyes to open wider. Still, dark and light blur my sight. I strain to get my bearings and hear the beeps of medical devices and see the IV snaking from the back of my hand. I search the corners of this white space. Am I in a hospital room? Is this real, or is this a dream? Did no one pay the ferryman? I close my eyes and try opening them again. I will blink my way into consciousness, wherever that leads me. There, in the corner of the room, is JP sitting in a chair and staring out the window. He cannot be on the River Styx with me. He dwells with the living. I mumble.

"JP." It's hard to get the words out. They feel stuck.

"*Ma chérie*, you are awake." He brightens, pops up from his chair, and those lovely creases in his face deepen. I can see it now. A smile forces his cheeks to appear rounder.

JP takes my hand and moves closer to me.

"Shh, shh, shh, do not try to talk." He puts his forefinger over my lips. "We almost lost you. The doctors were not sure when you would regain consciousness."

I feel disoriented. I'm still not convinced this is not a dream.

"JP," I say, clasping his hand. It feels solid. "What happened?"

"Lily. You decided to take a walk to the National Air and Space Museum. *Oui*, you must have heard Parker and me talking about it." He squeezes my hand again and kisses the top of my forehead. "*Mais*, Sergei is dead; you got to him before we did."

I'm quiet again. I remember now. That was the man who threatened my Rose.

"Jean Paul, I'm sorry. So sorry."

"This has to stop." His face looks tired and worn now. The brightness has disappeared.

"I haven't been myself lately. I lost my focus."

"*Oui*, my Lily. Let us talk about this later. I just buzzed the doctor, and he will be in here in a moment to discuss your, your situation."

My situation? Oh God, I hope all my organs are intact. I reach under the bedsheet and search my abdomen feeling for a clue. A large bandage around my belly greets my hand. That's where the pain started. I remember that. I try to wiggle my toes.

"Good morning, Ms. Laurent," says the doctor standing in the doorway, then turning to JP, he adds, "and Mr. Lavigne. How are you feeling?" His hair is gray at the temples, and he looks formal in his white lab coat, his hands in the pockets. I feel disoriented by those names. Is the doctor talking to JP and me?

"Still feeling confused? That's understandable after what you've been through."

"A little groggy. Please, what happened?" I search JP's eyes.

"Well, your husband brought you in after you were shot during an attempted robbery near the Air and Space Museum. The police assure us that they have the situation well in hand and everything's under control. The man was deranged from what we heard. Deranged people carrying guns is something this country has to come to terms with. It must have been very scary for you."

My husband, an attempted robbery? What's he talking about? I look over at JP, who has raised eyebrows indicating for me to follow along. Those names. Yes, yes, they are our code names for travel.

"We removed the bullet from your abdomen. You lost a lot of blood, so we gave you several units of red cells. You were already anemic before your gunshot wound."

A blood transfusion? This can't be good. All I can manage is "ahh."

"The bullet lodged in your liver. Now, we removed the damaged part. The good news about the liver is that it's one of the few organs that can regenerate."

His words fade in my ears as he gives me a lecture on liver regeneration. I close my eyes and try to focus—give myself a lecture. My liver. The liver owes its fame to its ability to detoxify those substances that enter our body—no matter how they get inside us. It holds the enzymes that champion drug metabolism. I'll worry about my liver later. I can hear again. I guess I'm lucky to be alive.

"You know, you're lucky to be alive. Lucky that your husband was right there soon after to call an ambulance and put pressure on the wound. Frankly, if he had not been there . . ."

Yes. If he had not been there, I would be dead. JP's right. I went too far. He rescues me once again. I squelch the thought. Focus, Lily.

"Thank you, doctor; when will I be able to travel and go home?" My voice sounds hoarse.

The surgeon looks at his bright white lab coat, flicks a bit of lint off the pocket, and arranges his pens. "There is one more thing," he says.

There's a long pause. So I wait while my heart rate picks up. I can see the images on the heart monitor as the gap closes between beats.

"I've already spoken with your husband. I'm very sorry, but you lost the baby," he finally says.

I'm stunned. Lost the baby? What baby? How's that possible? It's not possible. JP told me that he had a vasectomy years ago. Sometimes those reverse spontaneously or—oh God. This is Logan's baby! How could I be so stupid?

"Pregnant? Are you sure?" I spurt out in a tone of surprise and disbelief.

Yet, I can hardly get the words out. My mouth is so dry. Must be the atropine from the anesthesia, not the words I hear. I struggle to keep emotions under control, understanding that my hormones have had free reign these last weeks. I can't bear to look at JP's face. What must he think of me?

"Yes, your husband was surprised too," he says, looking over at JP. "You were only about two months along. The uterus was not damaged by the bullet, so you'll be able to have more children; that is if you want to," the surgeon says, feeling the tension in the room.

Thank God he stopped there. I don't want to hear anymore. I don't know what to say anyway. This is so unexpected but would explain the fatigue I've had and some of the nausea I experienced weeks ago.

"Thank you, doctor. If you don't mind, that's a lot of information, and I'm tired."

I am tired. I'm recovering from major surgery, a gunshot wound, and the loss of a baby I didn't know I was carrying. I'm desperately trying to block the tears that I feel welling in my eyes.

"Of course. I'll leave you two. You'll be here for a couple of days and then need some time at home to fully recover. If you like, I'll help with the transfer of care to a surgeon of your choice in Boston or wherever you go."

The man who has had to deliver all the news seems uncomfortable, shifting his weight from one foot to the other. He manages to nod his head and leaves my hospital room. I'm alone now with Jean Paul.

"JP, I don't—"

"Shush, you need to rest, my Lily. Close your eyes," he says and takes both my hands in his.

How is it that just the few words that took the doctor only seconds to say will change my life forever once again? Yet JP stands by my side physically, in this room, and figuratively, as my partner. The guilt I feel now, having betrayed our relationship, is overwhelming. I made an excuse of loneliness, of need, and of the anger I felt about Rose. I made an excuse. JP, I hope you can forgive me. You are my soulmate and the love of my life. I feel for you like no other. I will tell him all this when my mind clears, and my mouth leaves the desert to become an oasis once again. I will tell him all this when I can say that I am truly sorry and hope that he will forgive me. But how?

Now I feel myself drifting back into twilight, my mind muddled with pictures. I see the bright smiling child before he comes to rest on my autopsy table. He has a bat in his hand and stands at home plate. The baseball hurtles through the air at tremendous speed, missing the tip of the bat, and instead, strikes his chest dead center. Agitation of the heart—*commotio cordis*—a lethal disruption of the heart's rhythm. When a hard object strikes the chest just right, there's a 20-millisecond window to stop the heart. I can feel it. Another blow to my heart, just between beats. I've lost another child.

Chapter 33

Washington, D.C.

Ever since he landed in D.C., Dr. Leigh had been listening and watching. He had come to Washington to present a talk on mass spectrometry at the chemistry conference and had used the opportunity to follow up on his suspicions about the Tsar. The story about a madman with a gun who went on a rampage at the Air and Space Museum made front-page news. One innocent bystander was killed, another seriously wounded, and the gunman also died at the scene. In all cases, the names of the victims and the perpetrator were not disclosed. From all the chatter he gathered on the internet and from what he had learned of the recent events, Dr. Leigh was sure that the Tsar was right here. Ever vigilant, he continued to focus on people who fit the image he had crafted of the Poisoner-in-Chief.

A couple of days after the Air and Space Museum calamity, Leigh was on his way to attend the last day of the scientific conference when one man caught his eye. A thickset man with a long dark beard and dark hair wearing a brown suit and a satchel strung across his chest appeared along the path. His walk was not as energetic as it should be for a man only in the middle of his life, but his thick body and protruding belly reduced the pace he could otherwise manage. Leigh, appearing as a tourist, used the map of the Washington Metro to cover his face as the man came closer. The chemist could see that, despite the burly man's youthful hair color, he had a well-worn face and gunmetal eyes. Yet, it was his other distinguishing features that piqued Leigh's interest.

John Chi Leigh followed the burly man to the Metro Station Smithsonian stop. He was careful that he'd not been seen since he spotted his likely target on Independence Avenue after leaving the hotel. He widened the distance between the two of them, hoping his own dark glasses and baseball cap would make him a less familiar face. Leigh saw the man take his pass and swipe through the turnstile before heading toward the southbound Blue Line. Unsure of the man's final destination, the chemist followed suit, using the SmarTrip app on his phone to gain access to the train while keeping the burly man in his line of sight.

The two men took the escalator down to the platform housed within a cylindrical tunnel of cement squares and light. They waited at the stop standing one car's distance from one another, the burly man oblivious to his pursuer. Leigh kept his face down, focused on the terracotta hexagon tiles, only turning his head occasionally to make sure his target was still there. Soon he heard the roar of the train as it approached the station. Leigh made sure the burly man got on the train before he did and then entered the same car, but at the far end. He disappeared within the crowd, standing shoulder to shoulder with busy riders using public transportation to navigate the city. The chemist dipped his head down, staring at the floor, slipping sideways glances at his adversary while the train rattled on to the next six stops. Leigh checked the Metro map and saw that only five more stops remained until Reagan National Airport and wondered if there was a waiting connection there.

The train whizzed from Arlington Cemetery and headed for the Pentagon. When they reached the station, the burly man surprised Leigh and got off the train unexpectedly. Leigh, stuck in the middle of the car, pushed through the crowd to reach the exit before the doors closed. Determined to keep the burly man in his sights, his gut told him that the man he was pursuing was the Tsar. All the information he'd gathered over the years pointed to this man, and his reemergence on the scene gave Leigh another chance to bring him in.

The Tsar rode the escalator to the entrance and exited the station at the southeast side of the Pentagon. Since Leigh was flying without a safety net, he paused and thought about breaking protocol. Now more of a chemist than the stealthy operative he'd been in his younger days, he was still capable of tracking down a man who was in the process of disrupting the world order, but some additional coverage seemed prudent at this nexus. So, Leigh called Lily Robinson—and there was no answer. A sinking feeling entered his chest as he was about to replace his phone in his pocket. And then it rang.

It was JP who had seen the flash of Dr. Leigh's number on Lily's phone and called him back, thinking it could be critical. Surprised to hear JP's voice, Leigh nonetheless explained the situation and the urgency. He asked JP to come to the Pentagon—with backup. A car would reach this destination much quicker than the Metro, as long as the traffic cooperated. Leigh would do his best to keep his eye on the target and take action if he could. In the mind of John Chi Leigh, there were no lingering doubts about the identity of the man he trailed. Even with no confirmed sightings of the assassin known as the Tsar, many swore that he existed and attributed the plethora of assassinations that took place during the reign of the KGB to this mythical shape-shifter. And not until Leigh uncovered the curious article in an old newspaper from Moscow had he been so sure he was right on track.

Once outside the Pentagon, Leigh kept a

healthy distance from his quarry, quietly tracking his prey, looking for opportunity. They walked underneath the canopy along the concourse. Standing at the side of the gray-brown facade, the burly man stopped and waited. Within minutes, he was greeted by someone wearing an army uniform. Leigh could not clearly see the face of either man, but the person in the uniform stood taller. He edged a little closer to overhear their conversation, but without the cover of a crowd, the chemist was at risk of being exposed. Wait and watch would have to do.

After a few more minutes of exchange, a tour group strayed near the two men, and the Tsar took the opportunity to remove a small spray bottle and aim for the face of the military officer. Leigh could see the officer fall to the ground, startling the tour group, while the Tsar put the container in his satchel and moved back from his victim. Faced with a choice, Leigh decided on confrontation. He approached the burly man, keeping his distance, wary of the spray he assumed held poison.

"It is you, the phantom Tsar, come out of retirement?" Leigh asked, startling the man.

The brusque response was only in Russian, and rather than engage Leigh for fear that his time was running out, the burly man pushed him aside to move past, but not before the chemist grabbed at his hand and scratched him. After looking at the deep scratch, the Tsar turned around to Leigh, challenged his gaze, and then struck the chemist, knocking him to the ground. The growing commotion attracted more onlookers, and seeing his time ticking, the Russian man ran toward the Metro stop and disappeared down the escalator. Minutes later, JP and Parker arrived and found Leigh still down on the ground. He was catching his breath.

"Dr. Leigh, what happened here?" JP asked, scouting the scene and pushing the group of curious spectators aside.

"Do not worry about me. Follow the thickset Russian man with a long dark beard. I believe he will escape to Russia. Check all the airports. He is wearing brown pants and a brown jacket, and he has a deep scratch on his hand. Find him; he is the Tsar," Leigh said, still breathing hard.

JP understood immediately. If he could catch the Tsar, he could bring him in for the deaths of Senator Steinman, President Khan, and even Pixie Dust. He asked Parker to call for medical help and stay to look after the military officer and Dr. Leigh. JP got back into the car and, thinking Leigh could be right about the Tsar's escape plans, he headed straight for the Dulles International Airport. But the morning rush hour slowed his journey, causing him to curse at the traffic and pound his fist on the horn. He called Chad and asked him to put out a description of the burly man and have all flights to Russia held until he got there.

JP reached the airport in time to catch one flight about to leave the gate for Moscow. Using his authority, he managed to delay the plane until he checked all the rows of passengers. No one fit the description. Disappointed, he left the A Gates section and headed toward the B Gates to check on the next plane to Moscow. His eyes scanned for beards, glasses, and even all the thickset clean-shaven men. He walked past a gate for a flight to Jokovikstan when it occurred to him that maybe he was thinking of this all wrong. He followed his instincts and boarded the plane.

JP passed through the first-class section eyeing all the passengers, and then proceeded to the middle of the cabin. Still, no one fit the description until he came to the rear of the plane. There, in a window seat, was a large, bearded man wearing gloves and a light overcoat. JP requested his passport, which specified he was from Belarus, and then asked him to remove his gloves. The agent held his breath, thinking it had been a long time since Pixie Dust's death, and finally, he would exact revenge for his former lover. Leigh had indicated that the Tsar would have a large scratch on one of his hands, and JP waited impatiently while the man took his time to remove the gloves.

"Oh, *allez*," he said, waving his hand in rapid succession.

JP grabbed the remaining glove and pulled it off. He examined both hands carefully, turning from the palm to the dorsal surface. There was nothing. No scratches of any kind.

JP's face dropped. "Christ, *merde*," he said. The woman in the adjacent row flinched at his loud voice.

The agent decided to take a picture of the passport with his phone and, discouraged, left the plane. He monitored the airport for several hours, and empty-handed, he called Parker for an update. Accepting temporary defeat, JP returned to the operations base in the city.

With the plane now safely on its way to Jokovikstan, the flight attendant in first class apologized for the delay and indicated that a cocktail would be served shortly before the meal. She'd be coming around to take orders. The old woman in the fourth row leaned her seat back and looked out the window, her stomach feeling queasy. Her blue-gray hair curled around her ears, and her lipstick was unusually bold for someone that age. The flight attendant took her order for a meal—dry crackers and a ginger ale. She wasn't feeling well enough for anything more. Once the seat belt light went off, the elderly lady excused herself from the window seat, her cane in hand, and limped to the lavatory near the cockpit door. After closing the door behind her, she removed her gloves and saw the oozing scratch. She had done her best to rinse it with copious amounts of water, but she understood fully that there was no guarantee she had gotten all of what her adversary had given her. She could feel the irregular heartbeats within her chest and generalized weakness closing in. With a stopover in Istanbul, she wasn't sure there was enough time to make it back to Jokovikstan before the poison would take its final toll. Yes, poison—a strategic scratch might just cause her to die on the flight.

The old Hong Kong chemist, she thought. *He is still around.*

The woman sniffed and pulled the tourniquet a little tighter around her wrist. Better to lose her hand than her life. She put the delicate gloves back on and left the lavatory to return to her seat. She wobbled slowly past the flight attendants who were tucked away on the other side of the space outside the cockpit, working on preparing meals. She nodded, clutching her chest.

"Are you feeling all right?" one of the attendants asked the old woman.

In a frail voice, she answered, "I have some difficulty breathing. Do you have oxygen on board?"

"We do. Why don't you sit up here near us, and we'll set it up. Should we see if there's a doctor on the flight?"

"No, I just need to stay still and close my eyes." Her heart rate had slowed, and there was a creeping pain in her abdomen.

The two flight attendants smiled, got out the oxygen cylinder from the overhead compartment, and helped the old woman put the mask on over her nose and mouth. They notified the captain that they might have to make an emergency stop for a medical intervention. Once the woman closed her eyes and leaned back in her seat, the attendants spoke to each other in low voices about the frail, thin old woman who had uncommonly large feet.

Chapter 34

Boston and the Cottage

Chad told me he would come by the condo today to let me know what's happened. I'm staying in Boston to have my wounds taken care of locally. The story my hospital has is that I was the unfortunate victim of an attempted robbery on the streets of Washington, D.C. My colleagues are quite shocked, told me I travel far too much, and said they would help cover my clinical duties until my return. Dr. Kelley was particularly shaken given the experience he and Rose had. He's convinced that D.C. is just too violent and attributes its chaos to the political upheavals we have experienced over the last few years. We both agreed not to tell Rose any of the details just yet, because she's coping with so much now. He tells me her depression's improved with medication and therapy and that she looks forward to meeting with me. I'd be more than happy for her to come by my place so I can get a chance to know her better.

My medical leave will be for at least eight to twelve weeks. I could use the time off to get my life back together. Chad isn't the only visitor I can expect. I've had many calls since my return.

JP told me he'd take me to my cottage for the weekend before he disappears again, and Logan's promised to give me the details of the recent autopsies he's done for us. My phone's ringing, and I see it's Chad. I can get up from the couch to meet him at the door. My incision's sore but manageable.

"Chad, so good to see you again."

"I'm glad to hear you say that, Dr. Robinson. After everything we put you through, I wasn't sure if you'd ever talk to me again." He's wearing a soft smile, working his way up to something bigger. I think he's tentative regarding my response.

"No, look, I'm fine. My body's still intact," I say, holding my hand over my abdomen, "and in time, I will be good as new. My mind, on the other hand, may need a little more work." I return the soft smile and show him to the gray chenille sofa. "Can I get you something to drink?"

"Just a glass of water. Should I worry about drinking anything in your presence?" he laughs.

"Stay on my good side, and it shouldn't be a problem." He gets it and relaxes back into the couch while I return to the kitchen. I have some bottled water on the counter so I can avoid reaching and stretching for glasses. "Here you go."

"Thanks, Robinson."

"So, I know I missed a lot. What can you tell me? Did we get all the bad guys?"

"Yes and no. From what we were able to piece together, and much of this, you already know. President Khan was about to finalize a deal with the U.S. regarding the rare earth minerals, and Deputy Secretary Andrews was the contact as a member of the Interior Department. But the Russians wanted the deal stopped so they could control the minerals at their source. They paid off Andrews to stall the deal on our side until they killed Khan."

"And Trileaflet?" I ask.

"That's where it really gets interesting. Trileaflet was a convenient subsidiary of Global Tectonics that gave the masterminds of this plot a way to eliminate Khan, then later Steinman. Marina likely slipped the information about her husband's planned surgery during pillow talk to Thornton, and Thornton leaked that info as a matter of gossip. That gave Khan's adversaries a means for assassination that would have appeared as a natural death. Since Trileaflet was a company they also controlled, they had access to their weapon of choice—a poison-ridden valve implant. They banked on a quick cremation, but Marina's steadfast refusal was something they didn't anticipate."

"And Thornton?"

"Our president fired his ass. Frankly, I don't think he knew what he was in the middle of."

"Poor Steinman. Once he found out what

Andrews was up to, Andrews had to eliminate him, or the plot to stop the deal would have been exposed. From what I learned, the senator threatened to take the matter to Intelligence and have them investigate Andrews," I say.

"We believe Ambassador Taz Chernsky was the middleman who arranged to have the tainted valve implant for Andrews to use in the case of Senator Steinman. Probably carried it in his diplomatic pouch and gave it to the sales rep."

"Right, we can attribute the death of Steinman to Andrews. But the death of Khan was orchestrated by the Tsar. Well, in some regards, he's responsible for both deaths. The Tsar created the encapsulated scorpion toxin."

My mind drifts a little. It's always about greed, power, money, or revenge.

"So, where do Sergei and Alexis fit in with this scheme?"

"Well, you figured out that they were the two who visited Omair and likely left him the suicide pill. They were sent to the Middle East on a mission by the person we assume was in command of the bigger picture—the master puppeteer himself—the Tsar. Alexis was by this time just a flunky in the organization, perhaps a cover for Sergei. Sergei's job here was to eliminate Andrews and Taz Chernsky. Loose ends."

"But JP said Chernsky was not harmed in the

Air and Space Museum, and you had to release him given his diplomatic status. He's back in Jokovikstan, yes?"

"Oh sure, he went back. But we heard through the grapevine that he was killed in a terrible auto accident. Bullshit, of course."

"I guess in a sense, he was assassinated too."

"We believe the ultimate goal was to slip a Russian sympathizer into power in Jokovikstan, and that person or persons reports to the Russian consortium that oversees Global Tectonics. Another one of its primary companies makes communication satellites. Remember we discovered that the metal in the implanted valve was manufactured using a newly discovered rare earth mineral called ziyantium?"

"I do. Logan was all over that."

"Yes he was, and it turned out that he was really quite helpful. Anyway, whoever gets a hold of the ziyantium in the mountains of Jokovikstan, controls the future."

"That was the bigger plan that Sergei alluded to. So are we going to track down this consortium to try and find the Tsar or the master puppeteer, as you say?"

"At this point, I'm happy to report that I feel confident in discussing the case more openly; I don't mean publicly, but at least pushing the ball into the court of another group at the Agency to follow the progress of Jokovikstan. Did you know that their new president will be sworn in at the end of the week? It should be interesting."

"Did Dr. Leigh return to Hong Kong?"

"Oh yes. You were not there for his little adventure."

"What do you mean?" I must have missed this when I was in the hospital.

"Leigh knew about the Tsar, maybe even crossed paths with him in his lifetime, but he, like everyone else, had not been able to identify him or track him down, and as you know, the Tsar went to ground like a fox ages ago."

"Yes, Leigh shared some of his recent findings with me. He felt certain he was on his trail."

"Exactly. But no one in the espionage community had heard about the Tsar for decades. However, Leigh was convinced he spotted him around the Smithsonian and tracked him to the Pentagon."

"What would he be doing at the Pentagon?"

"Turns out there was one more loose end. Maybe that was Sergei's job too, but since you killed him, someone else had to do it."

"Who was the person at the Pentagon?"

"A military officer who'd been in charge of some U.S. troops over in Jokovikstan keeping tabs on that lucrative mine in the mountains. We don't know for sure, but we assume he was either in on the deal somehow, but again, loose ends."

"What did he say?"

"He didn't. Dead. Another Novichok spray in the face. Good thing Leigh wasn't hit with that. We piled up enough bodies in Logan's shop."

"Jesus!"

"Yeah, right. Leigh swears that it was a hit by the Tsar. Put him right under our noses in the center of all the action. JP was on his tail too, but goddamn it, we lost him. Don't know how we screwed that up, Robinson, but we lost him." Chad shakes his head in disgust.

I'm quiet now, thinking about all that Chad's told me.

"So you don't know where the Tsar is? If, in fact, that's who he was."

"Leigh swears he was right on the Tsar's butt. JP chased him to the airport since we assumed he'd be heading back to the motherland. Sent out his description and monitored all flights leaving for Russia. Came up with a blank."

"Maybe he never went to the airport or Russia. Maybe he's laying low until things cool down."

"Maybe, but I think if he had the chance to get out after all this mess, he would," Chad says, sweeping his hair over his crown.

"It does sound like I missed so much," I say, truly sorry I wasn't there for all the action. Wait, am I really thinking that? Why am I not railing against the dark tide that I claim draws me out into a bottomless ocean?

"There's just a few more things. I'll let Logan

tell you about the autopsies. He can give you all the gory details. By the way, Lily, I'd like to keep him working with us. It makes any autopsies we need a little more undiscoverable, if you know what I mean. You don't object, do you?"

"Me? I can't believe I have a say in this, Chad. It's your shop. I'm just an occasionally hired hand."

"About that. JP thinks you need some time off. He said we're putting too much pressure on you, and you need more time to heal yourself and heal patients." He can see my eyes open wide and lips part. "Now, hold on. You're still part of the team, and we'll use you, but maybe in a different capacity. Just hold off for now and get better."

"Chad, no, please, let's talk about this." I protest.

"Not now, Lily. I promised JP you and I wouldn't have this conversation. I think we all need to be in a better frame of mind."

It's not often that Chad calls me Lily. I'll talk with JP about this.

"Ah, listen. I better get going now. You need to rest, doctor. My orders."

Chad shows himself to the door, and I'm left here to ponder. I know there's more to the story.

This morning, Kelley's promised to bring Rose over to see me. I'm excited to get to know this young woman beyond her role as a medical student. She has her whole life in front of her, and I hope to be there to see her grow. Serendipity that she attended my talk at a career fair in high school, which laid a path before her that she's chosen to follow. Finding out that she was thriving all the years I thought her dead, shows that she has stamina and strength. One day very soon, I'll tell her the story of her biological parents, two scientists who shared a strong bond of friendship and respect. Her father, a Nobel laureate who worked to make the world a better place, and her mother, well, her mother, is complicated.

They're at my door now.

"Hi, Dr. Robinson," Rose says, giving me a hug. I wince just a little. "Oh, so sorry. Kelley told me you got knocked over in a robbery near the museum and got hurt."

I can't even remember if I told Kelley that the robbery involved a gunshot wound to the abdomen. That's the trouble with lies. You have to keep track of them.

"It's okay, Rose. Come on in." I wink at Kelley and thank him for the flowers.

I show them into the living room and go to the kitchen to find a vase. Kelley comes to my rescue, finds one in the lower cabinet, fills it with water, and arranges the flowers before setting them on the coffee table. Rose is standing and looks lovely, her dark hair falling past her shoulders and her pale complexion highlighted with a neutral blush and lipstick. God, I think she's wearing stilettos.

"You've got a really nice place here," she says, twirling around the living room and looking out the expanse of windows overlooking the Boston skyline.

"Rose, how are you feeling? How's your head?"

Her eyes dart to Kelley, and he nods his head, indicating for her that it's okay to speak. Thank you, Kelley.

"Much better, thank you. I seem to have recovered from the mild concussion I got in D.C." Rose looks down, her voice becomes quiet, and I can see her hand shake a little. Kelley latches on to it. "Dr. Robinson, I'm sorry for all the tears these last few months. It's just been so hard with my mother's illness and—"

"How's your mother, by the way," I interrupt.

"Well, that's the good news. Her health has really improved. She's left the rehabilitation hospital. Of course, she'll need more therapy, but she can get that as an outpatient. Père Berger has arranged for some of the village ladies to help her, and of course, I've arranged for some additional live-in help. I'll visit whenever I can." She looks over at Kelley, and I notice they are now firmly holding hands.

"I'm glad for her, and for you, Rose. And

before I interrupted you, you were going to tell me how you're doing."

"Yes, well that. I'm much better. I started taking an antidepressant and going to regular therapy. It's really helped. Made me think about going into psychiatry."

I shoot Kelley a look from my side of the couch. "Rose, give medical school a chance to present all the options to you. But just so you know that from my perspective, your keen ability to observe details, solve puzzles and think a problem through would make you a wonderful pathologist. Don't give up on Kelley and me just yet," I say with a large smile.

"I know. Just a thought," she laughs.

I decide not to bring up her abduction by Sergei Petrikov. I'll take my cues from Rose going forward, and I'm reluctant to discuss her sister Bella or Alexis as she was known to us. It would be hard to tell Rose what I know about Alexis's life after the plantation. The details of that tale will have to wait for another time and place. If at all. And even then, who tells her the story or the lies. I can't be a party to that.

The three of us enjoy each other's company, and Kelley tells us that his parents will move closer to Boston. Right now, they're living in Pennsylvania but want to be closer to their son, and a daughter who happens to live in Brookline, just outside of Boston proper. Now that Kelley will become an attending physician next year, he wants a solid home life for himself and his family. I can only hope that Rose will be part of the plan.

After an hour, they depart, but not before I remind Kelley to contact me with any complex cases or if he just wants to talk. Not that I worry, he has a good head on his shoulders, and I'm confident that the service is running smoothly. I suppose that I'm feeling a little useless now because of my health. Not working in the lab or working for Chad's left me a little down, but I expect I'll bounce back mentally after I mend.

Another day of rest, and I'm already feeling stronger. I should be finishing up my course of antibiotics before the weekend, and the visiting nurse said my wound looks clean. I'm impatient to move on from this. Too much time on my hands to ruminate about what has been. Logan's driving up this morning. He's planning to see me on his way to Maine to wrap up the case. Looking back on our relationship, I'm disappointed I let anger cloud my judgment. Sometimes we do things in our lives out of exasperation, or loneliness, or just because we want to. I see I have a call from Kelley.

"Hey, everything all right?"

"Of course. I just want to run a quick case by you."

"Sure. What is it?"

"It's a pediatric case. A one-year-old came in with severe developmental delays. Over the past year, mom described the baby as a fussy eater, with occasional vomiting and not meeting the normal developmental milestones. There appeared to be some muscle weakness. The pediatrician got a CBC and found the baby was anemic. A microcytic anemia. We tested for lead, among other things, and the blood lead concentration was greater than 45 μg/dL."

"Oh wow, that's lead poisoning for sure. Has the child been admitted for chelation therapy?"

"Yes, absolutely. I explained to the parents that with levels this high, their child will need to have medicine that can grab onto the lead and remove it from the body."

"And they've located the source of the lead and had it removed."

"Well, that's why I'm calling. The house is not old and wasn't painted with lead paint, the faucet water tested negative, and the family's at a loss for how their child got lead poisoning."

"Those are the usual sources of exposure." I start to think back to Grigory Markovic's plan of replacing a large feeder pipe at the New York Hillview Reservoir with one lined with lead. The contamination of the water caused the death of a child named Evy Chandler, who was already burdened with sickle cell disease. It gives me an idea.

"Kelley, find out how the parents prepared the bottle with baby formula and get back to me."

"Okay. Will do," he says and hangs up the phone.

I'll wait until he calls me back to see if my hunch is correct.

That must be Logan at my door.

"Hey, come on in. Oh, thank you for the flowers. I'm afraid you're going to have to reach down and get a vase." Logan kisses me on the cheek and gingerly hugs me, knowing I'm still sore.

"No problem. You look good for a lady who was shot just a few weeks ago."

"Thank you. You can find the vases in this lower cabinet," I tell him, pointing out the way in the kitchen.

Logan helps himself and gets the flowers in water. He brings them into the living room and finds a bouquet already on the coffee table courtesy of Kelley and Rose.

"Ah, huh. I see I'm not your first admirer." He winks, breaks into a warm smile, and finally walks to the dining room to place the vase there.

I laugh.

"Those are from my fellow and one of the medical students."

"Sure, sure. So how are you feeling, Lily?"

"Much better, thanks. Tell me, did the autopsies reveal anything more than we already know?"

"The autopsy of Alexis Popov was one of the sad ones. Gunshot wound severed her hepatic artery, and she bled to death."

I'm not sure if Logan realizes that the bullet that struck my abdomen also sailed into the liver, but without hitting any vital arteries. I lost a lot of blood, and much more.

"The young woman was also addicted to cocaine. She had an enlarged heart, which goes with the territory, and there was just a start of some damage to her nasal septum from snorting the powder. Otherwise, she was pretty healthy. Oh, one other thing, she had a tattoo of a spider just below her right hip. Don't usually see too many spider tattoos."

I think back to Rose's story of the day she and her sister got their tattoos. I feel sadness. So many people died needless deaths.

"And Sergei Petrikov?"

"That's a little more complicated. Whatever you gave him, and I won't ask, caused a lot of internal bleeding. He was a mess when I opened him up. I told Chad I was going to sign that one out as death due to unknown poison."

"Thanks, Logan. In Petrikov's case, there were actually two poisons—one slow-acting and one quick-acting. He really didn't stand a chance."

"Remind me to always stay on your good side, Lily." There's a twinkle in his eyes—a color that compliments his blue jeans and sage green T-shirt.

"And one more thing, if I can be blunt. I still have the hots for you if you ever change your mind. But I have a feeling that you already have a guy."

My heart just pulls. I'm feeling vulnerable now, so Logan's revelation feels like getting wrapped up in a warm blanket. For a short time, I carried his baby—another secret buried in my soul. I think it would devastate him to know the truth.

"Logan, I don't know what to say. We've had this conversation before. I would still like to work with you. If you feel you can. I don't want either one of us to get hurt." I feel my face flush. He can see it too.

"Listen, I better get going. My *Rogue Angel* is waiting for me. Anytime you want to sail those intrepid waters, my friend, give me a call." He leans across the couch and kisses me softly on the lips. He and I both know that the chemistry's still there, but the flask must be stoppered. No more vapors can escape.

"Thank you, Logan."

He lets himself out, and once again, I'm all alone in the condo. I'll give Kelley a call to see if he's found anything more about the case.

"Hi, Kelley. It's Dr. Robinson. Were you able to get additional info on our baby with lead poisoning?"

"I was just about to call you. I did connect with the mother, and she said she's been boiling water for the powdered formula in an antique tea kettle."

"One that's lined with lead?"

"My thoughts exactly. I asked her to bring it into the lab, and we can find out for sure. Mom was kind of devastated. Here she thought she was doing a good thing by boiling the water first and getting rid of any bacteria."

"I hope baby does well, but there'll probably be long-term damage. And mom will feel guilty about having done this accidentally to her child."

Mothers nurture a child within their womb for nine months before birth and then for every day of their life until their last breath. It's our job to protect, love, and see that our baby thrives in the world. While every mother has that desire, sometimes circumstances interfere with that objective.

"Thanks, Kelley. Keep in touch."

I spend the rest of my day reading and catching up on all the academic work that has accumulated. Lisa's sent over much of the paperwork I need to attend to, and working off my laptop from home, I can keep up with email and my writings. I'm ready to sleep now. I expect JP will be up here tomorrow. Can't wait to see him. I'm just about to get under the covers and pull the sheets up to my chin when the phone rings. Who'd call me at this late hour?

"Hello."

"Dr. Robinson, did I wake you?"

"No, but I was just about to turn out the lights. Is everything all right?"

"Everything is fine. I am sorry I did not see you when you were in the hospital, but I had to get back to Hong Kong. I wanted to wish you well."

"Thank you. I heard you were chasing down the Tsar."

"Yes. Thank you for the San Bushman inspiration. I developed another poison, a cardiac glycoside, a bufotoxin to be exact, that can also be introduced through an innocuous wound, like a scratch. Only one field experiment. Not yet perfect."

"Only one field experiment? Ah, huh. How'd you know it was the Tsar?"

"Detective work, Lily Robinson. I shared with you the newspaper article about the Markovic family. How you balance on those slim heels is beyond me. It would be hard to step into your shoes."

"What, I don't follow you?"

"Change your clothes, your hair, your make-up, even your nose, but you cannot change your feet. Good night, Lily Robinson. I will see you at your cottage next summer. Your poison garden awaits me."

"Good night, John Chi Leigh." I hang up the

phone and wonder what that was all about. I'm tired, and I'll think about it tomorrow.

This morning brings sunshine and renewed energy. I remember getting a strange call from Dr. Leigh last night. I'll have to catch up with him next week. Umph returns to my body, and today I will go all out on my hair and make-up. There's a billowy summer skirt I can wear even though it's the end of the season. Paired with a blue polka dot blouse, the blue circles, bold and bright, catch the light. JP should be here in an hour.

"Good morning, my love." He's barely through the door, and I'm engulfed in his arms, our lips meeting in space. He pushes me back slightly and looks into my eyes.

"*Ma chérie*, you are looking well. Are you ready to go to your cottage for a quiet weekend with your spy?" He laughs, picks up my bag, and we take the elevator down to the garage. He'll drive my car to the coast.

The drive is punctuated with music, soft music from the Boston classical music station. Our conversation's mostly gossip. He tells me Agent Parker says hello, and he can't wait to go on another assignment with me. I'm curious to know more about my agency teammates. I ask him if Parker's married. JP says no, most of the men he works with aren't married. The risk to their partners or offspring would be too great. I'm quiet when he tells me this because I catch his meaning.

We reach the cottage and bring our things inside. JP's brought a cooler of food. I'll be interested to see what he's planned. After unpacking, we go out to the deck. The sky's so blue, only interrupted with a few puffy clouds that cloak the horizon. Now still and smooth like a mirror, the water bounces the sun onto our faces and a slight breeze picks up my hat. I grab it just in time and laugh. JP smiles; those creases on his cheeks deepen while his eyes sparkle.

"My Lily, do you want to go inside and sit down?" he asks, taking my elbow. We pass through the French doors and sit in the living room. White sofas flank both sides, and pillows provide the blue-green pop of color needed to spark joy.

"JP, we never really talked about the pregnancy." The words fall out of my mouth and almost startle me with their boldness. He moves closer to me on the couch and takes my hand.

"You asked me once if I ever loved anyone else. I did. I loved a woman who was bold and beautiful, smart and talented. But that relationship was not to be. I never imagined that I would ever find her match again. But I have, Lily. I found you. From our first assignment in Cambridge, where your doubts were all over your face, I think that was when I fell in love with you."

"What happened to the woman you loved before?"

"She died. I have kept her memory alive in my heart, but our love had burned out long before I met you. She told me that someone like you would come along, and she was right."

"Thank you for telling me this. It makes me feel closer to you. I'm so sorry I betrayed your trust."

"I have forgiven you, Lily. I already told you that. What I love about you is your free spirit. And I believe that you love me, too."

"More than anyone," I say, kissing him ever so softly, our hands intertwined.

He lifts me up, a thing he likes to do, and carries me into the bedroom. Sunlight beams through the air, a light shaft landing on the bed. JP unbuttons my blouse, taking his time. His hand delicately pushes my white lacy bra to the side, and his lips gently take my nipples into his mouth. My skirt comes off, and he traces my incision with his finger, followed by the touch of his lips. I feel him swell next to my body. He's ever so gentle, knowing that my wounds are not fully healed, so we satisfy each other with our hands and our mouths. After, I lie on his back, smelling his hair, feeling the heat from his flesh, and rest my head between his shoulder blades. I love this man—a special kind of love, bonded through danger and a shared sense of purpose, and of course, chemistry. Life's all about chemistry. Every thought, every emotion, and every feeling are merely a string of molecules put together in such a way that only God knows the code.

JP makes us a simple meal with a French baguette, *Fromager d'Affinois*, fruit, salad, and a quiche Lorraine that he picked up in a specialty shop on the way up.

Afterward, we have a coffee and relax, pretending to be an old married couple.

"Lily, I would like to watch the news. Would you please turn on your television?"

This is a first. "Good Lord, you really do sound like a normal man."

He laughs. "They have confirmed the new leader of Jokovikstan, and he is going to greet his people. We have been so involved with them, I want to see the newscast."

"Oh, of course. I'd like to see how that turned out, too."

We turn on the television, and I click through the stations until I find one that carries the latest international news. JP's calling Chad to make sure he's watching too.

"Good timing, but then you knew this would be broadcast about now, didn't you?"

He just nods, telling Chad what channel to watch.

We can see the dais, a podium where the new president's speaking from. To his left, I see Marina, happy to know that she's well enough to make the ceremony. By her side is an old woman wearing a single glove. On the right, I see a senior man with gray hair and a mustache—and surprisingly large feet. I move up closer to the screen to get a better look.

"JP, who's the man just to the right of the president? Gray hair and mustache."

He squints at the TV and says, "I believe he is one of the Cabinet members or perhaps an advisor." Then he also moves closer and takes in the whole picture.

What was it Leigh said to me the other night? "Change your clothes, your hair, your make-up, even your nose, but you cannot change your feet."

"JP, the man you say could be an advisor, is the same man I saw pass by me before I was shot by Sergei Petrikov. His hair is different, and he doesn't have a beard, but he has those unusually big feet. Rose also told me about a man watching her while she and Kelley were on the carousel ride at the National Zoo. She commented on his enormous feet. There's something familiar here. You know, Grigory Markovic had big feet too. Rose saw him when he abducted Bella. And Leigh said something to me last night that now makes sense when I asked him about the Tsar. He said you can change so many things about your appearance, but not your feet. You don't think that could possibly be the Tsar on that dais, do you?" I'm catching my breath now.

JP takes another hard look at the screen and puts the call on speakerphone.

"Chad, the man with the gray hair and mustache. Who is he?"

"That's Vickor Rogmia. He's the advisor to the newly elected president. Been kicking around for years."

"Robinson thinks he could possibly be the Tsar, *oui*? He fits with Leigh's description."

"I doubt that. This guy's been a second player for some time. Guess he's finally moved up the ranks to the big tent."

"Chad, this is Lily. Who's the old woman next to Marina? I didn't see her while I was in Jokovikstan," I ask, my voice filled with excitement. "She looks like she could be Rogmia's twin." I'm trying to get a look at her feet, but they're blocked.

"Jesus, Robinson. You're supposed to be recuperating. You pathologists just can't get enough detail. And, I sent JP to Boston to check up on you, not stimulate your imagination." Little does he know what else JP stimulates.

"Her name, Chad, and her relationship to the new president?"

"That's Katarina Assimovca. She's the new

president's wife." JP looks again and scrutinizes the TV screen.

"Chad. I have seen that old woman somewhere before. I cannot recall yet, but I agree with Robinson. We have to go back to Jokovikstan."

"Sorry, JP. No can do. Diplomatic relations with Jokovikstan are shut down for a while with the new regime. I suggest you and Robinson look somewhere else for excitement."

We hear the phone go silent, and I click off the television.

"Perhaps, Chad is right. Our imaginations working overtime, *oui*?" JP squeezes my hand.

I shake my head, get up from the couch, and walk to my desk, forcing my brain to focus. I pick up a pen and paper and write down the two names. Vickor Rogmia and Katarina Assimovca. Hmm, such odd names, and then I write out the name of my nemesis, Markovic. I start to rearrange the letters— and it hits me. "JP!" I yell. "The names are anagrams."

Acknowledgments

Thank you to my colleagues from Encircle Publications for their support, and to the Encircle Publications team: Eddie Vincent, publisher; Cynthia Bracket-Vincent, editor; and Deirdre Wait, cover artist.

My colleagues, who were my first readers and consultants—your comments, as always, help to enrich Lily's story, and my life. Special shout out to Matt Cost, Yim Tan Wong, Dr. Tai C. Kwong, Karen Krajewski, Dr. Rebecca Hamilton, Dr. James Caruso, Tom Demarest, Linda Fisher, RN, and Annabel Dizon.

I also would like to thank Anne Brewer (annebrewereditorial.com) for her incredible help on the project. Her suggestions only made this a better book and me a better writer.

Rare Earth Elements

Rare earth elements or REEs are a group of metals that are of strategic value geopolitically. China dominates the world market. REEs are of critical importance in military defense applications, aviation, electronics, medical devices, and high-tech consumer products.

There are seventeen rare earth minerals, and they are divided into two groups: Light REEs (low atomic numbers) and Heavy REEs (high atomic numbers). The light group consists of the lanthanides, elements including lanthanum (La), cerium (Ce), europium (Eu), gadolinium (Gd), praseodymium (Pr), neodymium (Nd), scandium (Sc), samarium (Sm), and promethium (Pm) while the Heavy REEs include terbium (Tb), thulium (Tm), ytterbium (Yb), yttrium (Y), dysprosium (Dy), holmium (Ho), erbium (Er), and lutetium (Lu).

There is no REE called ziyantium. This was created for the fictional country of Jokovikstan.

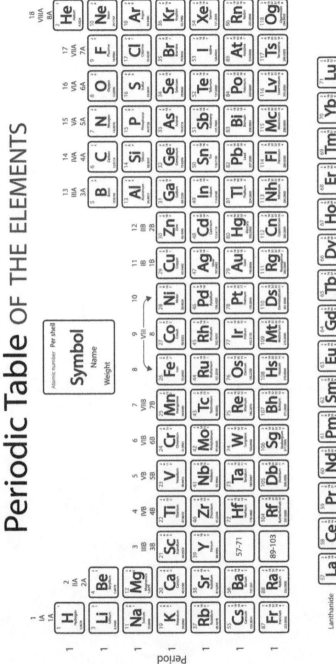

About the Author

BJ Magnani (Barbarajean Magnani, PhD, MD, FCAP) is the author of the Dr. Lily Robinson trilogy: *The Queen of All Poisons*, *The Power of Poison*, and *A Message In Poison*. *Lily Robinson and the Art of Secret Poisoning* is the original collection of short stories featuring the brilliant, yet deadly, doctor.

Dr. Magnani is internationally recognized for her expertise in clinical chemistry and toxicology, has been named a "Top Doctor" in *Boston* magazine, and was named one of the Top 100 Most Influential Laboratory Medicine Professionals in the World by *The Pathologist*. She is Professor of Anatomic and Clinical Pathology (and Professor of Medicine) at Tufts University School of Medicine, Boston, MA, and the former Chair of both the College of American Pathologists (CAP) Toxicology Committee and the Department of Pathology and Laboratory Medicine at Tufts Medical Center. Follow BJ Magnani on Twitter, Facebook, and LinkedIn.

Center Point Large Print
600 Brooks Road / PO Box 1
Thorndike, ME 04986-0001 USA

(207) 568-3717

US & Canada:
1 800 929-9108
www.centerpointlargeprint.com